I Love Me
(Who Do You Love?)

I Love Me

(Who Do You Love?)

Gordon Legge

Polygon
Edinburgh

© Gordon Legge 1994

First published by
Polygon
22 George Square
Edinburgh

Set in Palatino by ROM-Data Ltd, Falmouth, Cornwall.
Printed and bound in Great Britain by Short Run Press Ltd, Exeter

A CIP record for this title is available.

ISBN 0 7486 6184 0

The Publisher acknowledges subsidy from

THE SCOTTISH ARTS COUNCIL

towards the publication of this volume.

The Author would like to thank the
Scottish Arts Council for a bursary he
received which helped him out during
the completion of this book.

For everybody I ever had anything to do with during my stint as Writer-in-Residence at the Royal Edinburgh Hospital.

The sun was shining like a new bar of soap as the lassies from Robbs International Textiles sprinted, strode, sashayed and shuffled their way into town for their chip-shop dinners.

Gary sat back on his bench, spread his legs in a loose and ready kind of way, sucked air like he was sucking something else then indicated with a nod and said, 'Bet she does dirty things, eh?'

The guy sitting next to Gary didn't answer, though, just leaned forward so that his elbows were resting on his knees and shook his head, slowly.

This was Graeme's first day off in his nine-month stint as warehouseman, and out of a sense of duty that had a wee bit to do with old times' sake – but a whole heap more to do with job-induced guilt – Graeme had decided to spend the day hanging around the town with his old mate Gary: an experience which had already caused Graeme to reconsider his self-imposed ban of five weeks standing that prevented him from smoking outdoors.

'Well, what d'you reckon, then?'

Had to be the one with the leather jacket, the one he was on about, had to be . . . *and, come to think about it, what exactly were dirty things, anyway?*

'Eh, aye,' said Graeme. 'Aye, suppose so.'

'Bloody stunning,' said Gary. 'Telling you, see the best time to get yourself down here – Christmas, when you've got all the students and all that back, all the folk that've left. Plant myself here for hours, man.'

Graeme nodded. Outwardly to express gratitude for the information, inwardly, though, to confirm a longheld suspicion that poor Gary was going a wee bit seriously sideyways.

Graeme checked himself, though. Hell, why not, why shouldn't the guy have his wee bit daft fun? After all, when you started to think about it, was this not just another case of *and there but for the grace of job go I?*

For the sake of something to do, Graeme decided to do something and decided to ask a question. 'Eh,' he said, 'eh, you going the morrow night?'

But Graeme was wasting his time if he was waiting for any kind of response. All the attention that was on the go was for the girls with their orangey-browny overalls now making their back to their work, their methods of movement still a rare mixture of urgency, pace and poise.

'Come on,' said Gary, once the last of the lassies was out of sight. 'Time to shift.'

Graeme flicked some ash and did as he was told, following Gary round to the other side of the precinct pot plant, where the pair of them sat themselves down in eager anticipation of the skirt-suited office women going out for their baker-shop dinners.

The sight that greeted Hazel once she'd squeezed her way past the perfumed queue was not one she particularly cared for, and she barely acknowledged Gary and Graeme with the grudging half-smile she'd developed for the folk with their charity tins on Saturday afternoons.

No, Hazel wasn't what you'd call overly fond of Gary and Graeme. They were part of the baggage that came along with Andy, though, and going by what she knew of them – and what they were up to just now was pretty typical, leering away like that – it was likely that they would be around, like unwanted facial hair, forever and ever, amen.

Before she reached the door leading up to her office, Hazel did an about turn and stole a glance, a deliberate look back, trying to catch them staring at her legs.

And she did, she did catch them.

Graeme, at least, had the decency to turn away and look rather sheepish as he stubbed out his cigarette, but Gary, Gary just kept right on at it, like it was all part of some sort of silly wee game that she, Hazel, was supposed to appreciate, indeed was supposed to be damn well fucking grateful for this attention, this admiration; that she, Hazel, or any other woman come to that, should be grateful for this, this . . . Had the door into Hazel's building been a slammable sort, Hazel would have slammed it.

Back in her office, Hazel managed to calm down a bit, and soon amused herself with the daily ritual of watching her colleagues attack what passed for their dinners: Cath was on the boiled egg and half a banana; Helen was on the slim-a-soup with one slice of cold toast; Margaret was on the glass of water with cottage cheese; Alison, meanwhile, made do with the three coffees and five Regal. Every week brought along a new series of diets, each guaranteed to lose seven pounds by Saturday – not to mention free manic depression, barely suppressed aggression and the non-stop talking caused by lack of proper food. If Hazel had ever wanted to make millions she'd have moved into publishing with the launch of a new monthly glossy called *Diet*. Preferably with a telly tie-in à la *Food and Drink* or the *Clothes Show*. That was all this lot in here ever went on about. They didn't even have the sense about them to go on about the joy of food or the pleasure of clothes; it was only ever those daft bloody programmes that they went on about.

From her top drawer Hazel produced her bottle of ketchup, and smeared three dollops of its gooey wonderfulness onto her two rolls and square sausage.

'Would you look at Lady Beanpole,' said Cath. 'Does that just to annoy us, so she does.'

'Her time'll come, just you wait and see,' said Alison. 'When it goes through the lips, it goes to the hips.'

'Nah,' said Helen, 'it's when you start dropping weans is when you balloon. I used to be like that,' Helen held up her pinky, 'before my Michael, my Karen and my William came along.'

'Don't you listen to them, hen,' said Margaret. 'Enjoy it while you can. Treat every meal like you're going to the chair.'

Hazel nodded to indicate that this was the path she intended following. Anyway, child-bearing induced obesity wasn't something that particularly troubled Hazel. Point of fact, being a fat, cuddly mum was something Hazel was looking forward to, and something Hazel had been giving a lot of thought to of late, since teaming up with Andy, the man who was going to be the father of her children.

'How the fuck can he do that?' said Dunx.

'Fuck knows,' said Andy. 'Fuck knows.'

'Piece of piss, boys,' said Tony, supporting himself as he was with his outstretched legs wedged wishbone-style halfway up the corridor walls.

Trying to do the same, Dunx stretched his legs out. There was no way, though, he could even get near the skirting boards, let alone start to go up the way like Tony had done.

'Can you reach out with your arms?' said Andy. 'Like that, can you go like that?'

Still doing his wishbone bit, Tony stretched his arms out to the extent that he could lay his palms flat against the corridor walls. Then, showing off, he brought his legs out in front of him, at right angles to his body, so that he was just supporting himself with his hands, his hands wedged against the corridor walls.

'Fucking hell,' said Andy.

'This is fucking unreal, man,' said Dunx. 'Get down off there a minute, I want to try something out.'

Tony relaxed and fell to the floor, where he stood a good few inches shorter than either Dunx or Andy.

'Put your arms out,' said Dunx, 'like that. Go like that.'

Tony stretched his arms out.

'Right,' said Dunx and sized up, and, surprise surprise, Dunx's fingertips easily extended beyond those of Tony's.

'That's unreal,' said Andy. 'Let's see.'

Andy moved round the other side of Tony and did the same and Andy's fingertips extended beyond Tony's as well.

'Hold on,' said Tony, 'I'm no really trying but.'

So Tony tried. He grunted, he groaned, and first his fingertips, and then his palms, and then his wrists all caught up with and then shot out past the outstretched fingertips of Andy and Dunx like Tony was making use of some extra gear.

And then Andy and Dunx really tried, grunting and groaning like Tony, and really, really straining themselves.

'What the flaming . . . !!!'

Stan-Stan-the-supervisor-man gulped. Good God, that was it, he was fired, end of contract, out of job, get your cards, sign-on Monday, finito. Christ, all morning he'd been on at them to get themselves busy, or at least get themselves looking like they were supposed to be busy, because, as Stan had told them at least five times a day for the past five weeks, today was the day of the visit from the man from head office – the man presently standing there right next to Stan, and the man with the power to close down Stan's base and terminate Stan's contract, and what the hell were they up to but practising for a council crucifixion – three bodies, one cross.

Stan shouted, 'Get in there!' and Andy, Dunx and Tony duly untangled themselves and shuffled through the office where Heather, Julie, Wee Caroline, Big Caroline, Steve, Stevie and Steven were all at each other's throats over who's music was the loudest and the most irritating. The situation had arisen following Stan's attempt to end the tape wars by suggesting that everybody brought in their own personal stereos. What Stan hadn't anticipated, though, was that no one would actually own personal stereos, and what they brought in were radio cassettes with external speakers, so the place ended up sounding more like a record fair than a working office.

'Go and make us a coffee, darling,' said the man from head office to Julie. 'Three sugars, no milk. Ta.'

'Might as well,' said Julie. 'First time I'll ever have done anything in this fucking shitehole.'

'This,' announced Stan, 'hoy, you lot, listen up – this is the man from head office. He's here to hear your gripes. Off you jolly well go then. Gripe, gripe away to your heart's content.'

'When we getting a crêche?' asked Wee Caroline. 'Need somewhere for our weans. Know how much I'm shelling out for a sitter? Telling you, it's no worth my while coming to this place, neither it is.'

'Looking into that, sweetheart,' The man from head office made a note. 'Get back to you a week on Tuesday.'

'Equipment here's garbage,' said Steve. 'See up the college they've got these brilliant fucking. . . .'

The man from head office interrupted. 'New stuff arriving week after next, pal. Up-to-date as you can get. Next.'

'What about the money?' said Dunx, putting on his serious voice. 'What about the fucking money? A tenner is nothing, absolutely nothing, nothing in this day and age.'

The man from head office just shook his head. 'You can fuck yourself sideways, pal, but that's all you're getting. Like it or lump it. There's the door, son.'

Andy said, 'But I mean, what's all this about, I mean, really, what's supposed to be going on here?'

'You were told at your induction, son, it's all in your file, do I have to go over this every single time?' The man from head office turned to Stevie (the quietest, least demonstrative soul in the office, and very possibly the quietest, least demonstrative soul in the world) and said, 'Get that look off your face, sunshine, or so help me I'll fucking wipe it off . . . Thanks hen.' The man from head office took a sip from his coffee and lit a cigarette from the one he was smoking. 'Anything else?'

Nobody said anything because they were either stunned, confused or had given up hope.

'That the lot then? . . . Aye? . . . My, what a nice quiet shower you've got yourself here, Stan. Fair impressed, son. Christ, that the time, got to shift. Nice to see you all doing so well, keep it up. I'll see you later then, Stan. You're doing a grand job here, son.'

'Am I?' Stan looked stunned.

'Christ, aye, son. You want to see some of them. Boy down the road there – zero trainees, I mean fuck all, every one of them left. Every week he gets a new fifteen, and by the end of the week they're all away. And, here, what about Brian MacKlintock? No hear about Brian? Aye, Christ, one of his boys set about Big Brian with an axe. Aye, a flaming axe, big fucker it was too, right in the old napper, fifty-seven stitches. Expected to be off his work for six months, no counting the trauma, like. Telling you, Stan, you've got a real, right cushy number here, son. Keep up the good work, eh.'

And with that the man from head office winked at Wee Caroline and was off.

Stan sat back in his chair, looking for all the world as though he'd just been told he wasn't going to die a week on Tuesday after all.

The smugness of the moment was somewhat disturbed, though, when Robbie, who had hitherto seemed quite content sitting at his corner table, away in his own wee world flicking a squashed up piece of paper with a straightened out paper-clip while commentating on an imaginary cup final – the moment was disturbed when Robbie started laughing.

Now, Robbie's laughter wasn't something the folk were used to, and to be truthful, since his start three weeks ago it was something the folk had never even so much as heard.

'You want to let us in on the joke, Robbie?' said Stan.

Robbie brought play to a halt in the cup final. 'An axe through the skull,' he said. 'That's a fucking sare yin.'

Trixie the cat had quickly been bored by it, but Recca was transfixed by her newly purchased full-length, frameless mirror.

God, she looked old, she looked wasted, she looked like somebody she wouldn't like the look of at all.

Recca pulled her hair away from her face to see if she could stand it.

God, no! The features still weren't all that bad but the details had all collapsed or exploded into disaster zones with the whites of her eyes like dirty dishwater and her mouth like somebody else's trampled orange.

Christ, it must've been 'cause she looked so bad that everybody was so pleased about her teaming up with Dunx – everybody was pleased, that was, apart from Recca herself.

It was Recca who'd told Dunx he'd have to go out and find himself something to do, so fed up was she with him hanging about the house all the time and doing nothing but running up her gas and electricity. It wasn't just the bills, though, Recca was a bit fed up with Dunx period, and had hoped he'd maybe just take the hint, take the huff and piss off permanently.

Dunx's tenancy had began following a drunken one-night stand when Recca had woken up to discover, as usual, that she'd been left on her lonesome. This situation, however, proved only to be temporary as Dunx promptly returned . . . complete with all his gear.

Debate was a bit difficult with Dunx, and not just because Recca was on shifts and hardly ever saw him, and when she did see him they were invariably either drunk or stoned and she was grateful of his cuddly company (he was good company when you were mutually out of it, she conceded, but then again so was her teddy bear) but arguing with him, arguing with him was like arguing with a four year-old blessed with a two hundred point IQ. The guy was stupid alright but, God, he was good at it. Dunx could justify everything because everything revolved around Dunx.

And the thing that had really got to Recca, the thing that scared her really, was that everybody was so damned pleased for them. Andy called it 'my two best mates getting the gether'. Carol and Deke had been dead encouraging. It was unbelievable. Dunx was horrible. He was an arsehole, he was a complete and utter spoilt bastard. Sexually, he was less demanding than her finger had ever been.

For a while there Recca had even begun to worry about herself – was it her, maybe it was just her? Or did folk really expect her to have such low expectations of life that she'd settle for Dunx?

Recca looked at her mirror again. No, regardless of wrinkles, potholes, crow's feet and the million other flaws, Dunx had to be gotten rid off. She could do better than that; Christ, anybody could do better than that. And he'd been here nearly a month now, a whole month. A month with him away borrowing her best jackets, a month of coming home to discover there was no bread and a month of returning to a home that looked like a big, bad bomb had hit it.

Recca gave herself a shake. She picked up the phone and dialled Carol, to tell her about the new mirror, and to tell her that she was coming round tonight.

Joanne's bag landed on the two-seater settee next to the fishtank; her coat landed on the three-seater settee in front of the hifi. She picked up the remote, planked herself eighteen inches from the screen and fired, a bottle of twist lodged in her mouth like Andy Capp's fag.

'Anybody awake?'

Carol stirred. 'Oh, hello, dad. Must've dozed off.' Carol gave herself a stretch and a yawn. 'Fancy a coffee?' she said.

' "Dozed off?" Christ, you were sound, Carol, hen. The blooming phone was ringing. Did you no hear it? Listen, is everything alright?'

Carol laughed. From the way her dad went on at times it was like it was him that was doing the looking after, and not Carol who spent more time than she could really afford running about on his behalf.

'Yeah, I'm alright,' said Carol. 'Look who's here to see you.' Carol tickled Baby Joe awake. 'Papa's here to see you. Wave to Papa. You want to go and play with your Papa? Go on.'

Baby Joe didn't wave to his Papa, but Papa was suitably distracted to allow Carol to get on with things.

'Hoy, you, madam.' Carol picked up the bag. 'This!' Carol picked up the coat. 'And this!'

'Few seconds,' said Joanne.

'Now!' Carol saw the twist in Joanne's mouth. 'Where did you get that?'

Joanne pointed to her Papa as she gathered up her stuff.

'Dad, I asked you not to do that. You know she's just about to get her tea.'

'Och, I had to go for matches and, well . . .'

'Och, well, nothing, you shouldn't.'

Joanne returned and planked herself in front of the telly again. Carol took the twist from Joanne's mouth. 'Homework?'

Joanne's head went from side to side.

'Sure?'

Joanne's head went up and down.

The kettle clicked and Carol made coffees for herself and her dad.

'Was talking to Bob Johnson earlier on there,' said Carol's dad. 'You'll probably no mind of him but he used to be a good pal of mine and your mother's.'

'I think I've heard the name.'

'Aye, well, seems he's no been keeping so well himself of late. Wee bit of bother with his ticker, you know.'

'He doing better now?'

'Aye, aye – well, he's getting about, anyway. "Never died a winter yet" he says. Aye, never died a winter yet.'

'You staying for your tea?'

'Eh, no. No, I'll just grab myself something out of the chippie, a bag of chips'll do me. No really been feeling that hungry the day.'

'You can't live off going to the chippie every other day, dad.'

'Och, I get by. Still got some of that soup your sister gave us, still some of that in the freezer. Maybe just have that instead.'

'Be better for you.'

'Aye. Listen, hen, I better get going. Just need to visit the old cludge first.'

Carol took his hardly-touched coffee through to the kitchen and started peeling tatties for the tea.

It had been Carol's idea for her dad to collect Joanne from school. Prior to that he'd always been calling round at nights. Half drunk he'd spend his time moaning about dizziness, tightness in his chest and pains in his stomach. Deke once threw him out because he was going on that much, telling him never to darken their door in that state again.

Carol thought it would be better this way: this way her dad got to see the kids and Carol got to see her dad. Once or twice a week he stayed for his tea but he never stayed beyond that, he never outstayed his welcome.

'Well, I'll away then, hen.'

'Right, I'll see you. Will you stay for your tea the morrow?'

'Eh, aye. Aye, I could. If you're twisting my arm, like.'

'Right. Take care then. Say "Cheerio" to your papa, kids.'

Carol saw her dad to the door then came back through to the living-room so she could wave to him, and see that he crossed the road safely.

'Papa's stinking,' said Joanne.

'I know,' said Carol. 'Listen, don't tell Deke, okay?'

'Okay.'

Once her dad was out of sight Carol went through the bathroom to see what sort of mess he'd left – everywhere bar the bowl just about summed up his efforts.

Deke adjusted his safety specs and gave the nod to Willie that he was ready.

The high-pressure hose gave a blast and the clogged-up catalyst pellets spewed out like midges from Hell with Deke chasing after them with the vacuum hose.

This was industrial waste disposal, cleaning out the tanks.

When the work used to take on more folk, it was their own men who did this job. Then some smart alec did some calculations and the work started laying off folk and getting contractors in. Often it was the same guys who ended up doing the actual job, because, despite getting a hefty early retirement wedge, folk were greedy and when they heard there was a chance of a quick few hundred smackeroos, the fortnight in Orlando went on hold in favour of the working trousers. These blokes, though, the blokes who'd done this before, could see the difference in the way things were carried out now, the difference in safety, supervision and standards.

Whatever this stuff was it was getting to Deke something rotten, tickling the back of his throat like a blade. There could only be so much of it, though, it had to be finite, and Deke swung his vacuum like he knew what he was doing, and anyway, if this stuff wasn't finite then Deke's hours were.

Deke was a scaffolder to trade, and loved all that climbing and shouting at folk. One time he'd nearly got his cards when they'd been sorting the steeple up the High Street and Deke had entertained the lunchtime shoppers with some singing and dancing, spliff in hand, only pausing to recite extracts from the collected works of Carlos Castenada.

Yeah, Deke wanted to get back to the scaffolding. He'd learnt his tools, he'd bought his tools, he had his card, now all he wanted was the opportunity to use them again, eight hours a day, five days a week. It wasn't too much to ask for. And if what they were saying was true then the chance was due soon.

The word was that work would start on the site for the new plant in four to six weeks, two months at the most. An eighteen-month contract with a thousand taken on for the duration. And, as scaffolders always said, the scaffolding would be the first to go up and the scaffolding would be the last to come down.

Deke had had it as far as working with these cowboys was concerned, anyway. It was all just hassle, hassle, all the time. Even on the first day there'd been a strike, with complaining about the overalls, the boots, the hard-hats and the lack of safety specs and masks.

Deke just got on with it, though. The way Deke had it, sitework, and this in particular, was like going out to clean the windows when it was lashing, just making a cunt of yourself. Except here you got good money – and Deke had done not too bad at setting up a few deals for himself. Nothing too big, you understand, just enough to make enough of a profit that meant he'd be getting his for free.

Willie was alright and Deke had paired off with him. A few of the younger ones had it in for Willie – for some reason they had Willie down as being a bit simple – and were forever asking about the size of his knob, when he last had a ride etc etc. Deke, though, had taken Willie under his wing. It wasn't so much that Deke was Mr Macho, but what folk tended to know about Deke tended to make folk frightened of Deke – for Deke was known to one and all as The Poof Called God.

The blasting stopped and Deke and Willie started brushing up.

'What plant is this, anyway?' said Deke.

'Eh,' said Willie. 'Hold on, there's a sign over there. I'll go and have a look ... Says hydrogen cyanide, the hydrogen cyanide plant. Whatever the fuck that is.'

'What?' said Deke.

'Hydrogen cyanide,' repeated Willie. 'No believe me? Come here, come here and have a look for yourself.'

'It's alright, Willie. I believe you.' Deke went back to his brushing again and then started laughing. 'Eh, Willie,' he said, 'you've never heard of a place called Bhopal, have you?'

The one on the left had the borstal dots, dots that were supposed to translate as 'all screws are bastards'. The one on the right had the crosses, that were supposed to indicate the number of folk he'd killed (although Graeme wasn't too sure about that). The one in the middle, though, he was obviously the one blessed with the sense of humour: his left knuckles read 'kill', his right knuckles read 'fuck'.

There were two folders on the table next to Graeme's seat: 'Commis Chefs in Oban' and 'Other Vacancies'. Graeme opted for the latter, looking to see how many of the jobs paid more than his did.

Gary was still at his Restart. For somebody who'd said he'd only be ninety-seven seconds, he'd so far underestimated his interview time by a good five minutes.

The three tattooed-knuckled boys, all of them kitted out in matching black shell-suits, lit up, squashing up their faces as they inhaled.

God, thought Graeme to himself, this was what smokers really looked like: horrible, rotten, ugly, stinking, smelly...

Graeme panicked. For a second there he thought one of them was looking at him with a look that implied mind-reading ability. Graeme went through his pockets and brought out his fags and matches and lit up in a life-saving show of empathy.

Graeme read the posters as he puffed away. He was soon finished, though, and struggling for things to do. He gave some thought to going over and getting a few leaflets. But that would mean movement and he might slip, he might slip and fall and land in the lap of one these right dodgy-looking cunts.

Graeme settled instead for reading the graffiti on the DSS sign on the outside wall: 'If God had wanted us to work he'd have given us jobs'; 'Get Really Stoned – Drink Wet Cement'; 'Knowledge Reigns

Supreme' (reigns spelt wrong); 'Welcome to the Daisy Age'; 'Castrate the police and have a ball!'; 'Sign on, You crazy diamonds!'

'Mr Bampot, please.'

The three black shell-suited tattooed-knuckled boys all half stood up and Graeme shat himself the most serious hedgehog this side of Sonic.

'Mr. B. Bampot.'

The one in the middle ('kill' and 'fuck') got up and went over.

Mega shitface, man, said Graeme to himself. That's who this shower were, them with their black shell-suits and their squashed up faces and their tattooed knuckles and their tiny wee eyes set half a mile apart, pelmeted by the single caterpillar eyebrow. Wow, the Bampots, man.

All his life Graeme had heard about this lot, and how they were like the local Royal Family, a shower of serious, thieving, murdering, stabbing so-and-so's if ever there were.

Graeme had heard about them alright, and all his life had lived in the same town as them, but up until this moment he wouldn't have known them if they'd stopped and stamped on his face – which, funnily enough, was the sort of thing they were famed for.

Folk said there was a whole clan of them in the town but these three, these three had to be the main men, these three had to be the baddest bastards, these three had to be the terrifying triplets – Rab, Boaby and Robert.

These bampots killed folk. They sliced up their victims and stuffed the bits into polybags and buried the polybags under the floorboards of the house over the old town where the old grannie had murdered the old grandfather, the gardener and the gardener's two brothers; a house that had lain empty from that day on, and would continue to remain empty so long as there were those to pass on the tale of what had happened there on that fateful day. That was what folk said, anyway.

This was horrible. Graeme was going to see this shower everywhere he went. It would be like falling out with someone, you'd bump into them all the time. It would be like at school when the nutters who terrified you were always the ones that ended up sitting next to you in maths and woodwork, sharpening their compasses and priming their chisels.

Graeme looked over at Gary again. Good, he was getting up, he was going. Graeme ground a long stub into the ashtray and scuffed his way over to the door, arriving there just ahead of Gary.

'What about that in there?' said Graeme. 'No fucking real, eh.'

'Too right,' said Gary.

'Should've seen the looks I was getting.'

'Aye right,' said Gary.

'Aye right, your arse. I was fucking terrified.'

Gary looked puzzled. 'What you on about?'

'What you think I'm on about? Those Bampot cunts in there.'

Gary laughed.

'How?' said Graeme. 'What you on about, like?'

Gary was beaming. 'No see that new lassie doing the Restarts? Bloody stunning. Bloody fucking stunning.'

Stan-Stan-the-supervisor-man was so concerned about his numbers that come the end of each and every day, he piled the trainees, the lot of them, in the back of his van and provided a door-to-door shuttle – the incentive being the weekly tenner fiddleable in travelling expenses.

Andy and Dunx got dropped off at the traffic lights, assured Stan they'd be there at the pick-up point, quarter past nine in the morning, and headed off down the road.

'Hey, listen,' said Dunx, 'I want you to do something for me, right. I want you to do something for me the morrow night.'

There was a hint of caution as Andy replied. 'What, like?'

'Look,' said Dunx, almost giggling, 'I'm seeing that Heather the morrow, I've arranged to go out for a drink with her.'

Andy didn't say anything, just shook his head.

Dunx started laughing. 'You're not going to believe all this. This is what happened, okay. Mind when I was away at the bog earlier on there? Well, that's when I bumps into her, as I was coming back. And what I does, right, I sees her slowing down coming along the corridor towards me so I slows down and all and just says "Alright" and starts talking to her, like. And she's into it, aye she's well into it, alright. So I takes it a wee bit further and starts flirting and chatting with her, you know, going on about what she's wearing and all that, what she does with herself. And she's still right into it, still well into it, giving it the eye and that, and I can tell she's right into me, aye well into me alright, so I just thinks, ah fuck it, just ask her out – so, there you go, I just asks her out. Tell the truth, right, I'm sure she planned it so she'd bump into me, I'm sure she did. Positive, in fact. It was her that slowed down first mind.'

'What 'bout Recca?' said Andy.

'Nah,' Dunx was laughing. 'There's nothing going on, like, nothing in it, nothing like that. Just going out to see her, just going out to see her and have a wee drink and a blether and that. Just going for a drink.'

Andy wasn't so sure. 'So what's it to do with me then?'

'Right, here's where you come in – dead easy – all I want from you is to meet up with us the morrow after the game and we'll head off up the quiz, 'cause I'm supposed to be meeting Recca up there.'

'Where you going to be?'

'Don't know yet. Just out for a drink somewhere.'

Andy sighed.

'No,' said Dunx. 'Just a drink somewhere.' Dunx started laughing. 'Mind you, I get a couple of bevs inside me, you never know.'

'Fucking hell, man.'

'Nah, just joking, just having you on. All it is is I like female company. I like talking with women, I've got a special kind of way with them. You can say certain things to women, you can open up a wee bit with women. I'm interested in them.'

'Invite her round to meet Recca then.'

'Nah, don't be stupid, that'd never work. We're just talking one-to-one here, just one-to-one. Just like we're doing the now. I like things like this. You know I like walking down the road with you like this. It's alright this, eh.'

'So, wait a minute,' said Andy, 'what exactly is it that you want me to do again?'

'What I said. Just meet up with us after the game. I'll meet you outside the ground at full-time. And you can let us know everything that happened and we'll head over to the boozer, just like I'd been at the game.'

'What if Recca's to see you up the town with this lassie?'

'Nah, no chance of that. We're staying in ET City when we're going out for the drink, then getting a bus back.'

'And where are you supposed to be when you're supposed to be home from your work?'

'Don't know,' Dunx laughed, 'not thought about that yet. Ach, I'll just say I bumped into somebody or I went round to see one of my aunties, something like that. Recca never bothers us with hassles like that, anyway. Got a kind of open relationship, we have.'

This came as a surprise to Andy. He suspected it would come as a surprise to Recca as well. For all Dunx was going on about this being nothing of any consequence Andy was starting to get those itchy heels of his, usually a pretty good indication of trouble ahead.

'Should be worth it, though,' said Dunx. 'Aye, should be worth it, alright.'

Andy kind of shrugged.

'Aye,' said Dunx, as if imagining to himself, then he snapped out of it. 'Christ, better be. Hey, mind, I'm missing the game for this as well remember.'

They went their separate ways with Andy going over, but never quite getting to grips with what Dunx had been going on about.

What was he meaning by "Just going out for a drink?" Was that meaning what it was supposed to mean, or was that meaning what it was supposed to imply?

Andy was confused. And when Andy got confused, Andy got those itchy heels of his. And when Andy got really confused, Andy's conscience took on another voice. Specifically the voice of Iain Cuthbertson doing his Charlie Endell and terrifying the life out of poor Budgie, or as it was in this instance, Iain Cuthbertson doing his Charlie Endell and terrifying the life out of poor Andy.

'Fuck! Fuck! Fuck!'

Andy stopped in the middle of the street.

There was him forgetting about Hazel again. Not that there was anything special Andy was supposed to be remembering about Hazel today, it was just that he'd made this pact with himself to spend more of his time thinking about Hazel. Andy was always thinking about his mates all the time when he should have been thinking about Hazel.

Hazel was a bit touchy about Andy and his 'mates'. Even the word got on her nerves, the word 'mates'. It was too non-committal, she said, like in 'one of my mates', 'a mate of mine', or you 'hung around with mates'.

Trouble, though, was as much as Andy understood what she meant, he was never too successful when it came to doing anything about it. Things were just so difficult. Like whenever anything went right, then something else just went wrong.

And that's exactly what happened when Andy got home.

Things started well enough, unbelievably well in fact. Hazel told Andy she'd phoned up Carol to see if it was alright for them to go round there that night. Andy was chuffed to bits.

Hazel was never one for going out at all and for her to suggest going round to Carol and Deke's, friends of Andy's and possibly the last place Hazel would suggest going, was just so fucking brilliant, it was like her scoring her first goal. Then she said . . .

'I'll take a couple of my tapes round.'

'What?'

'My tapes, I'll take a couple of them round.'

'Eh, why?'

'What d'you mean "why"? To listen to. To let them hear them. What d'you think?'

'No, eh,' Andy was getting into trouble. 'It's just that . . .'

'They like their music round there. They're always playing music.'

'I know,' said Andy. 'But, I mean, they're really serious about it. Deke's got this really expensive tape-deck, yours'll maybe no play right.'

'You mean I'll break his machine.'

'God, no. No, I mean, what do I mean, I mean . . .'

'You mean I'll be embarrassing?'

Andy responded with the most honest expression he could muster. 'No, love,' he said. 'That's not what I mean. I swear that's not what I mean.'

'What d'you mean then? Tell me.'

'Look, listen, I know a bit about these things, right. I know that

your tapes won't play on that tape-deck, it's all to do with these
things called azimuths, right. We just play them on that wee punky
thing, that can't do them any good.'
    'If they don't play properly then they can just be taken off.'
    Andy sighed. 'Look, Deke's really serious about his music, This
stuff's a bit . . . bland. I like it, I really like it, honest, I like it, it's just
that I don't want you to get upset if nobody else likes it.'
    Hazel put on her either/or face. Hazel's either/or face was like
having Andy's family, teachers, friends, all the big boys and all
the bad boys, all rolled into one. It was a look that demanded
mercy.
    'Sorry,' said Andy, 'I was just wanting us all to be happy.'
    'No, let's just start with *us*,' said Hazel. 'We two, just the two of
us. Okay?'
    'Okay.'
    'Fine then,' said Hazel. 'We're going, and I'm taking my tapes.'
    Andy nodded. Typical of Andy, though, he wasn't nodding
because of Hazel, he was nodding because he'd come to a decision:
he was going to tell Dunx that he wasn't going to do what Dunx
had asked him to do.

    'You going to go halfers then or what?'
    Deke had the eyes of a spaniel, Carol the brow of a bank-man-
ager.
    'Well?' said Recca.
    'Ach, go on,' said Carol, going into her purse. 'Here, take it.'
    'Yes,' said Deke, and went back to bathing Baby Joe.
    'Right,' said Recca, 'Just let me finish this coffee then I'll head
off.'
    'No hurry,' said Deke, meaning the opposite.
    Recca gave him a squashed up face of a scowl. 'See if you were
a man, a real man, a proper man, a real proper man, you'd offer to
go instead of me, or you'd at least have the decency to offer to come
along and protect me – 'stead of just staying here washing the
wean.'
    Deke held up the sponge and squeezed it dry like he couldn't
be bothered one way or the other; which was as big a lie as any lie,

but Recca was going to go, she always did, and the sooner she got off her arse and top-geared it, the better for all concerned.

'Aye right, Derek Henderson,' Recca was giving it an old guy's voice, 'Ah tell you, ah mind the day, aye ah mind the day, and it was never that long ago, ah can tell you, when you'd've chapped half the doors in this town for your wee bit blow. You're getting past it.'

Deke laughed. 'That's not getting past it, that's getting sussed when there's daft mugs like you going about taking all the hassle and all the risks. Come on, shift.' Apart from going to see his brother over the old town, Deke never went out for a bit. Not for five years had he ever went out chasing it.

'I forget to tell you,' said Carol, 'your friend's coming over the night.'

Recca gave birth to a look of dread-induced disgust. 'Who? What friend?'

Carol smiled.

'Not Fids? Please no, God no, don't let it be Fids.'

Carol shook her head. 'No, you're alright, not Fids, not the night.'

'Who then?'

It was Deke who did the honours. 'Hazel and Andy are coming round.'

'Come on, please, not her, anybody but her.'

Carol nodded. 'Bout eight, she said.'

Recca's brain got to the thinking. 'Right, I'm working the night mind, so I'm not driving, definitely not driving, so I'm going to have to leave 'bout when?' Recca juggled her knees and pursed her lips. 'Bout nine, say nine, call it nine. Right. Get home, get washed, get changed, give myself time enough to get down the road; aye nine, nine'll do.' Recca stuck out her jaw and puffed out her cheeks. 'So I should only have to put up with the little snotrag for an hour or so. Heh heh. And if I get myself right wasted, I won't even notice her.'

'Recca,' said Carol. 'Your work, mind.'

'Well,' Recca looked pissed off, 'can't stand her. Can't stand it when you go round there and she's got this tiny, tiny, tiny wee toaty thing she calls an ashtray that you're all supposed to use. And here, listen, that's not the worst of it, the worst of it is once you've stubbed your fag out, she's, whoosh, out that wee seat out of hers like a rocket and away through the kitchen. Next thing all you hear's the tap going and she's back through and putting the bloody thing in her flaming cabinet. Telling you, see for her Christmas, I'm doing a spot of thieving and lifting her one of them big ones out The Duck.'

'You are not,' said Carol.

Recca got up and got her coat on. 'Nah, don't suppose I ever will, trouble with being a nice person. Still, don't like her, mind, don't like folk like that.'

'Just a young lassie,' said Deke, pat-drying Baby Joe. 'She's just a young lassie.'

Recca scowled. She didn't like that bit, that bit about the brat being young. Recca let it go, though. It wasn't something to draw attention to.

'Well,' said Deke, holding up Baby Joe for inspection, 'how's about that then? Who's the handsomest wee shite in the world?'

Baby Joe smiled and put his hand between his legs.

'That's right, son,' said Recca. 'Just you cover it up. Causes nothing but trouble, it does.'

Carol and Deke laughed.

'He's not covering it up,' said Carol, 'he's playing with it.'

'What?'

'He is,' said Deke. 'Go on, touch it. Telling you, it's hard.'

'Aye, right.'

'True,' said Carol. 'Even at that age they're at it.'

'Aye, right. Look, I'll be back in 'bout an hour or so, okay.'

'Dunx be coming?' said Carol.

'Yeah, suppose so.'

'Here,' said Deke, holding out a book with babies on the cover, 'take this away with you and have a look. Page eighty something or other, can't find it the now but it's here somewhere. Take it and have a read. Fascinating stuff.'

Recca declined. Once they got started on the trainspotter baby bit it was time to hit the trail.

Damn this fucking daylight. If he could see them then they could see him – the kids outside, that was, climbing up on the garages.

Gary moved himself away from the window, stuck himself in a shadow, and readjusted the focus.

The room was blue so the sunbed was on – that much was certain. If she was using the sunbed then she was naked – that much was probable – no, hold on, that wasn't a mere probable, that was a definite certain, yeah that was a certain as well. There was no point in her going to all the trouble of houfing up a sunbed if she wasn't going to get the maximum benefit from it, was there? No. Now that much was logical.

Folk liked wandering about naked, anyway. If for no other reason than just for the fun of it, it was a natural kind of thing to do. Gary himself, even he liked wandering about naked. It was a good feeling you got, a sort of primitive feeling, like shouting or climbing. Aye, you couldn't shuffle about with your hands in your pockets when you were naked, no there had to be a more organic method to the movement.

And when you were a few storeys up, nobody could see you, 'cause nobody could see in. Nobody that was apart from those on the same level from the block across the court – specifically those with fifty quids worth of binoculars.

Gary'd been here the night for two coffees now and still she hadn't made an appearance. In the three months since her and her six-tube sunbed had moved in Gary hadn't seen so much as a bare shoulder.

For all his mags and for all his films there was something that wee bit special about this lassie. Never in Gary's term of tenancy had the women of the court united and shown such venom and spoken such spite towards a new neighbour as they'd shown the lassie with the six-tube sunbed. Convicted murderers, rapists, child-molesters, thieves and dealers all lived here – and more than a few unconvicted – but the women of the court had this poor lassie down as the lowest of the low.

They said she was a dock-fairy; they said she liked her men; they said she'd been with this one; they said she was after that one; they said that she was filthy; they said her house was black; they said that she was on drugs; they said she wasn't all there, that she wasn't the full shilling, you know, a wee bit funny, like. On and on they went on about her, the unspoken fear, the shame that their men would dare darken her door.

That wasn't what Gary saw, though, no, Gary never saw any of what was supposed to have been going on. Not that he kept a twenty-four hour surveillance or anything like that but if she was anything like what they made her out to be then surely to God he'd have noticed something. But no, he'd never even seen anyone coming or going, just the lassie herself.

The blue light went out. Gary scanned.

. . . The kitchen light went on . . . She didn't appear . . . The kitchen light went out . . . The toilet light went on . . . The toilet light went off . . . All the lights on this side were off . . . The living-room light went on . . . She walked across and put the telly on . . . She was wearing a robe.

Gary lowered his binoculars and wiped his slobbers. Fucking hell, this was unreal. God knows what he would have been like if he ever actually saw anything.

That would do for the now, though. No point in standing about here all night. He wasn't that much of a perv.

Anyway, this was Tuesday, and Gary had his work to do on a Tuesday, 'cause on Tuesdays Gary had himself one last look through the wee paper, the local rag, before it went in the bucket, cutting out the reports of the games, and any bits of news with folk he knew, places he knew or even just things he liked the look of.

Gary'd started making scrapbooks when he was a kid, keeping a record of his goals in the football reports. There were also the school trips, the outings, the exhibitions and all that. Then the first of the wedding photos appeared, and Gary cut them out as well: wedding photos of folk he'd known or even just photos of folk he'd remembered from school. Then there was the folk in the news: the folk doing well for themselves, the folk in bands and the folk in trouble.

There'd been a while there when there hadn't been much happening in the paper with folk of Gary's generation. A few still cropped up in the court pages, of course, but that was a bit like a soap opera, seeing all the same faces all the time, always apologising for something or other, and saying how they'd never get in trouble again blah blah blah. There was a lack of surprises going on, though.

Then, within the space of a month, three surprises did appear – three deaths. The deaths of three guys Gary had gone to the school with, three guys Gary had known and who he regularly saw stoating about the town. One had died in a road accident, one had died following a prank and the third had killed himself. Since then another two had died. Guys the same age as Gary, guys that young.

Gary had had reservations about starting a scrapbook on death. It seemed a bit sick. But all this, his binoculars, his mags, his scrapbooks, all of it, it was all just for him, for him alone to look at and for him alone to look back on.

There was nothing to clip out the paper, though, just a photo of the new signing on the back page.

Gary cut it out and stuck it in volume five of the team's scrapbook. The team's scrapbooks covered all the games for the past twenty-odd years.

Gary put the scrapbook back in the drawer. Things were getting a bit tight, though, and Gary decided he would be just as well to spend some time and get them all sorted.

So Gary pulled out the drawer and lifted out the scrapbooks. As he shook them straight and tapped them on the carpet one of the scrapbooks fell apart. Gary laughed when he saw which one it was, the thinnest one, by far and away the thinnest one, and set it aside for a look-through once he'd got the others organized.

On the front of the scrapbook Gary'd set aside were written the words, 'Captain Trip'.

'I'm not going to do what you asked me to do.'

'What?'

'I said,' said Andy, 'I'm not going to do what you asked me to do.'

Recca returned from the toilet and Dunx whispered, 'Look, we'll talk about this the morrow, the morrow, right.'

Andy shrugged while Hazel, Deke and Carol were all sitting there wondering what the hell was going on.

Recca was too busy hunting out her matches to notice anything strange.

'Mind you've your work,' said Carol.

'Just a wee one for the road,' said Recca, 'just a thin one.'

Recca'd made this great big joke of being out of it for when Hazel arrived. It really all was just a joke to start with, but there was this kind of compulsion in Recca that told her that if she was out of it when Hazel arrived it would be like a victory, a slap in the face to the little runt. Recca's grannie, though, had a better name for it – cutting off your nose to spite your face. Now Recca was smoking out of another daft notion of hers, the one that told her how the more she smoked, the more she was able to control it. Stupid, but she believed it to be true.

'You off tomorrow?' said Carol.

'Yeah,' said Recca, 'start back the day after, overtime, an early.'

Deke couldn't help but notice how daft it all was with them all sitting there; Dunx staring at Andy; Andy staring intensely at nothing – so as to avoid having to look at Dunx; Recca concentrating on her thin one; and Deke, Carol and Hazel watching them, like they were sitting in on some kind of performance.

Deke caught Hazel's eye then slapped his hand across his gob as if to stop himself from giggling. Carol, who was sitting at Deke's feet, pinched the loose skin behind his heel to let him know it wasn't funny.

'I know what we can do,' said Deke, 'we'll stick that tape of yours on and see what it's like.'

'You probably won't like it,' said Hazel.

'Nah, you never know till you try. Hold on, here we go.'

They managed about ten seconds before Dunx erupted.

'That is just dreadful, absolutely fucking dreadful, get that garbage off.'

'Hey,' said Carol, 'less of it.'

'Well,' said Dunx, 'I hate classical music, hate all that stuff. And that's not even good stuff, that's shite stuff.'

'It's not classical music,' said Hazel. 'It's not called classical music.'

Dunx sniffed. 'Whatever it is it's fucking dreadful.'

Hazel went over and switched off the machine.

Recca said, 'I've got to get going now.'

'Hold on,' said Dunx, 'I'm coming with you.'

They all kind of mumbled their cheerios and then that was that.

'Eh,' said Deke to Andy, 'and what was all that about?'

Andy scratched at his itchy heel and said, 'He was wanting to go out with this lassie from the work the morrow night, and he was wanting me to say that he was at the game with me when he was out with her.'

'Christ,' said Carol, 'he's just a stupid wee laddie that. Will he ever grow up? Right, who's for coffee?'

'I'll get it,' said Andy, going through the kitchen so as he wouldn't have to talk about Dunx.

'She's just as bad,' said Carol, 'Recca's just as bad, that's how I was thinking they'd actually be good for each other. And did you see her, going to her work in that state?'

'She could get her cards for that,' said Deke. Deke went over to Recca's chair and put his hand down the side of the cushion. He held up a crumb and said, 'Ya beauty, a two-er.'

'What is it?' said Carol.

Deke passed it over.

'That was nice of her,' said Carol.

Andy returned. 'Eh, who takes what again?'

Carol said, 'Strong, one-and-a-half teaspoons, no milk, no sugar, half boiling water, half tap water.'

Deke said, 'Stronger, two-and-a-half teaspoons, milk and five sugar.'

Hazel didn't say anything, just had that look on her face that said something along the lines of 'If you don't know what I take in my coffee by now I'm going to fucking kill you, ya bastard.'

'Eh,' said Andy, 'it's milk and two sugar, eh?'

'One-and-a-half, and I like it weak. Just a half-teaspoon of coffee.'

'Aye,' said Andy, 'that's right' then disappeared back through the kitchen again.

'Mind like a sieve,' said Deke, 'it's 'cause he's an Aquarian. Can't help it. Great for the insights and that, but not the type of folk you'd want doing your rewiring, know what I mean.'

Hazel laughed. Despite the fact he was a total fruitcake, Hazel was quite fond of Deke. It was all a show he put on, of course, all an act, but she had to concede he was good at it.

Because Hazel felt so comfortable, Recca and Dunx having left, Hazel decided to do something Andy had always warned her against doing – she decided she would ask Deke a question. Andy called it 'interrogating folk and putting them on the spot'. Andy said mates didn't do things like that, mates ranted. Hazel thought fuck it, and decided to ask the question, anyway.

'Deke,' she said, 'how come you tell everybody you're A Poof Called God, and yet you're sitting here with a wife and two kids?'

Graeme was hiding in the bushes next the car park up the Kirk of the Holy Rood.

He'd had half a notion himself of going round to see Carol and Deke, knowing there would more than likely be a smoke on the go and that; in theory, he wouldn't have to use up any of his fags. Never worked out like that, though. Nah, false economy. Trouble was Graeme preferred his filter tips to Deke's wacky-backie. It was like Christmas when you got this right mountain of a dinner, course after course after course, and when the first thing you wanted once you were finished was some real food, a couple of selection boxes or that.

So instead of going round Graeme had amused himself by making up a tape for Carol's birthday, and, to give him something to do while he was doing this, Graeme had been rearranging all the pictures, postcards and posters on his walls. But the thing was as soon as he put them up again – the pictures fell, the posters flopped and the postcards flew. Even vigorous chewing of the blu-tack hadn't managed to reactivate the stickyness. Fuck it, he'd thought, he was earning good enough money so he'd be as well to spend some of it. So the jacket went on and the trainers went on and it was over to Ali's with the intention of investing in some Prittstick.

On his way back, however, Graeme had seen Fids coming in the direction Graeme was going.

And this was how Graeme came to be hiding in the bushes next to the car park up the Kirk of the Holy Rood.

It wasn't that Graeme disliked Fids, nobody really disliked Fids, it was just that when you saw Fids you tended to end up seeing a lot of Fids. Next thing you knew he'd be round at your door all the time and wanting to hang about with you and all that carry-on, worse than the Holy-holys he was.

Fids wasn't what you'd call thick or dangerous or dodgy or anything like that. Fact he was a good sort to have around when there was a problem – 'cause he'd do anything for any cunt, Fids would – but he was always wanting to be friends, always wanting to be awfy pally, and wanting to be pally with your pals. Fids himself didn't have any pals. He had half the town as acquaintances but he never had any real pals. Were Fids to pop his clogs in the morning it would be a fortnight before anyone'd notice he'd gone, then all at once fifteen thousand folk would all think or say, 'Haven't seen our Fids stoating about for a while.'

Graeme hid himself low and out of sight but kept his head up, keeping his eye on the notoriously short-sighted Fids. Should by any chance Fids spot him, Graeme would just explain it away as having been caught short and taking a dump. It just about summed Fids up to say that if things came to the worst, and Fids were to run off and tell folk he'd seen Graeme taking a dump, next to the Kirk of Holy Rood car park (as Fids would be sure to do, cause Fids told everybody everything), then all the subsequent laughter would be at the expense of Fids, 'cause everybody would know that all Graeme had been doing was avoiding Fids – something they'd done at one time or other.

Fids was approaching. Graeme lowered his head and peered through the bushes, commando-style. Fids was mumbling away to himself, fair worked up about something. Then again, Fids was always worked up about something or other. This was the guy, mind, who started everything with 'You're not going to believe this . . .' and proceeded to follow it up with a pile of shite nobody ever had the remotest interest in.

Graeme held his breath. Fids was less than four feet away. This was terrible, a terrible way to treat a fellow human being.

God, the stink, the stink. It was like being on the platform when the Inter-City went bombing through; 'cept here it was half a ton of Old Spice, not half a ton of diesel.

Fids passed but Graeme remained where he was until he could

see Fids cross the road and then cut through behind the community centre, heading up in the direction of Gary's or, more likely, Deke's. The coast now clear, Graeme emerged from the bushes and dusted himself down. He allowed himself a smile of satisfaction and awarded himself a fag, not a justifiable fag in terms of someone supposed to be giving up, but one Graeme felt he somehow merited. A happy fag, Graeme called it; a commando would have lit one too.

The fag became less a happy one, though, and more a ground-open-up-and-swallow-me one as Graeme turned and saw that he was being watched from the other side of the Kirk of the Holy Rood car park by a carful of laughing and grinning, tattooed-knuckled, black shell-suited famously psychotic Bampot Brothers.

After what had seemed like years of stoned and smashed plotting, Deke finally secured the loan of a bass guitar for Graeme, Andy got money off his folks to go out and get himself a keyboard, and Dunx said he'd be as well to be the singer.

Captain Trip was very much Deke's band. It was Deke that taught Graeme what he was supposed to do with the bass, likewise it was Deke who did all the arranging, and Deke who told Dunx all about microphone technique and helped him out, ostensibly with the spelling, of his lyrics.

The only musician Deke hadn't had to bother about was Gary.

Gary had drummed in groups all through school and college. He'd been a punk with Banana Vomit, a mod with All or Nothing, a new romantic with Eulogy and a goth with Essence of Hamburg. He'd even sat in for a couple of sessions with the Crawford Hughes quintet; serious middle-aged, middle-class guys who got together when the mood took them to to play just the one tune, a forty-minute improv. on the Theme From Highway To Heaven, which required Gary only to brush the cymbals for the first thirty-five minutes, then for the finale to go for it like Animal out the Muppets had never been invented.

In between groups Gary earned a few bob by doing cabaret gigs with the Bob Smith Trio, the Tom Nicol Trio, Sunshine, the Miami Music Machine etc, keeping time to 'Feelings', 'If you leave me now' and 'Just the way you are' at various golf clubs, works clubs, weddings and the like. It was all right for eyeing up the talent, and the money was good, but Gary wanted to be in a real band again, playing gigs or even just rehearsing, but to be in a real band.

Gary laughed out loud as he went through the Captain Trip scrapbook.

The photos showed the band rehearsing at Deke's old flat and up the huts at the old high school. Then there were those from the recording studio and from all of the gigs (the one in Kirkcaldy, the two in Edinburgh and the four up the town). Gary, or at least a part of him, appeared in every shot. While the rest of them were all striking moody poses, Gary would be caught in mid-action, making faces and gestures well beyond the call of his exertion.

The clippings included reviews from *Sounds* ('taking a Moulinex to the maggots on the corpse of Elvis'), NME ('like sandpaper on a baby's face'), the *Scotsman* ('strange, vaguely compelling') and several from the local rag, who were always awfy supportive of the 'angst-driven sounds' of Captain Trip.

There was more stuff from the fanzine end of things, including Gary's favourite, a half-page feature in a short-lived glossy that had cut a C-90's worth of Deke's ramblings into just two quotes, the one about how they were all signing on and the one about how they didn't sound like anyone else, with the journalist spending the bulk of the article going on about the 'greyness' and 'bleakness' of the town, which had actually been quite hurtful when it appeared in print.

It was all worth it for the photograph, though, Gary's all-time favourite photograph, the five of them lying on the floor in a circle with their heads at the centre. The published photo showed just their faces. Gary studied each face in turn.

Deke – eyes popping out sockets and mouth forming an O. Dunx – furrowed brow and bottom lip protruding. Graeme – looking as if he was going to burst. Andy – face creased and tilted to one side. Gary – grinning from ear to ear 'cause he'd just let the big one. Fucking classic.

The most lateral of prompts was all it took for Gary to tell folk how the short-lived career of Captain Trip had been the happiest time of his life. Equally, Gary was all for reforming and getting them all going again. They were still young enough. Christ, half the new bands were older than they were, and they were all doing stuff that Captain Trip were doing years ago.

But with the closure of the rehearsal hut up the old high school and the arrival of Baby Joe (not to mention the death threats from Deke's new neighbours), The Trip had gone into a hibernation that had turned into a limbo.

Gary couldn't even land a gig on the cabaret circuit these days after the time halfway through a wedding reception when temptation had got the better of him and Gary left his drumstool to go and stick his head down the front of a bridesmaid's frock. The lass herself seemed quite taken by this show of affection but the other guests weren't so chuffed and Gary had to make like the Roadrunner, evading first the clutches and then the bottles and the cans of the evening guests.

He didn't even have his kit anymore, he'd had to sell it 'cause of the debacle in Kirkcaldy. Since then Gary had kept his hand in by getting his sticks out, arranging the cushions on his coffee table and hammering away to his heart's content. He maybe wasn't the greatest drummer in the world, but there was never anyone who put in quite as much practise when it came to making the faces.

Dunx was wild.

It was just so Andy to turn everything into a drama, typical of him. Had to give it his wee moralistic bit. Had to show-off in front of the sour-faced little sweetheart. Had to be Mr Morality, the man who could do no wrong.

Dunx turned the tap on to fill the kettle. He missed the spout, though, and the surge of water rebounded and soaked everything in sight. Dunx tried again, this time taking the lid off the kettle.

Make no mistake, had to be the little runt that had put him up to it, had to be. The conniving, stuck-up stunted little runt that looked like something out of a Poundstretchers Wendy House. *Her.* Christ, you didn't have to go all like that just 'cause you had yourself a girlfriend, you didn't have to get all jumped-up and jumpered like Tories on Sundays. Nah, not Andy, though, no not Andy, oh no, not Andy, Andy's got to be the little yes-man, Andy's got to be under the thumb, Andy's got to tuck his shirt in his underpants, Andy's got to . . .

Dunx looked in the cupboard to see coffee jars full of beans and pasta and spices that had lain there since the day Dunx arrived, and would probably still be lying there the day Dunx left for all the cooking she ever done for him, but no fucking toast.

And what the hell right had Andy to go off blabbering to the little runt for, anyway? What was Dunx just after saying to him the night walking down the road? Something 'bout friendship, wasn't it? Something 'bout mates, wasn't it? Christ, many's the time Dunx had done things for Andy, many's the time. The nights he'd gave Andy a shoulder to cry on, hundreds, hundreds of them. Well, never again. That was that. Him and his problems could bug some other space, and, Christ, Andy'd have to go a hell of a long way before he'd find anyone who'd put up with all that shit the way Dunx had.

Dunx looked in the freezer – no toast, only frozen veg and pizzas. Dunx screwed his face up as he considered the prospect of his first ever pizza. Nah, vile, disgusting things they were. Looked like beans on toast that some fat bastard had sat on.

And what was all this with blurting it out in front of everybody, anyway? What the hell was all that about? It was nothing to do with them, nothing to do with any of that shower. No, but Andy's got to be formal now, Andy's got to make an announcement, Andy's got to put a notice in the paper, Andy's got to . . . No, but that was it, Andy was getting seriously out of fucking order. The guy was needing to give himself the serious shake, not just any old serious shake, but the ultimate serious shake – he was going to have to dump her. That's what he was going to have to do.

Dunx looked through the fridge. In the tray at the bottom there was a selection of two-day old veg that had lost its shine so Dunx did his weekly housework and bucketed the lot.

Oh aye, and there had been Deke sitting there. Mr I-am-the-happiest-man-in-Christendom. How the blazes could he ever profess to be so fucking happy when Carol was only the third lassie he'd ever been out with in his entire life? The third, number three out of one-and-a-half billion and, there you go, hey, eternal bliss. Aye right. For a guy that was supposed to be so adventurous when it came to his pharmaceutical intake, he was helluva fucking conservative when it came down to settling down with a woman.

Dunx looked through what else was in the fridge: eggs – no toast; beans – no toast; peanut butter – no toast; jam – no toast; honey – no toast; pot noodle – no toa- . . . how d'you make a pot noodle?

No, no, this wouldn't do. It didn't matter what any of them thought. Let them tut-tut, let them moralise-moralise, let them all head down to B&Q on a Sunday afternoon, just let them. If that's what they wanted then let them get on with it. If that's what turned them on then fine, fine for them. There were better things to do in life. Dunx was going to go out with that Heather. Dunx was going to party with that Heather. To hell with them, Dunx was going to go and have a good time.

Dunx read the instructions on the pot-noodle . . . was that all you were supposed to do? Christ, any cunt could do that.

The kettle clicked off and Dunx made himself a pot noodle.

'It all came from when I was at the school,' said Deke. 'See I hardly ever went to the school, just hung about with my brother, getting into everything. Cause of that I was shunted into all the different classes, all the different streams as they were, and I ended up in what they called the C-stream, the C-stream with all the psychos of the day. And 'cause I had the hair down to the arse, the cheese-cloth shirt and all the beads and bangles and that they all started saying I was a poof; and I could never be bothered disagreeing with them 'cause all I was ever bothered about was no getting battered. Telling you, you ask any cunt, all you ever do at the school is spend your time avoiding getting battered, that's all you ever learn, should get certificates for it. Anyway, we never got proper classes in the C-stream, all we ever got were remedial classes and religious education with that old bastard from over the road there. And me and him just did not hit it off one little bit; 'cause I done all my reading back then, and I was asking him all these brilliant questions, and he just wasn't digging it at all. So I was telling him how I was God and that, started signing my name "God" all the time, and it stuck.'

'So it was all just a joke,' said Hazel.

Deke looked affronted. 'Was it fuck a joke. No, I was right into it.' Deke paused. 'Still am, to tell you the truth.'

'Aye, right,' said Hazel.

'Don't get him started,' warned Carol, shaking her head, 'just don't get him started. He is not joking.'

'No,' said Deke, 'there's a lot of cheapos going round these days, giving the old I-am-God business a bad name.'

'Come on,' said Hazel. 'you mean to say . . . .'

Hazel was interrupted by a knock at the door, a weak knock, a do-not-disturb of a knock. Then there was a loud whisper going, 'Deke . . . Der-ek . . . Deke . . . Der-ek . . . Deke . . . .'

Carol got up.

'Just leave it, love,' said Deke. 'He'll go away.'

'He'll wake the kids,' said Carol and went to get the door.

'It's rotten the way you lot treat him,' said Hazel.

Deke shook his head and pocketed his bit before Carol returned.

'Alright there,' said Fids. 'Hey, you been hearing what's been happening?'

'Hearing what?' said Deke.

'Bout Smiddy? Got busted. Quarter past six the night.'

'You're joking?'

'Aye, bad scene, Deke. Guess what? His folks were round.'

'No,' said Carol.

'Aye, got hauled down the station, the lot of them. Smiddy, Debs, Old Peggy and Geordie. John-Jo was there as well. I was round seeing Shona and Josey, it was them that was telling us, like.'

Deke laughed. 'God help the poor bastard that has to give Old Peggy the strip-search. She'll stiffen the fucker.'

They all laughed but Fids laughed like the thought of it was funny as anything. He pushed his hand through his long, greasy hair and smiled to reveal the worst set of dentures Hazel had yet come across. Hazel'd heard or read somewhere that all this smoking carry-on was really bad for the teeth, taking out all the calcium or something like that. The likes of Deke and Recca were dental disasters, but they were straight out a Colgate ad next to Fids.

No, Hazel decided, Fids really was a mess, the guy just hadn't a clue. He had on: a buttoned leather jacket that would have been far too wee even for Hazel; the tightest, most uncomfortable, almost indecent, pair of black drainpipes; the biggest and brightest high-tops this side of anything that had been seen at Cape Kennedy; and, because he was trying to be hip, although five years too late, a maroon, hooded top with a bronze sun motif peeling at the corners; and then the hair, the guy seriously had to do something with his hair – presently, it was half-in, half-out of a ponytail.

'You selling?' said Fids. 'I've money, like.'

Deke held up the crumb that Recca had dropped.

Fids laughed. 'Aye, I can see you've been giving it a good seeing to.' Fids sliced his arms through the smoky atmosphere. 'Any idea who might be selling?'

Deke shook his head and started skinning up the crumb.

Fids looked round. He still hadn't sat down. All the seats were taken and the floor was covered in fragile-looking toys. The only space available was the spot Fids was standing on, so, wiping his palms on his drainpipes, Fids went down on his haunches.

'Christ, every Cunt's sitting on it, Deke, and here's me with the money . . . Seen anything of Millsy lately?'

Deke shook his head.

'What about Heinz, you seen Heinz?'

'Just keep ourselves to ourselves, Fids.'

Fids went down so as he was kneeling and sitting on his heels. 'Who you getting your bit from these days, anyway?'

'Ho ho ho. Now that would be telling.'

Fids took the hint. 'Can't trust no cunt these days. See this town, Deke, this town is hoaching with the Feds, absolutely hoaching, they're everywhere. I tell you about what happened to me that time up the park when I was going over to see the Smudge-man? No? Well, I was going through the park, right, when I sees this council workie with a walkie-talkie, man. Now, tell us, when's the last time you seen a council workie with a walkie-talkie, eh? Cunt tried to hide it from us but I seen him, I seen him alright. Same with Fat George, he was saying he seen them and all. Know how the council've got them new vans, the blue VW's? Well, some of them's no the council, Deke; no, some of them's the DS. Aye, Fat George says he seen them piling out the station one day and piling into a van, with all the overalls and that on.'

Fids sniffed for the sixth time since he'd come in, wiped his hand across his nose for the fourth time, put his hand through his hair for the seventh time and rubbed his palms on his drainpipes for the twelfth time.

'You better watch yourself,' said Carol to Deke.

Deke nodded.

'Aye,' said Fids. 'Need eyes in the back of your nut.'

As Deke finally licked the rice-paper he spotted a bead of sweat forming on the left corner of Fids's lower lip.

'Perfect,' said Deke and held up his handiwork for all to see then put it on the mantelpiece, folded his arms and said, 'Well, that's my breakfast sorted – what we going to do now?'

And being an arsehole of number one proportions it was the bus that was the transport, not the train, which was now affordable, easily affordable in fact, or even the blooming plane which was within budget, no, got to be the fucking bus, the good old boneshaker, the good old rocking and rolling, freezing and boiling, toing and froing, scary and frightening built for folk under four foot eleven, bus. And why the good old bus? Cause the good old bus stops outside the mother's door, five hundred miles it goes and stops outside the mother's door. Fucking hell. Brilliant, eh? Takes five times longer than the fucking train, and's five times infinity more uncomfortable but, by God, it stops outside the mother's door. Fucking obnoxious, fucking unpleasant and genuinely fucking painful but it goes five hundred miles and, know what, actually stops outside the mother's door. That no fucking brilliant?

And the thing is all this is just to please other folk – aye, other folk. Got to go back to the old shitehole, the only corner of the cosmos where Runrig is cool, where smoking is cool and where the national drink is made from fucking girders, aye, all that just to go and please other folk. It was a case of this had to be done or else.

Well, once it was done, that was it over and done with, and never again. And if it ever was ever again it was definitely never again on the bus where it was always the fucking same, the exact fucking same, always getting seriously tanked up with the sole intention of being effectively unconscious for the duration, but, oh no, never quite manage to pull it off. No, just get stuck at the old incontinence stage, the old 'There will be an incredible urge to constantly empty the bladder, a function which will prove to be necessary exactly every thirty-seven minutes.'.

And it's off to the cludge, off to the cludge, off to the good old cludge every thirty-seven minutes. And every thirty-seven minutes it's time to trip over the outstretched limbs of the blue-eyed, blonde-haired Scandinavians, who, being born and brought up in the way they'd been born and brought up, are all either naked or near-naked, barely covered by their wee blankets and wee rugs, looking so fucking peaceful and so fucking content that they ought to be shot, yeah shot, shot several times through the head, shot with bazookas, really big bazookas, fucking huge bazookas, man, biggest fucking bazookas in the history of the bazooka-verse.

Anyway, next it's the old cludge, and the cludge is absolutely swimming in it, absolutely swimming, but there's no point in caring anymore, not worth a care, not an iota, nah don't care 'cause there's never ever been anyone else using the old cludge, has there? No, apart from number one arsehole, no one, so it's pretty obvious who's guilty of piddling the puddles, eh? And when the flush gets pressed the flush never works, it gets pressed again and again, but it all just swills one way then it all just swills the other way then – wheech – back over the pan and all over the feet and all over the jeans. Ha bloody ha.

Then it's back through the obstacle course of the gorgeous and naked limbs of the gorgeous and naked Scandinavians, thinking this can't be real, this just can't be real. Then it's stamped and sealed and delivered back at seat No 33, when there he is, he's still there, seat No 34, he's still fucking there, him holding his once-bitten cheese and pickle piece like it's been spiked with one of those superfast Thrush paralysing poisons – one bite and, phttt, dead, just like that. Madame Toussaud's, eat your heart out. Cause that's what he's like, him sitting there with his gob wide open, his gob wide open and making no sound, making no movement and making no sound whatsoever, none at all. Smelling a wee bit, mind you. And, hey, hold on, man, this was serious ... was he dead, or was he no dead? That was the question. Come on – surely when folk snuffed it there was some kind of audible or physical gesture they came away prior to actually snuffing it that translated as, 'Christ, son, the game's a bogie, I just thought I'd let you know case you wanted to shift your seat'?

But, nah, this old guy had never moved, never budged or never done a thing, just sat there, being really fucking irritating.

Just like the guy across the aisle with his personal stereo, he was really fucking irritating and all, him with his, guess what, yeah, Runrig, going on again and again and again – guess why? Cause he's got a really expensive personal stereo, that's why, and it's got auto-reverse, hasn't it, and this thing is never going to go off until he switches it off, that's why. And this guy, this guy is snoring like he ain't going to wake up till there's a fucking crash and St Peter tickles his fucking toes at the Pearly Gates.

And a fatal crash was the only thing that was ever going to shut up the four Japanese in front; from the way they were at it they were never going to shut up, never ever going to shut up. No, sirree, no way. What the hell were they on about anyway, what the hell could they possibly have to go on about that could be so terribly fucking enthralling that they could go on all through the fucking night about it? Not just what were they on about but what the hell were they on period? Had to be something. The four of them all whispering away, all whispering away apart from when they were fucking giggling, and, by Christ, they were fucking giggling a hell of a bastarn lot alright, giggling a damn sight more than any human being had ever earned the bastarn right to fucking giggle. Strange bastards, the Japanese. Had to be taking the piss, had to be. Mean had to be loaded to get over here in the first place so they could surely afford to be doing something decent with their time and with their dosh . . . and why were they taking the bus, anyway? At least there was a wee bit of a reason when you could tell folk that you'd been on a bus that had travelled five hundred mile and stopped right outside the mother's door.

The Japanese started giggling again.

Fids made out he had to go and see if he could find himself a bit somewhere else. It was Deke who saw him to the door, telling Fids it would be for the best not to call round for a while since things were a bit heavy. Fids said okay, and how he'd been intending keeping a bit of a low-profile, anyway, wanting to get himself sorted out a bit and that.

'Did you give him a row?' said Carol.

'Nah,' said Deke, 'didn't have the heart. We're all the poor sod's got.'

'Guy's a total cling-on,' said Andy, 'don't like him, don't like him at all.'

'All that stuff about the council workies,' said Hazel. 'He's off his head.'

'No,' said Andy, 'that's true, love, that's true.'

'Oh aye,' added Deke, 'every cunt knows that.'

It took a second for Hazel to realize that no, they weren't joking.

Deke lit up his breakfast then wandered over to the hifi. 'I'll shove your tape back on. See what it's like.'

'You probably won't like it,' said Hazel.

'Nah, I'm in the mood, in the mood for something different, for something new and exciting.'

Deke shifted some of the toys and lay on the floor.

The music went on for a couple of minutes before Deke finally spoke. 'You know what this is like?' he said. 'This is like the Dead Sea. No, it is. It's like floating on the Dead Sea. There's no current so you don't go anywhere, you just float. But that doesn't matter, no, that doesn't matter, cause where you are is just the best, oh, the best alright. Just so beautiful, just so peaceful, just so, so good . . . Minds me of that smoke we got off that Australian bloke with the wooden leg. Mind, Walter Whatyoumacallhim?'

Everybody laughed. Hazel was pleased, she could see that Deke was smiling and that he was really into it.

'Whose tunes are these?' said Carol.

'Mine,' said Hazel, 'all mine.'

'And you play them all yourself?' said Deke.

Hazel nodded. 'Just me, me on trumpet and piano. They said I was very good for my age.'

'How old were you?' said Carol.

'Twelve.'

'Twelve?' said Deke. 'Twelve year-old and playing your own compositions on the bloody trumpet. Christ almighty.'

Hazel laughed.

'Telling you, sir,' Deke addressed Andy. 'You should be bloody proud of this lassie. Bloody proud. If this was Carol doing this and some bloke made a joke of it, I'd fucking panel the cunt.'

Andy gulped and Hazel cast him a glance that said, 'See.'

'Just relax,' said Deke, talking to everybody. 'Just relax. Look, just imagine it. You're floating on these lovely, still waters. 'Member, you're not going anywhere 'cause you don't need to, you don't need to do anything, you can just relax.'

It would've taken a couple of bullets to the head to get Andy to relax. Here he was with his two best mates totally against him, Hazel looking at him like he was the antichrist. Well, so what if she was some kind of child genius, that wasn't necessarily everybody's cup of tea, was it? And as for the morrow, and what Dunx was going to be like, God knew. All Andy knew for sure was that he was going to be getting it in the neck all morning, all dinner, all afternoon, all . . .

Andy stopped. He couldn't believe what his eyes were seeing. She was taking a blast; Hazel was taking a blast. This was amazing. Deke never offered her a smoke, nobody ever offered a smoke. She always went on about teeth, and about Fids, Recca and Deke being the paranoid, the bitter and the refugee from the planet Freak-Out. Hazel took another blast.

It was with unabashed pride and joy that Andy watched Hazel take yet another blast, her third, then another, her fourth! Christ, she was hogging!

Hazel, though, coughed and spluttered after the fifth.

'Alright,' said Deke.

'A-ha,' said Hazel, 'Just had this wee panic attack about being strip-searched by my binmen on Thursday morning.'

Taking the Sauchiehall Street option, she took the left at the third roundabout. That was her on the Champs Elysees. Taking a right on the second roundabout of the Champs Elysees got her onto the neon lights of Broadway. From there it was on until the third on the right, the one she was wanting, Oxford Street.

About half a mile down Oxford Street she reached the plant

where she was supposed to be meeting up with her colleague, and Recca got off the works' bicycle and promptly coughed her guts up.

The factory was a fair size, twice the size of the town, and still growing. Recca could spend half her working day just going from here to there.

There were two ladders to go up and one to go down before Recca made it to the control room where she met up with her colleague, and where they went over all the readings with the process boys, seeing if there was anything unusual.

Recca hated shutdowns. It was a hectic time for folk whose work normally demanded little physical effort. That meant most of them and Recca especially, with everybody bombing about all over the place, up and down the ladders and opening and closing valves. Some of the older guys always needed a day or two off after a shutdown, complaining of pulls and sore backs. It wasn't just the physical thing, though, it was a mental strain as well. While shutting down one part of the work gave employment to some, like Deke, on the short-term cleaning and maintenance contracts, the folk who were full-time, like Recca, had to get everything ready, had to monitor everything that was going on and had to make sure everything else was unaffected. It was like doing something blind.

Shutdowns also meant Recca had to work nightshifts. Normally, she was just nine-to-five but now with the big-wigs all safely tucked up in their beds, she got a buzz out of knowing that she was the only woman in the factory, and also that she was the highest paid of anybody working at that time of the night, a joke she shared with others by wearing her spare hard hat, the one with the 'The Boss' black-markered on the front.

Recca was good at her job. She was good at getting on with the folk and she knew her stuff. Being a non-male brought problems, though.

A few of the blokes' wives were said to be having sleepless nights when they heard of this temptress being left alone with their feeble-minded easily-led spouses. The work being what it was stories circulated at changeovers and the like. The stories went round out of boredom, mostly, just the guys taking the piss out of each other. But try telling that to their wives. Who was this woman?

And why was it that they were always having these sore backs at the same time as she was around? Surely the work wasn't that hard. Up and down ladders for twelve hours non-stop? Aye, that'll be right.

One of the suits in executive corridor got to hear about all this and hauled Recca up to explain herself. Even though the guys had all stood up for her, saying it was all just a joke, Recca still got a ticking off like she'd did something wrong.

Recca and her colleague went out to take some readings of their own, and while the air couldn't exactly be called fresh Recca was grateful for it. God knows why she did things like this, getting herself completely wasted when she was supposed to be going to her work. It was stupid, really stupid; it was crying out for help, that's what it was. A sackable offence as well. She could get reported and, no questions asked, next thing she knew she'd be out on her arse. And there were enough misogynistic busybodies around only too willing to set the ball in motion.

Back in the control room, one such beast was in full flow.

'You see the state of that the night? High as a kite, high as a flipping kite. That's supposed to be our top engineer? Christ, that's not fit to lay the table. Telling you, Rab, I've a good mind to report that. Aye, I have. What d'you reckon, Rab? Think we should?'

Rab didn't answer, just shook his head. It wasn't so much a negative shake in response to the question more a response to the whole situation. 'Cause Rab knew that the lassie, whose name was Recca, was one of the crew that his daughter Hazel was mucking about with these days – and Rab was imagining the worst.

'. . . and it's really, really huge, you want to see the size of the thing, it's massive. And it's green, uh-huh, totally green, like really thick pea soup. And it's got these great big, blue plastic things sticking out its head, they're big and they're blue and they're plastic and they're like big, blue sticks of rock with silver stars on the end. And it's, and it's, and it's, and it's got one eye, just the one eye, and it goes up and down, the eye just goes up and down like that, goes up and down like that. Just up and down, doesn't go across, but it's a great big eye, the size of a football, so it doesn't need to go from side to side 'cause it can see everything 'cause the eye's that massive. And it's got these great big monster feet, three of them. One there and one there and one there and all. Three great big monster feet with these great big, fat hairy toes, like sausages. And when it's angry, when it's angry, when it's really angry, its face gets bigger. gets ginormous, and its mouth opens right up and you can see right down, right down its throat, right down to its belly-button, the inside of its belly-button. Uh-huh. And its got these teeth, right, these teeth, and these teeth are green, these teeth are really dark green, bottle green, really dark, and they're really sharp, like a shark's, sharp like a shark's. And it's gonni, it says it's gonni, it's gonni . . . It says it's from the centre of the earth, a place called Hooliahoopialand. Uh-huh. And it says it's come here to steal me and take me back to great King Harrow in Hooliahoopialand. And that, and that, and that great King Harrow is going to make me do all the horrible things and make me be a slave. Oh, and it's really stinking, it really stinks, it's ponging really bad, like dog's dirt. And it's all slimy and greasy and dripping on the carpet. And it's . . .'

'Wow,' said Deke, 'total wow. And this thing's through in your room?'

'A-ha,' said Joanne.

Deke couldn't have been more impressed if Joanne had recited Shakespeare backwards in Latin.

'Come on,' said Deke, 'I have got to see this. Lead the way.'

'Hurry up,' said Joanne. 'Oh, and can I have some juice, please?'

It was Carol who replied. 'No!'

Joanne screwed her face up and her and Deke went through to see the monster that had taken up residence in her room.

'Does she do that often?' said Hazel.

Carol shook her head. 'Nah, she's just showing off 'cause you lot are in. She's just a little Miss Show-off. Wonder who she gets it from?'

The air was tasting of stale chewing gum – the way it always tasted first thing in the morning – and the folks at the bus stop were standing about looking like they were auditioning for parts in a

new Russian film, *Queueing For Cabbage* – the way they always
looked first thing in the morning.

All that was apart from Andy – poor Andy, who through the
night had only managed to amass a total of fifteen minutes of sleep,
but somehow in that fifteen minutes had contrived to contort
himself in such a way so as to jigger his neck.

Andy had jiggered his neck 'cause Andy had spent the night on
the settee.

Andy had spent the night on the settee cause Hazel had told
him to spend the night on the settee.

It all started when Andy'd said as how he was really pleased
for Hazel for having taken a smoke. Hazel had asked why it was
that Andy was so pleased. Andy'd said he was pleased 'cause
Hazel had done something that couldn't have been easy for her.
Hazel pointed out that it wasn't difficult, and that all sorts of
morons did it. Andy'd said that that wasn't what he'd meant, what
he'd meant was that she would no longer be feeling left out. Hazel
had wondered aloud as to whether she'd been left out before.
Andy'd told her to calm down and not to go into one of her moods
. . . and that was Hazel started: going on about how Andy wasn't
pleased for her at all, how he was pleased for everybody else 'cause
she would no longer be an embarrassment. Then she went on about
how Dunx and Recca had been rotten to her, and about how Andy
hadn't stuck up for her. Andy'd said yes that was true and that he
was sorry but that she was being unreasonable in not allowing him
to say so. *Ouch.* Unreasonable was not the right word to use, Andy
told Hazel he was sorry again and asked her to calm down and
went over to give her a cuddle. It was then that Hazel picked up
the ornamental knife she used for opening envelopes and said,
'Come near me and I'll stake you, ya bastard.'

So Andy had spent the night on the settee.

'Alright.'

It was Dunx.

'Alright,' said Andy.

Dunx sniffed. 'I'm saying nothing about last night,' he said. 'I'm
saying absolutely nothing about you last night. I'm saying nothing.'

Andy sniffed.

'That was fucking out of order, though, seriously out of order. Absolutely shocking.'

Andy scuffed his feet and lowered his head as far as it could go. 'I just want you to know that what I do with my private life is not for public broadcast. And I'll party with who the fuck I want to party with.'

Andy sighed. This would go on all day. The sarky remarks and the Richter Scale silent treatment, the self-pity and the you-know-what-your-problem-is, the defiance and the assaults. It was all a waste of time. But try telling him that. Try telling him anything. He was hurtful, Dunx was, he was cutting. He'd slag off Andy and he'd slag off Hazel, and Andy would never respond. It was like last night with Hazel. Hazel had been wrong. Dunx was wrong and all. But Andy couldn't explain it to them 'cause Andy couldn't explain anything to anybody.

Andy's trouble with his neck meant he could only look in the direction he was pointing in. Which meant that when the London bus pulled in across the road Andy had no choice but to watch the folk getting off. First there was a fat woman with t-shirt and jeans who went round the back to get her luggage, then a couple got off, then an old guy, fag in mouth and carrier-bag clutched to his chest, and lastly a bloke with a sports bag and a serious leather jacket.

'Fucking hell,' said Andy. 'Check that, see who it is.'

Dunx looked over. 'Oh yes,' he said. 'ALRIGHT THERE, SIR!'

The bloke with the leather jacket waved across then got down on his hands and knees and kissed a puddle before giving it the I-am-not-worthy bit a couple of times. Finally, he got up and delivered a healthy 'WE'RE BLUE! WE'RE WHITE! WE'RE FUCKING DYNA-MITE! . . . .'

So next thing Eddie knew he was being introduced to a bloke called Stan and travelling out to a place that went by the name of ET City.

The way Eddie told it, London was made up of Nigels, Simons and Trevors, none of whom could understand any cunt that talked faster than the Queen on mogadon. The saving grace was the dosh, coming out with five hundred in your hand each and every week.

'Five hundred?' Dunx was in awe, and going by the way the van swerved, so was Stan.

'Christ, man,' said Andy, 'you could've flown up.'

'Nah, slight shortage of funds at the moment.'

'Ih?' said Dunx. 'Come again?'

'Well, look at it this way, what would you do if somebody gave you five hundred a week?'

The response was automatic. 'Spend it.'

'Exactly – and what about the bills?'

'Ach, fuck the bills, man.'

'Right again – 'cepting the bastards've been catching up with us. Nothing serious, like. Just got to be careful.' Eddie hated having to lie about all this but the truth of the matter was just too stupid, and, anyway, there was an extent to which bumming about the amount of money he had would be a bit sick. It wasn't just that he had money they didn't, he had money in his pocket that they didn't, money in his bank that they didn't and even money he didn't really need that they didn't. The joke was that Eddie worked the same hours as Andy and Dunx, the exact same hours.

The van stopped and they picked up Heather, Big Caroline and Tony. Heather smiled at Dunx and gave a big 'Hiya.'

'How's the good Captain these days?' said Eddie. 'Still striving away?'

Dunx laughed. 'Nah, The Trip's in a state of permanent hold, jacked it in.'

'What, how come? Deke too busy away suing that David Icke bastard for nicking his act?'

Dunx and Andy laughed.

'Was round seeing him last night,' said Andy.

'Aye? Still stinking of incense and patchouli?'

'Nah,' said Dunx, 'no quite that bad.'

'Christ,' said Eddie, 'mind the night I went there? The most boring fucking night of my life. Can't handle all that crap.'

Dunx laughed. 'Deke's too into all that. Going on about using drugs all the time, using them, no just taking them and partying, but using them.'

'Fucking pish, man,' said Eddie. 'Was the same down our bit

with all the rave scene. All started out with just the kids getting out their faces and partying, fucking brilliant, then along comes the rent-a-hippy crew with all their pish. A free mind never pays the bills, man. See them crusty bastards, line them up and shoot the fucking lot of them.'

'Too right,' said Dunx. 'How long you up for, anyway?'

'Heading back Monday night. Work Tuesday morning. You still staying at your mam's?'

Dunx blushed. 'Nah, I'm staying at Recca's . . . living with her, like.'

'What d'you mean "Living with her"? Aye, living off her more like. Christ, you never change. Mind at the school when every other cunt was sticking their rulers up lassies' skirts, you were after them to do your fucking homework.'

Dunx let loose a nervous giggle. He was a wee bit hesitant 'cause of Heather being there, not something he was really wanting at this moment in time.

Eddie clapped his hands then rubbed them. 'Right,' he said, 'all set for the night then? Up see the game then out for a few bevs, aye?'

'Sounds brilliant to me,' said Dunx, 'sounds brilliant to me.'

This wee exchange between Eddie and Dunx didn't provoke any spoken reaction but in terms of body language Andy's brow was going, 'You're just after saying . . .' and Heather's eyes were pleading, 'But what about me?'

It was breaktime and apart from Ped, the health fanatic with the porn obsession, and old Dickie, who'd stopped at seven minutes past six on Tuesday the thirteenth of February, 1973, affording himself an annual trip over to see his daughter in Canada with the proceeds, the rest of them were smokers.

Greg withdrew his chair from the table, planked himself down then reclined it on two legs so as he was leaning against the wall. Then he lit up what he called, 'the only pleasure I get in life'. A series of smoke-rings followed each inhalation. He did that all the time, right down to the cork.

Usually Robert, who was the chain-talking chain-smoker, just

smoked roll-ups but when the bosses were around, Robert said a
lot about himself by producing a packet of B&H. Presently he was
rolling a thin one.

Phil was the boss, a serious forty-a-day man till his kid was
diagnosed asthmatic. Since then his wife had banned him from
smoking in the home and he'd had to halve the habit. Phil was
always lighting up, and this was always annoying Graeme, who
didn't smoke at work, 'cause whenever Phil would light up, he
would get called up the stairs or have to go and do something,
leaving his fag to burn away in the ashtray, and leaving Graeme
drooling.

But for Graeme, the fascinating one was Glasgow Kenny who
each and every day brought in a different brand of fags. It wasn't
even as if there was one particular brand of fags he favoured, no
brand of fags appeared two days running and no brand of fags
appeared more often than any other brand of fags. Now this was
weird 'cause smokers were loyal folk and stuck with their brands.
Okay, they occasionally checked out the new cheapos, but they
never bought flaming different packets every day.

The funny thing about all this was that when Glasgow Kenny
had with him one of the less common brands, Graeme would catch
a whiff and recall to mind some long-forgotten acquaintance
who'd smoked this brand. Not only that but each time this brand
reappeared, Graeme would remember more and more about this
person or other. Like today Glasgow Kenny was on the Winston,
and Graeme was remembering an Italian guy at college who'd
came through to the Captain Trip gig in Kirkcaldy and had tried it
on with Carol in the back of the van on the way back when
everyone was out of it.

Glasgow Kenny lit up. As the smoke swam over the name that
had been on the tip of Graeme's tongue for the past few weeks
finally dripped off. Andrea, the guy's name was Andrea.

The warehouse held and dispatched electrical components. Most of
their orders went to the north of England. Some, though, went
abroad and when Graeme joined he'd been disturbed to find out
that their regular shipments to France were immediately rerouted
to South Africa, thereby passing the trade barrier. That was a bit
nasty, but ethics went out the window when it came down to work.

Graeme liked it here, and if it wasn't for the Ministry of Defence they'd lose half their contracts, anyway.

The tea-break over, Phil headed upstairs and everybody went back to work. When Phil wasn't around Robert oversaw the paperwork and answered the phone. Robert fancied himself for the promotion when Phil went upstairs permanently. Phil, though, had told Graeme that when this happened, and it would be soon, very soon, that it would be Graeme who would be getting the job 'cause the bosses all knew that Robert smoked roll-ups when they weren't around.

As it was, Graeme was nearly running the place. Whenever Ped or Greg had a problem, it was Graeme that they asked. It was the same with Glasgow Kenny and Old Dickie, neither of whom cared a lot for Robert.

A wee bit of friendly commotion started up on account of Ped and Greg discovering they'd made an arse of it when they weighed one of the outgoing parcels only to discover they'd packed what appeared to be twice the number of components they were supposed to have.

The subsequent battle with the polystyrene filling subsided when Phil returned with the new bloke, the bloke that was supposed to be starting the day.

'Fuck, look who it is,' whispered Ped.

Graeme looked. He watched the guy withdraw the packet from his pocket and he watched the guy light up.

You could tell a lot about folk from the way they smoked, and equally there were times when you could tell a lot about folk from what they smoked. Such was the case in this instance – cause everybody knew all the Bampots smoked wee Regal.

'Could you tell me please why the fuck Dunx's clothes are lying all over the living-room floor?'

Recca yawned a big one then lifted up the covers to look at the clock. 'Half twelve. Fuck the fuck off, will you.'

'Nah,' said Carol, 'I've had one of those days and you're going to hear all about it. Wanting coffee?'

A groan came from under the bedclothes.

Carol went downstairs and stuck the kettle on. She looked for bread to make toast but there wasn't any so she used some slices from the loaf she'd bought for herself.

While the kettle was boiling and the grill was grilling, Carol went through and had another look at the living-room. Sure enough, clinging to the furniture, covering the floor and curled up in the corners were a decade's worth of jackets, t-shirts, jeans, tops, trackie-b's and footwear. It looked like a teenage party, only the bobbing bare bums were missing.

'Rhubarb and ginger jam on toast, served with black coffee. Right, wanting to hear all about the day I've had?'

A hand came out from under the covers and grabbed a bit of toast. Then one of the hands' fingers made stabby points in the direction of the dresser.

'In a minute,' said Carol.

A puppy-like whine came from under the covers and Carol went over to the dresser.

'Got it,' said Carol. 'Just be a minute. You mind of that cow Lizzie-Anne McBride? Her that used to go out with your Martin? Well, at the school this morning she comes storming up to me, and I'm thinking to myself, oh-oh what's going on here, and up she comes, bold as you like, and says, "Mrs Henderson", she says, "Mrs Henderson, I don't appear to have any record of you paying up your shoe menage last week". Telling you, right in front of all the mothers, she comes away with this and brings out her wee note-book. And I'm like this, I'm just mortal. "Oh," I says, "I'm sorry, I completely forgot, I'm terribly sorry, Lizzie-Anne." And so I gets my purse out and pays her right there and then. And you know it was just as well it was the day she asked 'cause I was just heading up the town for messages, and that's why I had the money. What a brasser to give somebody, though, eh? Right in front of every-body. Could tell she never believed me, just looked at me like I was muck, but I'm no caring. See the likes of her, she's one of them that's life's that boring they don't actually realise that it is actually possible to actually forget things, that it's a fairly normal thing to do.'

The whining noises under the covers became more desperate, almost coyote-like.

'In a minute, in a minute. You try feeding a bairn and skinning up at the same time.'

Recca keeked out to see that this was indeed the case.

'Anyway,' said Carol, 'then I goes over the town and takes Baby Joe down for his check-up. He's alright, by the way, but I asks Dr Naylor about all this with Joanne getting up in the middle of the night and coming away with all these stories of hers, and guess what he puts it down to? What else, diet, of course. Too many sweets, he says, too many sweet things. And he's looking at me like it's my fault, like it's all my fault. Well that's that little madam on carrots till she's earning. Then I'm off to the bank for money . . .'

Carol lit up and the whining started under the covers again.

'Bide your time,' said Carol. 'I need it more than you do. Anyway, I goes to the bank and tries to get some money out, but there's none there, none coming out the machine. So I goes in and asks to see the manager, and I'm told he's too busy to see the likes of me, and they ask what my problem is, so I tell them what my bloody problem is and they go away and check. And you know what they're saying, they're saying Deke's wages haven't been paid in, and I'm saying that they have 'cause they're always paid in the day, and I'm telling them I've got two bairns and a man to feed and that I'm needing the money, and that I'm needing it right now, but, oh no, I'm not getting any. They're saying the wages haven't been paid in, and there's nothing in the account and all I've got's the money in my bloody purse and there's fuck all of that 'cause I gave Lizzie-Anne McBride a blasted tenner for that blooming shoe menage.'

The puppy's whine changed to a rottweiler's warm-up growl.

'Here,' said Carol, 'here you are then. Take it.'

The covers flew off and Recca lunged forward, resplendent in her limited edition Captain Trip t-shirt.

'Stop moaning,' said Recca, 'I'll give you money. I'm loaded. How much you wanting?'

'Look, I don't want your money, I want our money. Where's it got to?'

Recca shrugged.

'I've got two bairns to feed,' said Carol, 'I've got . . .'

'I told you I'd give you the money,' said Recca. 'How much you needing?'

'That's not the point,' said Carol.

'For the moment it is, how much you needing?'

Carol said she needed thirty quid for the messages.

'Right, we'll go over the town and get your thirty quid. Now, listen,' said Recca, 'you think you've got problems, wait till you hear this one. Know how I was totally wasted last night, totally out of it? Right, well when I comes in this morning I was shattered, absolutely shattered, I wasn't really feeling too clever, and, hey, you'll never guess what? But I could have sworn Dunx's clothes were lying all over the living-room. That no fucking daft?'

As the morning wore on Eddie's normal motormouth persona had all but gone mute, and as he, Andy and Dunx waded their way through greasy fish suppers in the wee park next the chip shop, Eddie wanted for nothing more than a bed, a feather bed.

'So what d'you make of ET City then?' said Andy.

Eddie shrugged. 'It's like a university campus for bugsy folk. All you see is prams out here. You never see prams down my bit.'

'They shove all the training schemes in some out of the way place,' said Andy. 'It shows you're willing to travel and it puts the nutters off.'

'Funny,' said Dunx, 'I was just thinking 'bout you last night.'

'Oh aye,' said Eddie.

'Nah, no what it was was Recca got us this smart new mirror, right, and last night,' Dunx laughed, 'you'll never guess what I did last night?'

Eddie shook his head.

'I got all my gear, right, all the old stuff, all the classic looks; I had it all on, all of it. That's how I was thinking bout you. Had on those black Wranglers you gave us, them that were too wee for you. Had them on. Looked well smart. And, guess what, guess what else I had on? That old black bomber of yours.'

Eddie laughed.

'Telling you,' said Dunx, 'it was alright. I'm thinking about going back to it, seriously thinking about going back to it. Aye, turn a few heads that would.'

'All your stuff was nicked off folk,' said Eddie. 'Like that jacket you nicked off that lassie's old boy. You fucking nicked that.'

'Did I dan, her old boy gave it us.'

'Aye, gave it you as a loan, aye, and you never gave it back. That's called thieving.'

Dunx looked puzzled. 'Nah, he gave it us, I could have sworn he gave it us. Anyway, it was good having all the old stuff on and putting on all the old sounds. Brought back a lot of memories, a lot of good times.'

'It's gone, Dunx, it's gone.'

'I know that, I know that, but I can still think about it, Christ, still mine to think about. And see back then things were different. Back then your mates really were your mates.' Dunx cast a scathing glance at Andy. 'Back then folk did things for you, they gave you clothes and that, records, they did things for you.'

'Aye,' said Eddie, 'and it was you that never gave them back. By the way, those black Wranglers weren't too wee for me. I gave them to you for a loan.'

'Eh?' Dunx looked surprised. 'You sure?'

'Aye. Positive. Got witnesses.'

'Well, eh, you wanting them back then?'

Eddie laughed. 'Nah, don't be daft, you're alright.'

'How much that jacket skin you, anyway?' said Dunx.

'Ton-fifty, and no, you're not getting it.'

'It's alright,' said Dunx, giving it his mildest seal of approval. It looked expensive alright but it looked an impulse buy, the sort of thing that looked good in a shop but not the sort of thing you've ever actually ever seen anybody wearing: thereby breaking Dunx's Number One rule when it came to buying clothes, only ever get things you've seen folk wearing.

Eddie looked at his watch. 'God, I'm fucking shattered, boys. Think I'll just get a Joe back to my mam's and crash out.'

'Be as well just to stay here,' said Dunx. 'Just crash out back at the office.'

'What?' said Eddie.

'Aye, be as well to. Christ, every other cunt does.'

Eddie laughed. This place was daft. This whole place was just plain fucking daft.

Laughter, like daftness, was contagious, and Andy and Dunx joined in, and soon Andy was so away with it he didn't even realize his head was now moving without restriction.

Dunx laughed along with them. He didn't know what was supposed to be so funny, but he knew one thing, he knew you only ever laughed like this with your mates, only with your mates.

'Oh aye,' said Willie, 'you get hydrogen cyanide in fags.'

'Eh?'

'I'M SAYING, YOU GET HYDROGEN CYANIDE IN FAGS. SO THIS IS LIKE ONE BIG FAG, EH?'

Willie laughed.

Deke could hardly hear him, though, and, anyway, Deke was wanting to concentrate on what he was doing so as not to get caught unawares with the catalyst flying out.

The pump cut off and somebody shouted up to them that they were stopping for twenty minutes for a meeting about something.

'Thank fuck for that,' said Deke. 'Right, listen, I've to go and see a couple of boys. I'll be back in twenty minutes, alright?'

'Alright,' said Willie.

Deke climbed the ladder to get out of the tank then went along the walkway and down the steps to get to his bike.

With his eye out for the works' black Escorts and blue vans Deke sped his way through the complex, taking care not to exceed the ten mph speed limit. If your face didn't fit, that was the sort of thing you could get your cards for.

Deke was wanting to get out and about to find out what folk were saying about last night's bust, and he was wanting to know what the latest was on the big contract.

There was good and bad news about the bust. The good news was that Smiddy would probably just get off with a fine. The bad news was that nobody knew why Smiddy had been singled out. Busts usually followed folk flaunting it or when there were gangsters involved. Smiddy fell into neither category. The police knew about him, alright, they knew about damn near everybody, but as to why him and as to why last night, nobody really knew. All they did know was it was enough to put the wind up folk. Deke took the hint. There was no way he'd be setting up any more deals for himself in here.

The news about the contract was that they were now taking on 2500 and it was for two years, and with all the inevitable problems you were looking at the best part of thirty months work. The guy seemed to know a lot about what was happening, but not the important bit, not when. He told Deke it would be soon, though, real soon, and promised he'd be in touch when there was anything definite. Deke trusted the guy but he knew that in this game it wasn't just who you knew, or how well you knew who you knew, a lot of it was just down to luck and just chasing things.

When he got back to the plant the degree of inactivity seemed that wee bit more assertive than Deke was used to. It was like the first day with the company's union man, who looked like David Bellamy with rolled-up sleeves, green wellies and green hard-hat, and the works' union man, who looked like David Bellamy's identical twin brother, except his wellies and hard-hat were yellow, with the pair of them holding court.

'What's up?' said Deke to Willie.

'Eh, no sure, but I think we're on strike again.'

Deke sighed, sat himself down and accepted a polo from Willie. The ring-leaders were the guys that had been hassling Willie, local neds. It would be over once they'd exhausted their collective brain-cell and reason prevailed. A third of the men travelled in daily by coach from over the water. There was no way they would jeopardize their jobs, even with pay and conditions as shite as these.

'What is it this time?' said Deke to anyone that would listen, 'the bastards complaining about their shoelaces no being shiny enough?'

One of the boys from over the water turned to Deke. 'It's no laughing matter, son. They've stopped the wages, the bastards've stopped the fucking wages.'

'Ih?'

'I says, they've stopped the wages, laddie. The bastarn company's no got any fucking money to pay us cause the bastarn fucking company's went and got itself bastarn fucking bust, hasn't it.'

*

Like all great ectomorphs Dunx was easily located seventeen minutes after he'd eaten. Heather knew this and Heather was waiting
for him.

'Christ,' said Dunx, 'what you doing in here? You can't come in
here. This is, this is . . .'

'I need to talk with you. We were supposed . . .'

'Okay, okay, need to talk, right, aye, but you can't come in here,
for Christ's sakes.'

'What's going on?' said Heather. 'We were supposed to be
going out the night mind?'

'I know, I know, I mind alright. It's just that, well, fuck, you can
see for yourself, Christ, Eddie's back. Eddie's an old mate and . . .'

'You said you were finished with that lassie. You told me you
were. . . .'

'No, hold on, hold on, I never said I was finished with her, I said
I was finishing with her. I can't just up and leave. All my stuff's
there. Need to get things sorted out first. These things take time
mind. Look, I'm seriously dying for a shite, go and let us past,
please? Talk about this later, eh?'

Heather stood firm, blocking the access to the cubicle. 'No,' she
said, 'I need to know what's going on, Dunx.'

'What d'you mean "What's going on, Dunx?" Nothing's going
on. Look, I'm sorry. Honest. Some other time, right? Next week.
Promise. Next week.' Dunx put his hand on Heather's hip and
smiled reassuringly.

Heather sighed then coyly lowered her lids. 'Who is this Eddie?'
she said. 'You've never mentioned him.'

'Eddie? Eddie's a mate. Eh, he stays in London and he's a great
guy and, look, go and please let us past. I'll tell you all about Eddie
some other time.'

'All your friends sound great. I'd love to meet them all sometime.'

'Yeah, sure, surely, sometime, aye. Look. . . .'

'You don't mean that.' Heather sniffled. 'When then, tell me
when? Are you ashamed of me?'

'No, don't be daft. Look, don't start that, please. I can't handle. . . .'

'Can't handle what?' Heather was greeting.

'Hey, come on, this is getting a bit out of order. I mean, think about it, an old mate appears from out of the blue, I've no seen him for ages, he's only here for a wee short time. Christ, I could never have anticipated that. How could I have? Look, I'm sorry. It's the guy's holiday, he's come all this way just to see us. Come on.'

'I could come with you.'

'No, look, this is a bit awkward. It's complicated.'

'How?'

'Fuck's sake, it just is. Go and let us past, please?'

Heather was bubbling. 'You don't care about me, do you? What is it that's wrong with me?'

'Christ, fuck, nothing's wrong with you.' From experience Dunx knew folk never really wanted that question answered with any kind of honesty.

'I could just be there as a friend. Friends from work hang around the gether, don't they?'

'Yeah, but look, this is like a big special occasion. It's a mate's thing, it's a, it's a, it's a male thing. That's what it is, it's a male thing. Tonight is just going to be one serious bevvying session, and I'm one total bastard with a drink in me, there is only one thing on my mind, and that's to get more and more bevvy.'

'Will Recca be there?'

'Recca? Nah, don't be silly. She's going out with her mates the night. She wouldn't want to be with us, wouldn't want to be near us.'

Dunx gave it his best shot: total eye contact with the pinky tickle on the chin. 'Look,' he said, 'there's a time for us, there's a special time that'll be just for us, the future, our future.'

Heather smiled. 'Time,' she said. 'The future.'

Dunx nodded.

'Us,' said Heather.

Dunx nodded again.

Heather moved aside and Dunx sprang past and bolted the door behind him. Talk about exasperation.

As Dunx undid his belt he allowed himself a sigh of relief.

Unfortunately, though, the sigh came out the tangible end as well as the audible end.

*

It was one of those moments daytime telly flung forth with joyous regularity, one of those moments when you just go, 'Jesus fuck, I just don't believe it'.

Gary turned the volume up so as not to miss any of what the guy was saying.

'In the original packaging this would be worth, oh, a good few hundred to a collector, of course.'

'So the packaging's important?' said the hostess, Cathie Galbraith, ex-mistress of TV weatherman Ian Kettley and subject of the immortal tabloid headline 'Under the weather'.

'Yes, to a collector, yes,' said the expert. Then he hesitated, remembering what he'd been told about always sounding positive. 'Of course,' he added, 'even an old battered model without the packaging can still fetch a pretty penny.'

'Well, there you have it,' said Cathie. 'Time to check out those old toys in the attic. Now it's over to Glynn who's got with him today's special guest, serial killer expert Dr Bruce Sinclair . . .'

Gary turned the volume back down and picked up his white Man From Uncle car. His limited-edition-cause-they'd-run-out-of-blue-paint-ultra-rare-and-ultra-valuable white Man From Uncle car. A limited edition cause they'd run out of blue paint. Who'd have fucking thought it?

It was one of those moments that would have been good to have shared with a mate or two, arguing about whether he should sell it or hold onto it. You'd all be studying it and playing with it, wondering if any of the others were worth anything. And everybody would be going on about what cars they all used to have.

Any conversation about the past was alright by Gary, back when they were all the same, all in the same boat and all with the same money.

That's what it all boiled down to, money. Even if folk had been round and seen the bit on the telly about the car, they wouldn't have appreciated the moment, like being there when there was a really great goal, all they'd have been wanting to know was how much was it worth and where you could sell it, and what they'd do with the proceeds.

Anyway, it was time to shift. Gary put the telly off, did twenty hand-clap press-ups, then went over and checked out the window to make sure the coast was clear before heading out.

Gary didn't like bumping into folk when he went out. Didn't like hearing about them going on about their jobs, their cars and their girlfriends. Gary would rather be ignored. He could walk past folk he knew and never say a word, just shuffle on with his head down, 'cause all folk with jobs, cars and girlfriends ever went on about were their jobs, their cars and their girlfriends. Folk with cars were the worst. When Gary seen someone he knew in a new car Gary prayed for malfunctions on the mechanisms and watched it only to see if it would crash.

All these folk just didn't have a clue. Sure, they would pass some crappy wee comment telling you how they voted, or go on about nationalism or that crap, but they would never say 'Look, we're bringing in about twenty quid every week more than we're needing – would it be alright if we gave it to you? Fridays do you?'

Nah, they never said that, did they? And it wasn't a joke, they never did that, and it wasn't as if they couldn't afford to, they could all afford it alright. They just went on and on about how the more money you brought in the more you spent and all that absolute shite, and all you wanted to do was put a brick through the nearest shop window and nick yourself an ice-cream Bounty just to show them how it was you were really feeling.

There was no one going about so Gary got his jacket and trainers on, picked up his sportsbag and left.

While Gary could time things so as he wouldn't bump into the folk with their jobs, their cars and their girlfriends, he could never not see the tricky little shites, the tricky little shites whose sole purpose in life seemed to be to hang about in wee clusters between the flats and the shops.

Mammies' boys, spoilt gets. Gary hated folk in gangs. Sure some of them had only just grown out of being kids but there were certain faces you could pick out and take a real serious dislike to, certain faces you could just walk right up to and just smack right in the gub.

The route over to the launderette was quiet, though, and Gary managed to get his washing in his machine, third machine along in the left-hand middle-lane, without having to entertain too many violent thoughts.

It was a costly venture, the launderette, and Gary could only afford to visit twice a month – once for everything that said wash separately and once for everything else – but, God, it was worth it.

Big women, huge women, massive women, women with tattoos, women with muscles. Stretching and bending, and sweating and just plain bloody stunning. Clothes clinging to them as they showed off more cleavage than you could ever dream of in a month unconscious and massaging their sopping armpits like it was the most natural thing in the world. Which, let's face it, it was.

Gary could even put up with all the 'This you with your washing, son' and all the 'You're Elsie/Irene/Isa's laddie, eh?' carry on. Gary even played on that and used his cheek to join in. Gary loved it but, loved it all 'cause here the two things that mattered most to Gary, the fact that he was young and the fact that he was male, were the two things that got him noticed.

Graeme told the others he had paperwork to catch up on and said he'd see them in the morning. Once he'd given them enough time to clear the grounds, however, Graeme went bombing upstairs and along to the cleaners' storeroom at the back for a keek out the wee window.

Good, everything was cool: the Bampot boy was heading right where Graeme went left. Probably heading for the Haggsknock. That's where he would be off to. The Haggsknock had been the original drop-off point for the Glasgow overspill, and still held the worst reputation among older locals who shed tears and held wakes when their holidays clashed with fair fortnight.

Graeme came back down again and lit the fag he'd stolen from Phil's packet, put his feet up on the desk, his desk, and settled back in the chair, his chair.

The arrival of the Bampot boy, Stuart his name was, had meant the promotion of Graeme. Everybody had been pleased, even Robert had congratulated him. So that was Graeme in charge now, in charge of downstairs at any rate. The money was handy and meant that Graeme could now seriously think about buying a place. He'd need to stop smoking, of course, but that was well in hand. This one was a bit of a daft one, he'd call it a daft one, a reaction to the appearance of the Bampot. Graeme never smoked at his work. He considered it a new environment and it was easier not to smoke in a new environment. Like if you went for an hour-and-a-half to Belgium, it would be easy enough not to smoke. Having cut out all the non-essentials Graeme was down to five a day now. The last non-essentials had been the ones after meals and the one before bed-time. The ones after meals were 'reaction cigarettes', like public transport. Circumstances dictated you smoked these. The thing was that about half an hour later you craved another one so the one after meals clearly didn't work. Graeme never really liked the one before bed either, he knew this because he always seemed to hurry it and, the giveaway, he left a long-stub. He couldn't have liked it if he'd left a long stub.

So since he'd started work he'd gone from twenty down to ten down to five. These were the hardcore: first thing in the morning (the ultimate reaction cigarette); half an hour after tea (by now a desperation cigarette, and an experience so wonderful as to be beyond orgasm); mid-evening (essentially a craving to recreate the effects of the previous one); the one with supper (fag, Mars Bar and coffee – Godlike); and the one half an hour before going to bed.

The trouble was Graeme was really into this five. He suspected these were the same five Princess Margaret got stuck at. Cutting down anymore was pointless, the next step had to be the big nothing. Yeah, the only thing left would be just to jack it in altogether – and that, as Graeme reminded himself for the millionth time, was what all this malarky was supposed to be about, anyway.

Graeme reached the cork and ground his fag out in the ashtray. He'd give it half an hour before heading home. Time enough to make sure the fag was out and time enough to check all the windows were shut and that all the plugs were unplugged.

God, this was going to be hellish. It would be like leaving the house. It would be even worse when winter came round and they all got out their own wee fires with their cables going all over the place.

Graeme was getting a bit nervous. There were fag-ends everywhere. Graeme went round checking none of them were still going. Nobody ever used the ashtrays. They ground them out on the floor or they left them upright on ledges. They'd even had complaints from customers that fag-ends had made their way into the orders.

The cold sweat of responsibility or the onset of paranoia was getting to Graeme. He was normally bad, but he was never as bad as this.

Graeme picked up his ashtray to see if there was any smoke coming from it. None, none that he could see. That didn't mean there wasn't any there, of course, it just meant he couldn't see it.

First day nerves, Graeme told himself, just first day nerves. Graeme said this aloud, 'First day nerves.' Then he wondered why that guy he'd heard on the radio who'd said you were supposed to talk aloud to yourself when you were by yourself had actually said that?

Then Graeme wondered if the Bampots were plotting to kill him. Then he wondered . . .

Right, that was enough. Time to go. Graeme collected all the fag-ends he'd gathered and put them in the bucket. It was only then that he noticed something really weird – there weren't any wee Regal butts. Graeme looked through them all. No, none. Graeme said 'Fuck it,' got the jacket off and went in search of the wee Regal butts.

'Yes, dad . . . Yes, dad . . . Look, dad, I'll need to be getting back to my work, okay? . . . Listen, you know I'm not supposed to take personal calls unless it's an emergency . . . Yes, dad . . . Right, I'll see you Sunday then . . . Bye . . . No, I won't forget . . . Cheerio.'

Hazel lowered the phone and got back to her typing.

He wasn't even acting as if he knew what was going on, he knew alright, he knew what was going on. It was only an act in so much as he pretended to be giving warnings rather than rebuking actual behaviour.

Drugs, he'd mentioned drugs. Said it like it was a tabloid headline. Drugs! Years of Hell!

All that nonsense he'd come away with, all that about sorting them out, coming away like some sort of gangster.

Hazel could've argued, could've said it was no worse than cigarettes or alcohol. But Hazel could never outargue her dad, even when he was wrong he ended up being right, so Hazel had just lied and denied.

'That shower of dunderheids,' he'd called them. 'That shower of weirdos.' Assumptions based on prejudice, and assumptions that were ten out of ten accurate, but that wasn't the point. In a million ways Deke was a million times better at being a parent than her dad had ever been. Deke made meals, Deke washed the dishes and Deke looked after the kids so Carol could have a night out. Hazel's dad had never done things like that. When her mum had been in the hospital, her dad hadn't had a clue and they ended up having fish suppers every night like it was some kind of treat.

So many of the things that Hazel hated about Andy and his 'mates' were the same things she hated about her family. It was all so cliquey. You could never really get to know folk and you could never really say what you meant. That's what was wrong, wrong, wrong with it all. You couldn't tell Deke he was havering pish and you couldn't tell Recca she was a total mess in the same way you couldn't tell Uncle Bert that his stories weren't funny and Auntie Beth that she should try keeping her legs the gether when she sat down.

Hazel sighed and went through what she'd been typing, marking the mistakes with her pencil.

Andy still hadn't rung yet. She gave him the benefit of the doubt cause they'd been busy. He'd maybe tried and hadn't got through. Hazel'd phoned at dinnertime but he was out and she left no message. Since then she'd tried twice but it was engaged.

Hazel had wanted to apologise for last night, and, as a means of making up, she'd decided she was going to go up to that stupid bloody quiz with Recca and Carol, something Hazel had only ever done the once before and had hated with a ferocity she normally reserved for slit-skirts and long skirts. There was nothing worse than looking thick in front of folk who didn't like you.

But this was Hazel apologising, and when you were apologising it was best to have a peace offering, it was best to show she could give a little. It would show she was willing to try and get on with folk.

Hazel looked through her desk-top directory but it was Andy's number she dialled. It was engaged. She hung up.

Apologising for last night wasn't going to be easy and Hazel was going to gloss over it, 'cause Hazel was by and large unrepentant.

Okay, she'd gone a bit far with the envelope opener, but she'd been wild, she'd been raging. Andy going on at her like she'd just scored a goal or something stupid like that.

While Hazel got back to her work and tried to figure out what it was she was supposed to be doing, (if it's Wednesday it must be accounts) it got to her that what she was really doing was just waiting, just waiting for Andy to phone. If he just phoned it would be alright. If he made the effort. If he did something.

Andy was getting to Hazel like a really bad toothache. And when you had a really bad toothache there were always times you could forget about it then, ouch, pangs of pure pain, it would, he would, be back again, only worse.

All Hazel wanted was some consideration, not necessarily always consulted but always considered. To have her views and her feelings considered. That wasn't too much to ask for, was it?

As though in response, the lead at the tip of Hazel's pencil snapped.

Carol and Recca were in the queue for the cashline machine.

'Your wee pal took a smoke last night.'

'She what?'

'A-ha,' said Carol. 'Should've seen her, eyes all over the place and cheeks out like that.' Carol made like a hamster.

'What brought that on?'

'Don't know. Turned into a really good night once you left.'

'Thanks.' Recca sniffed.

'Come on, you were being obnoxious. Should've heard the slagging you got.'

'What? What was the little bitch saying?'

'Uh-uh, not her, me. It was me that was slagging you. All the usual stuff about you making a mess of your life and all that.'

'Hold on, I thought you were supposed to be really pleased for me, the way you were going on about me and Dunx.'

'Nah,' said Carol, 'we were just giving it a try to see what would happen, I think we can safely say it's a . . .'

'Fucking disaster,' said Recca. 'Hey, I was really worried about the way you were going on at me like that.'

'Just trying to give you every wee bit help and encouragement.'

'Well, thanks for nothing. I go and make the biggest whopper in the world, and you're there cheering me on.'

'Well, we were worried that maybe you'd fallen for him or something.'

' "Fallen for him", that's a joke. He's a selfish prick, he's useless in bed and I'm paying for all this. What less could you ask for?'

'As long as you're sure?'

'Course I'm fucking sure. I have not fallen for him. I have not fallen for him.' Recca was almost singing. 'I have not. I will not. I can not. There you go, that good enough?'

'If you say so.'

They reached the front of the queue and Recca said, 'How much you say you were wanting?'

'Thirty. No, hold on, you better make it forty.'

'*Forty*?'

'Recca, I've got two bairns and a man to feed, my cupboards are bare . . .'

'Alright, alright, there's no need to go giving it your wee wifie routine.'

'There's nothing wrong with being a wee wifie,' said Carol. 'Do you the world of good to get yourself a decent man and a couple of weans.'

'Oh aye, and stopping to have serious conversations with every paid-up member of the pram-pushing posse about council maintainance and the death of the decent lettuce. No thanks. Wife stands for Wash Iron Feed Etcfuckingetera. That's you twenty-four hours a day. Me, I'm just fucked-up – but I could be well the morrow.'

Carol ground her teeth. 'If that's true then how come you were so happy that time you thought you were pregnant.'

'Cause, at that time, I was being a stupid wee lassie and cause, at that time, I was on one-and-a-half wee dovies.'

'Aye, right,' said Carol.

Recca withdrew fifty quid from the jaws of the machine and handed forty to Carol.

As they turned to go a smartly dressed middle-aged woman grabbed a hold of Recca's sleeve. 'Excuse me, dear,' she said, 'but

I couldn't help but overhearing, and, well, if you could just hold on a minute I'll . . .' The woman let go of Recca and looked through her handbag.

'Ah, here we are,' she said. 'You'd maybe like to take one of these. Take your time with it, dear. There's always someone who cares.'

The woman smiled politely. An expression somewhat in contrast to that of Recca's when she read the words on the leaflet: 'Christ, he is your lover.'

'Alright. Carol not home yet?'

'No, son,' said Carol's dad. 'I've no seen her. Can't think where she'd be at this time. She's always in for when I get here.'

'Must've got held up.' Deke took the small bag of messages he was carrying through to the kitchen. The foreman had given those who wanted it an advance against their wages once they'd got everything sorted out and the company went solvent again.

'Fancy a coffee?'

'Aye, well, if you're having one yourself.'

Deke stuck the kettle on. 'Us lot nearly got paid off the day.'

'Aye?'

'Aye, was a bit scary for a while there, never knew what was happening. The company went bust and never had any money to pay us.'

Carol's dad laughed. 'Heard that one before,' he said. 'Bastards'll do anything no to give you your wages.'

'Aye,' said Deke, 'You staying for your tea?'

Carol's dad looked at his watch. 'Well, ach, since your twisting my arm, go on then, just peel another tattie. Just peel another tattie.'

Aye, thought Deke, and grill another chop, and open up another tins of peas and serve up another four slice of bread and wash up another set of dishes and put up with you for another hour. Just peel another tattie, your arse.

Carol's dad stubbed out his fag then took his ashtray through the kitchen where Deke was peeling the tatties.

'Did you notice anything different out front?'

'What different, like?'

'Have a look.'

Deke leaned over and looked out the window. 'What have I to look for?'

'The Escort, the blue Escort.'

'Aye, what about it?'

There wasn't a reply so Deke had to work it out for himself. 'What? You bought that, it's yours?'

'Ach, well you know what they say about taking it with you. I thought I could maybe take Carol and the kids out for the odd run or that.'

Deke was counting to ten so as he wouldn't explode . . . one two . . . there is no way that my kids are ever going to be in a car driven by you . . . three four . . . I am fed up to the back teeth with you getting them things I can't afford . . . five six . . . and what happens if you have a bloody heart attack and my kids are in that car . . . seven eight . . . stop butting in, just stop butting in, they're my kids, not yours . . . nine ten . . . you're not on, you're just not on.

Recca's car pulled up outside.

'There's Carol now,' said Deke.

Carol's dad waved to them from the window. When he saw them opening up the back to get the bags out he went down to lend a hand.

'What's up with your wages?' said Carol when she came in; a bag of messages in one arm, Baby Joe in the other.

'It's alright. It's all sorted out,' said Deke. 'Be in some time the morrow.'

'Better be. D'you know I've had to . . .'

'Papa's got a new car,' said Joanne.

'What?'

Deke nodded.

Her dad came in behind them, carrying Baby Joe's buggy and a bag of messages.

'Is this true?' said Carol.

'Is what true, hen?'

'Don't fucking hen me, is this true you've just bought a bloody car?'

'And what if I have? It's my bloody money and I'll do whatever the hell I want with it.'

'For Christ's sake, dad, have I not got enough to worry about without knowing that you're out there looking for an accident.'

'Carol, love . . .'

' "Carol, love" nothing. You get that thing and you take it back to wherever you got it from, you hear me?'

'Calm down, hen.'

'No, I will not calm down . . . Did you have Joanne in that?'

'Just down the road, hen.'

'Listen, don't you ever take either of my kids in that again, you hear me? I'll collect Joanne from school the morrow.'

Carol's dad pocketed his fags and matches. 'I know when I'm not wanted. I'll not stay where I'm not welcome.'

Carol just stood there as he left. But when she heard the slamming of the front door she went chasing out after him.

Deke went over and shut the living-room door then turned up the telly so as Joanne and Baby Joe wouldn't hear the slanging match.

'Alright if I stay for my tea?' said Recca.

'Might as well,' said Deke. 'Seeing as how I've peeled the other tattie.'

A comic strip illustrating a second in the life of Andy would run five identical frames. In the first four frames a thought bubble would display a different worry. In the fifth frame, however, there would be a speech bubble containing the words, 'See my fucking brain, man.'

Time and time again Andy ended up thinking about things he wasn't even thinking about. And it wasn't just Charlie Endell.

Hazel would be home soon. Andy put on some music to make it look like he was busy then sat back down again, leaning forward, elbows on knees, like he was in a waiting room, a dentist's waiting room.

Andy was forcing himself to think about why it was he had to force himself to think about Hazel. Even at this time, and after last night's set-to, he still had to force himself to think about Hazel. It was like he kept forgetting about her, but it wasn't like forgetting a birthday or a programme on Channel 4. No, this wasn't a mere slip of the memory, this was deeper, like blocking out something, something you feared or something you dreaded, there had to be a word for it. Like Tuesday afternoons when you had double PE and double woodwork with the big boys and the bad boys who you were always frightened would turn round and kill you.

Not so long ago, thoughts of Hazel had been a joy, like finding a fiver or beating the Fifers. Andy could find pleasure in looking back on being with her, or he could look forward to seeing her. But now it was all so different, and now it was all so wrong.

It was all so wrong 'cause Andy loved Hazel, loved her more than everything and everybody in the world added up and multiplied by the biggest number anybody'd ever thought of. Andy was terrified of losing her. Terrified she'd go off with some guy who had a proper job and a car. That's what they said about Hazel. That she was just waiting for somebody better to come along. Dunx had said it. Recca had said it. And Charlie Endell had said it millions of times.

This, though, didn't have the effect of making Andy more determined. No, it only made Andy more despondent. Like bookies being richer than punters, the opinions of others ganged up on Andy and his dreams and kicked shit out of them. Other folk were always right. Like the time . . .

There it goes again! Damn it!

Andy cursed himself and tried to focus his thoughts on Hazel. What should he say to her? . . . And then? . . . And then? . . . What? Think! Think! Say sorry. Wow, that's a good one, top of the class. Tell her she was out of order. That's the truth so tell the truth. The truth never hurt anyone. Well, it probably had done at some time or other but Andy didn't want to think about that. Honesty, that was the word. Honest. Nah, not honest. Honest sounded dodgy. Honesty and love, that sounded good. Honesty and love.

Andy checked the time. Tonight was the start of the season and Andy would get to bawl and shout his head off for the best part of ninety minutes. All the frustrations, all the rages, all the everything would come pouring out of him and vent themselves on that most deserving of creatures, the lowest scum that had ever walked the face of the earth – the standside linesman.

Shit! Andy chastised himself again. He was supposed to be

thinking about Hazel. There was him thinking about something else yet again. Think about Hazel! Think about Hazel! For God's sake, man, think about what you're going to say to Hazel!

Click. Click. Click. Click.

That was her coming up the stair now.

Shit! Think! Think!

Click. Click. Click. Click.

Andy paced about. Look, it's not important. Don't go over the top. Don't mention it. That's what lands you in trouble. That's what Dunx always says. Hell, Christ, don't think about Dunx, just don't think about him. Don't think about anybody. And don't be too melodramatic. Hazel had said he was too melodramatic. Then what exactly the fuck had she been last night then? Shut up, don't think like that. Just forget about it. Make light of it, if need be then lie. No, don't, don't lie. There were major penalties associated with lying, don't lie. Just behave like a forward-thinking, positive-type person.

The front door opened.

'Got it!'

Andy had the brainwave. It sounded brilliant. A diversion tactic. Andy clapped then rubbed his hands. He knew what he was going to say, he knew exactly what he was going to say. As the living-room door opened Andy went over all the possible ramifications. Nah, it was alright. It was perfect. Enthusiastic! Positive! And completely and utterly absolutely nothing at all to do with last night.

Oh, come on, if there were freshly toasted crumbs on two wee plates then there had to be bread. Surely to God she hadn't bought and scoffed a whole bloody loaf.

It had been the smell that had first got Dunx going, that lovely sweet smell, then when he'd seen those two wee plates with their wee crumbs there followed a ransack of the kitchen the CID could've used for a training video.

But the ransack proved breadless so Dunx had to consider the alternatives.

There was still time to go round to his folks – but that was way

out of the way and wouldn't leave him long enough for a shot of
the greatest thing since sliced bread, namely Recca's electric
shower. Likewise, buying something was out of the question, Dunx
would be needing his money for later on.

The thing was that Eddie liked his Indians, so they'd probably
all be ending up at the Take Your Nose Off Tandoori, so all Dunx
wanted was something to tide him over. Something to keep him
going. Something like . . . Got it!

Dunx picked up the phone.

'Hello. That you, Auntie Bella?'

'Oh, hello, Duncan. Not heard from you for a while. How you
keeping, son?'

'Fine, fine. Yourself?'

'Oh, doing away. I was just saying to . . .'

'Listen, Auntie Bella, reason I'm phoning, right, is I was thinking of maybe dropping in on you on my way up to the game the
night. Just to say hello and that.'

'Now have you had something to eat, Duncan?'

'No, I was just going to get myself a pie or something at the
ground.'

'Och, no, I'll make you something proper. Tell you what, I'll put
your favourite on, will I?'

'Alright,' said Dunx, 'that'd be great. I'll see you later on then,
right?'

And with that Dunx hung up and Auntie Bella rushed away to
bake some pancakes before preparing Dunx's favourite – poached
eggs on toasted rolls.

The sight of Dunx's clothes still spread all over the living room
brought to mind another problem – what to wear.

It was too hot for the leather jacket . . . or was it? Dunx pondered.
Christ, he didn't know, though, many's the time he'd suffered for
his look. Like being a twelve month a year overcoat man with
sweaty fringe, itchy brogues and smelly black trousers. Aye, he'd
suffered alright. Those were the days of a lassie called Kate who'd
gave him that ghetto-blaster, a lassie called Susie who'd gave him
his favourite checked shirt and a lassie called Liz who'd shown him
how to apply foundation properly.

Those were the days, those were the glory days, the days before

Deke and the big slipper (c. B. Connolly.), when mates were mates and all you did was party.

That didn't solve the problem of what to wear, though. What to wear? Had to be the look, had to be the classic look: black t-shirt, black 501's and bikers jacket. It was a bit faggoty for summer but it was definitely the classic look. Eddie would mention Pete Best. Dunx bet himself he would.

No!

Pete Best bit the dust and Dunx made up his mind to do something he'd been told not to do, something he'd even been warned with malice not to do – Dunx was putting on Recca's brand new green Levi jacket and damn the consequences.

Green levi jacket with white jeans, white baseball boots and either the baggy-necked white t-shirt or the tight-necked white t-shirt.

Dunx tried out the look and the baggy-necked white t-shirt got the nod. It would have been better if the jacket was a red one, mind you; the red ones were better. But, anyway, he was getting it for free, so who was he to complain?

Dunx phoned Eddie to be sure of what was happening. Eddie was expecting to meet up beforehand but Dunx hadn't the time so they arranged just to meet in the ground.

Dunx wanted another shot of the phone. Right: three minutes for the shower; four to do the hair; five to get dressed; six to look in the mirror; seven, say seven, to get down the road. Call it twenty-five. Dunx dialled the numbers.

'Auntie Bella, me again. I'll be there in twenty-five minutes.'

'I'll be ready for you, Duncan.'

'Eddie's here!'

Hazel looked round.

'No, well he's not here, like, but he's home, he's back here.'

Hazel said, 'Oh' and wondered why Andy looked as though he'd been holding his breath for the last fifteen minutes. She didn't mention it, though, just kicked off her shoes, sat herself down, stretched herself out and said, 'Eddie?'

This was as far as Andy's plan went. Andy stuttered. 'Eddie? Oh, Eddie, aye, Eddie's a mate, he's from London, he's living in

London now but he used to muck about with us. He's fucking mental, you'll love him.'

Hazel smiled. A strange recommendation. But Hazel had decided she wasn't going to give Andy a hard time so she said, 'I tried phoning you but I couldn't get through.'

Andy laughed. 'Aye, Stan took the phone off the hook so Eddie could get some sleep.'

'Eh?'

Andy explained what had happened.

'Listen,' said Hazel, 'I've decided to go up to the quiz tonight. Will I see you later?'

'Yeah! Yeah! Yeah!' Andy was barking with delight. 'Yeah, that'll be great.'

Hazel smiled. 'Will I get to meet Eddie?'

'Eh, doubt it, no the night at any rate. Eddie's a bit of a serious bevvy merchant. Him and Dunx are likely going out on a bender.' Andy shook his head. 'I won't be going, though.' Andy nodded his head. 'After the game I'll be coming straight over to the quiz to meet up with you.'

'So Eddie won't even be popping over to say "Hello"?'

'Shouldn't think so.' Quick, Andy thought to himself, another diversion tactic. When in doubt, gossip. Hazel liked her gossip, so gossip!

'Eh,' said Andy, 'Eddie and Carol used to be pretty close, you see.'

'Really?'

'Oh aye, I think she freaked him out a bit.'

'Is that why he left?'

Andy shrugged. 'Who's to say? But if things had worked out different, well you never know. Don't say I said anything, though. Old wounds and that.'

'No,' said Hazel, 'of course not.' But she was thinking to herself how that would be a good name to bring up the night.

'My dad phoned the day,' said Hazel. 'Gave me a right rollicking.'

'Aye? What about?'

'Drugs.'

'Eh?'

'He was being very intrusive. Asking about you lot. To tell you the truth I don't know why he even bothered asking, he seemed to know everything.'

Andy sat down beside Hazel. 'What exactly was he saying?'

'Oh, just slagged you lot off to a tee. Said he'd sort you out.'

Andy looked wary. 'He's just being overprotective. There's no way he knows anything.' Andy picked crumbs off the covers to mask his concern.

'You don't know him,' said Hazel. 'He could batter you – and he would. He said he would.'

Andy shifted so that he was stretched out with his feet over the edge of the settee and with his head in Hazel's lap. 'Christ,' he said, 'that's nothing to mouth off about, any cunt could batter me.'

Hazel smiled and ran her fingers through Andy's hair.

'So I'll see you at the quiz after the game?' said Hazel.

'Aye,' said Andy, 'I'll be there. I'll mention it to Eddie and see if he wants to come over and meet you. Doubt it, though. I'll be there, though. I'll be there.'

'Dad! Dad! Listen, will you. For God's sake's listen!'

Even though they'd had this same scene a hundred times before, everything would have to be gone over as though it was for the first time, 'cause for him nothing, absolutely nothing, nothing ever changed.

'Dad, listen to me, you're not well enough to drive that car. You've got to think of other folk.'

Carol's dad swung his arm as though swatting a fly. 'Carol, hen, I'm not going in for Brands Hatch, I just want to take you and the kids out for the odd run. I'm not a flaming invalid.'

'But, dad,' said Carol, 'you are, you are an invalid, you are a flaming invalid, you get invalidity benefit, you are an invalid, you got paid off your work for being an invalid. We worry enough about you without this thing as well.' Carol pointed at the car.

Her dad was going red in the face, he was fuming. 'You know, it's you that's the one that needs the looking after, it's you that needs the worrying, you and the kids, you and that bloody clown in there.'

That was it. Carol had had enough. 'Dad, you're not fit to drive that car. If I can't trust you to go and get Joanne from school without getting yourself flaming mortal, what like are you going to be with this flaming thing. If you get in that car I'm going straight up that stair and I'm going to phone the police and I'll tell them that you're not fit to drive. I'll tell them that, and so help me I'll keep telling them. I mean it, I'm warning you.'

Carol waited for the reaction, but it didn't come. His rage had built up but then it had just come straight back down again. He just looked lost, lost and deflated, like all of something had just drained out of him. Carol had seen that look before, when the nurse had told them that the condition of her mother had deteriorated, when he seemed to realise just what that meant.

Carol's dad looked away so she couldn't see him. 'I'm frightened, Carol,' he said. 'I'm really scared . . . You know I don't enjoy living anymore, I don't enjoy it. I'm no good at it, I'm just no good, I'm no good to anyone. Carol, love, you're all I've got. Don't turn against me.'

That wasn't true. Carol had a sister up the braes and a brother in Germany, but it was her that had to put up with all this, all this carry-on.

'I just want what's best for you, hen. To know that you're okay. I thought you'd be pleased when I got the car. I really thought that. I shouldn't have got it, I shouldn't have. I'm sorry.'

Carol held back the waterworks and said, 'Look, come on in and get your tea. Come on.'

'Do you want it?'

'What?'

'The car, do you want it?'

If she'd been thinking, she'd have anticipated that.

'We'll see,' said Carol. 'I'd need to discuss it with Deke. Could you not just get your money back?'

'Ach, Carol, what do I want with money at my age?'

They'd been here before as well. Carol could list a million things her dad could do with his money, a lot of them things that actually needed done.

'You know Deke gets upset when you give us things we can't afford,' said Carol. 'I get upset too.'

Carol's dad didn't say anything.

'If Deke gets on this new contract,' continued Carol, 'we'll be able to do all these things for ourselves. You appreciate things more when you go out and get them for yourselves. We'll think about getting a car then. It's good money, dad.'

Carol's dad shook his head, as if his daughter was just being daft. 'Carol, hen, that's all just pie in the sky stuff. Half the town's waiting for this contract, they've been waiting for years.'

Eddie lowered the phone. Shit, damn and blast.

Somebody had seen him getting off the bus. Said somebody had been telling another party about this when a bypasser happened to overhear the conversation, a bypasser that went by the name of Fids.

Oh God, Fids. Eddie had forgotten all about Fids. He'd never even thought about the guy, not once, not since the last time he'd seen him. Now he was going to have to spend time with this guy like he was some kind of mate or something. It was like seeing shit on your shoes, and then shit on the carpet, and then shit on the . .

It had taken all of Eddie's powers of persuasion to prevent Fids from coming up to the game. Eddie emphasised the cost and Fids's poverty. Eddie also reminded Fids that Fids didn't like football, and how he wouldn't be wanting Fids to feel left out.

Fids had complied, he always did.

Eddie promised he would go round and see Fids on the Sunday afternoon. Eddie stressed this, that Eddie would go and see Fids. The last thing Eddie wanted was Fids turning up at his door. His folks would have a hairy fit.

Fids had hung up when his money ran out. Eddie was rather touched – the man who never had any money had spent his money phoning Eddie. Fids wasn't all bad. He was just too petty, pathetic, paranoid and poor, just like the town, so small-minded, all the things had driven Eddie to seek his fame, fortune and happiness elsewhere.

Eddie went back up the stair and started getting himself the gether for going out. His old room was looking so much smaller these days. It reminded him more of all those hotel rooms he'd been in when he was away on courses. So neat and fresh and tidy was it that it came as something of a shock to see that the cupboard wasn't empty, but was filled with the neatly stacked remnants of a child and a teenager: shoeboxes full of pendants and postcards and photos and badges; some embarrassing LP's, a few tapes and most of his books.

Pride of place, though, went to a fort his dad had made for him, complete with inaccessible walkways cause the ladders had been broken off and used for something else. There was a poly-bag from the old pet-shop filled with hatless and headless cowboys and Indians. Eddie's favourite was always the cowboy that had his hands tied behind his back. He was the one that won all the fights and did all the rescuing.

Eddie laughed. The other day he'd just been talking with someone about the relative merits of Sonic the Hedgehog and the toys of his generation. Sonic had won hands down, of course, but now Eddie wasn't so sure. There was something intensely personal about all this.

Eddie checked the time, it was getting on. He put everything back in the cupboard and got himself changed into his jeans and football top.

The top had prompted a few reactions down south, a few greetings, a few puzzled looks and more than a few sneers. One of the latter had come on the tube from a Jambo saddo who started haranguing Eddie about a dodgy penalty a few seasons back. They got to talking and the guy invited Eddie up to Hyde Park on the Sunday afternoon where a group of ex-pats challenged and thrashed all-comers from itinerant Australians to Rolls-Royce driving Arabs.

Sounded alright to Eddie and he'd gone along and quickly established himself as a regular. One week they'd played against a team from the Dorchester. Afterwards they'd all got the gether for a chat and a bev, and Eddie got talking to this boy called Simon, and, to cut a long story short, Simon had gone on to become Eddie's flatmate.

And that's what this trip was all about. This time he wasn't just going to use the word flatmate. Like he'd said flatmate about Brian at college and like he'd said flatmate about John through in Glasgow. That's all he ever told anybody. Everybody that was apart from his folks, who he'd told years ago, and who'd been pretty good about it, although his dad had said that if Simon was to visit it was to be separate rooms – he'd said it would have been the same if it was a girl. Eddie had also told Carol, shortly after telling his folks, half-hoping she'd tell everybody else. She hadn't, though; Carol liked her secrets.

Eddie pocketed his money and went back down the stair. He wanted to phone Simon but there was no news so he didn't. It was Simon that had told him he was to stop making a cunt of himself and to come up here to tell folk, to come out.

Eddie looked in on his folks before he left. They were curled up cosy on the settee, getting stuck into the box of Thornton's he'd got them, and watching a video of Daniel O'Donnell.

Not since the heyday of Sydney Devine had his folks got so worked up about a singer. The living-room was a cross between a shrine and a warehouse: records, tapes, calendars, pendants, everything.

'Right,' said Eddie, 'I'm off then.' He thought for a second then added, 'What is it that's so special about this Daniel O'Donnell, anyway?'

'Oh,' said Eddie's mum, 'he's got a beautiful voice, a lovely voice. I like his songs, too. Aye, I like his songs. And he's got a wonderful personality, and oh he's just lovely. And, here,' Eddie's mum whispered, 'he's got a lovely wee bum.'

Eddie's mum and dad started giggling and cuddling up to each other.

On the screen Eddie got a glimpse of the tightly packed O'Donnell hind-end. Like two peas in a pod, as they said.

The sound of a speeding fire engine was followed by another, then another.

Three barriers along and two barriers up from the stand-side corner flag, Graeme was shuddering.

He'd never found any wee Regals. He'd searched the place from top to bottom and then back again but he'd never found any wee Regals, not a butt.

So that was it, that was the work up in flames then.

Shit, don't be stupid, fires always caught quickly. He'd stayed behind for an hour, if it was going to take it would have started by then.

Then he'd went home and had some cheese on toast then just came straight out.

Shit, the grill! No, he hadn't come straight out. No, he'd got washed and changed, then he'd washed and dried the dishes. There was a gap of about half an hour from when the grill went off, or should have went off, and when he went out the door. Enough time for any discernible rise in temperature to have been noticed . . . wasn't it? Had the place been hotter than usual when he left? And then, of course, there were the two scariest words in the English language to consider, spontaneous combustion.

Graeme shrieked internally. There was nothing like spontaneous combustion to scare the living daylights out of you.

Fuck, this was getting out of order. At least Graeme hadn't had a fag, that was smart. And for the first time ever Graeme could recall locking his door 'cause after he'd set the propellers of the nutter-proof booby trap to six then closed his door behind him one of the kids had said to him, 'Is that you locking your door and going away out, Graeme?' whereupon Graeme had replied 'Aye.'

Shit, probably the wee shite was just casing the joint, making sure Graeme was going out, then going off to tell all his pals and they'd all come round and do the place over.

Graeme said 'Fuck it' to himself and got the fags out. If there was a fire or a break-in then there was nothing could be done about it, all he could do was pray no one was hurt and that there wouldn't be a really embarrassing message over the tannoy asking him to contact the nearest police officer.

Still thirty-five minutes till kick-off. Graeme was one of those folk who never had anything better to do in life so he was always early. The only times he was ever late was when he arrived ridiculously early and went for a wander to kill some time and got lost. This had happened memorably at three away games and two job interviews.

The football was like the seaside and like the hills, it was always cold, and as Graeme cuddled up to himself and leaned on the barrier, he looked round, casting an eye over all those old familiar faces in their old familiar places, all these folk he'd forgotten about, all these folk he'd seen growing from boys to youths to men, many of them he'd never even spoken to.

Male-bonding, that lassie on the telly with the big jaw had called it. Instead of folk opening up to each other they acted out rituals with each other. She may well have been right, but by God when it was good it was just the best, as sport, as entertainment or as achievement it was simply the best.

The pre-season opposition, the once mighty Sunderland, came out for their warm-up to be greeted by great cheers from a healthy travelling support. Healthy, that was, in numbers, not in appearance. Away supports were always ugly. The same way that refs were always biased and other teams always cheated. Just one of those things.

The home side came out and what crowd there was went mental. Graeme clapped quickly with his hands close together. He felt his eyes glistening. He didn't stop clapping until everyone else had then let loose a whistle which he could hear but which he hoped no one else could.

The tears were now flowing from Graeme's eyes; the hell that was summer was over and life could get back to normal.

The lads, though, weren't looking too good. Suntanned from Mediterranean holidays they proceeded to do a series of exercises only the clinically dead would've found any difficulty in coping with.

Graeme braced himself. Warm-ups were dangerous and pre-season warm-ups were the worst. Players afforded themselves the luxury of a few long-range shots. These were only ever attempted in the warm-ups. Reason being the high percentage of efforts which failed to find the target but somehow, and with a miraculous degree of consistent accuracy, managed to pick out the bloke three barriers along and two barriers up from the stand-side corner flag.

There were four balls in motion.

Whoosh! Straight out the ground!

Smash! Into the advertising hoarding up the top of the terracing.

Thwack! The new signing stubs his toe, the ball travels all of twelve feet, and there's calls for the stretcher to be brought on.

Crunch! Elephant Man hits the bar from all of forty yards and the home crowd starts singing 'We're gonni win the league!'

Graeme relaxed. This was it, this was the place to be. This place was safe. No hassles from work, no hassles about bumping into Bampots, no . . .

It was then that Graeme got grabbed from behind, Graeme got shaken about and Graeme heard the fearful words 'What fucking dozy bastard went and left their fucking grill on then?'

'Eddie! Fuck, man, what you playing at? Damn near gave us the fright of my life.'

'How come, gangsters after you or something?'

Eddie laughed but Graeme didn't. Some things weren't funny. Like pretending, however unwittingly, to be a black shell-suited, tattooed-knuckled, Regal-smoking famously psychotic Bampot.

'Hey,' said Graeme, remembering what Eddie'd said, 'you're joking about that fire, eh?'

'Nah, you're alright, the engines went past your bit. What did we go and sign that useless bastard for?'

'Nah, he's a good player, always caused us a fair amount of problems.'

'Christ, if that's your criteria, you could sign half the cunts in the league. COME ON, ELEPHANT MAN. LET'S SEE A FEW BASTARDS GETTING THEIR LEGS BROKEN THE NIGHT, RIGHT UP TO THE ARMPITS!'

'Eddie, come on to fuck, man.'

Eddie laughed. 'Gary coming the night?'

'Nah, it's just money, he says,' Graeme did his Gary impersonation. '*It's just money.*'

'Still the same, ih. Here, you wanting one of these?'

'Thought you were supposed to have stopped. Last time I seen you you said you'd stopped.'

'Aye, six months it lasted. Six months with waking up in the morning and dying for one, every single bastarn morning was like that. So I just says to myself fuck it, and starts again.'

Graeme tutted. 'Should've stuck with it.'

'Nah, think about it, six months, man, never got any easier. Guys like us'll never stop.'

'Nah, Christ, I'm stopping,' said Graeme. 'Got it sussed.'

'Your arse, you'll never stop.'

Aye, I will, said Graeme, but only to himself. Eddie was not the

sort of smoker Graeme wanted to discuss this with; Eddie was too
unrepentant, a failed giver-upper, as they were known. Graeme
quickly changed the subject.

'Some support these cunts've brought up, eh.'

'Aye,' said Eddie, 'right shower of bruisers.'

'You seen this lot?'

'Aye, should take four of us easy. You still go to all the games?'

'Oh aye. Close thing last season, half them could've went either
way. Mind you, the other half we were seriously shite.'

'Same old story. Funny, in Europe you've got all these crappy
wee teams like Sampdoria winning the league but over here nothing ever changes.'

'One day it'll be different,' said Graeme.

'And you can nail jelly to the ceiling. You coming along to get
slaughtered later?'

'Eh,' Graeme'd have to get fags. He'd have to buy twenty,
maybe forty. 'No,' said Graeme. 'No, I've got work the morrow.
Early rise.'

'How's the job going?' said Eddie.

'Alright, got promoted the day.'

'Aye? That you getting to use the scissors on the sellotape now?'

Graeme laughed. 'No quite that bad. Got a bit of a rise.'

'Should get yourself down south.'

Graeme pointed to the pitch.

'Sad bastard,' said Eddie. 'Hey, I thought you said Mr Smart-
but-casual wasn't coming the night?'

Graeme looked across, and there, walking down the front so as
he could get a good look at the WPC's behind the goal, was Gary.

'See his mam still buys his clothes, anyway,' said Eddie. 'Look
at him, just look at the guy, he's staring right through that lassie.
Watch it, watch it, here it comes!'

Eddie and Graeme burst out laughing as Gary nodded, winked
and smiled at the two WPC's.

'Poor bastard,' said Graeme, 'still trying to convince the world
he's no a poof.'

Eddie grimaced – that was what they called a sare yin.

Waiting.

Waiting for something to start then waiting for something to happen then waiting for something to finish.

Hazel checked the clock on the wall then the watch on her wrist.

The clock was winning but there was ages yet so Hazel started on her second mat, peeling and picking at the corners, trying to separate the label from the cardboard. If she could manage it in a oner she'd be the new world champion.

Hazel was early cause Andy'd insisted they'd have to take the same bus up the town. It was one of those times when he'd got all manly and masterful, like it was one of the rules laid down by Andy's own personal Moses. Andy wouldn't hear of Hazel travelling up on her own, even with this daylight you couldn't be too careful. He'd even offered the ultimate sacrifice – taking the later bus, which would've suited Hazel but which would've meant Andy missing the start of the game. The way he'd swollen those doleful panda eyes of his had been rather touching. Bless him.

Nah, stuff him. Missing the start of the game wasn't what had been bothering him, it was the explanation he'd had to have given good old Dunky Dunx.

The label came off in a oner and Hazel rolled it as tight as she could, then rubbed it between her fingers, taking off all the sticky stuff and leaving a nice smooth surface.

Sound, that was what he'd said, it was sound. That was the new word – that was the worst, that was just the worst, that was worse than mates.

Hazel didn't like waiting, and she sure as hell didn't like waiting in public. One of the things about having a live-in boyfriend was you weren't supposed to do things like this anymore.

The label on the other side wasn't coming off so easy. Hazel wasn't going to get anything even remotely resembling a big bit. First round elimination. The disgrace of it. Hazel decided she would change the rules once she worked out what the new game was, in the meantime she would just pick it to bits, excavating with her nails then parting with her fingertips.

That Eddie bloke, that was worth some contemplation. She could while away some time thinking about how she was going to bring that up. Something between him and Carol. That was a turn up for the book. Somebody'd got dumped then, somebody always got dumped, so somebody had been dumped. Likely candidate: Eddie. Either way it would merit a mention.

Hazel stopped. Something was wrong. She looked up and saw that that shower of perennial losers, the greasy-haired, appallingly attired, Fids-lookalikes, the thick-as-fuck Media Studies students, were displaying a collective amusement at her mat-destruction masterclass.

Bozos, thought Hazel. Yeah, it must be really smart watching somebody picking beer mats to bits.

As much as Hazel wanted to sneer she felt a bit flushed and suspected she was giving it her coy and cute look. Hazel got back to her mat and tried to remember the punchline to Recca's 'How many Media Studies students does it take to change a lightbulb?'

The door opened. But it was only the pensioners, Recca's *bête noir*. They coughed and spluttered before making an exhibition of shaking bone-dry coats and folding them neatly on the window ledge. The acknowledged champs of quiz night, they actually trained for this. They even cheated. They got disqualified once for sneaking in a reference book. It was Recca who'd grassed them.

Hazel looked at the debris on the table. She ripped up the biggest pieces so they were all about the same size and stacked them in the ashtray. Then she brushed up all the crumbs into her cupped hand and sprinkled them over the stack.

This was getting bloody stupid.

Hazel sighed and flattened out the stack then took the ashtray over to the bar and exchanged it for a clean one. While she was there she got herself another drink and on her way back swiped some mats from an unoccupied table.

The clock on the wall had advanced five minutes. The watch on her wrist had advanced six. Hazel cheered the watch.

A couple of minutes and several sips later the woman came round with the pens, notepads and scoresheets.

'Are you in the quiz?' she said.

Hazel nodded.

'Do you not want to move to another table so that you're not on your own?'

'No. No, it's alright,' said Hazel. 'I'm waiting, I'm waiting on people.'

Throughout the history of football there has never been a sighting of a linesman in civilian life, not one. Nobody has ever known a linesman, nobody has ever bumped into a linesman, nor has anybody ever known anyone who has ever seen, known or bumped into a linesman.

The only bloke in history ever acknowledged to bear any physical resemblance to the species linesman was him out the old Cossack hairspray ad whose photo still adorns the walls of old-fashioned barber-shops. That smart side-shed and chiselled jaw whose telly appearances were famous for the lack of synch that went on between what he was supposed to be saying and the way his mouth was actually moving. This fuelled the notion that he wasn't at all real and was actually a fucked-up computer. Funnily enough, folk said much the same about linesmen.

Sunderland were on the attack. A hoof up the park was being chased by a red-headed winger with Elephant Man bombing across to clear the danger.

Crunch!

The ball went out of play. The linesman raced to the corner spot, pointed his flag down on the quarter circle, and nodded to his referee.

Now while the angle of departure indicated the defender had indeed made the final contact, what the linesman hadn't seen was that although the ball had been *played* by Elephant Man, what he'd done was to *play it off* the red-headed winger. From his viewpoint the linesman couldn't really be blamed because he wasn't perfectly placed to pass judgement. Mind you, if he'd been keeping up with play like he was supposed to . . .

'JESUS FUCKING FUCK! CAN YOU FUCKING BELIEVE THAT!!' Andy was outraged. He looked to the others to share his disgust, but only Eddie was vocal, and he was getting on at Elephant Man for leaving the red-headed winger fit enough to walk.

The red-headed winger got himself up and went over to retrieve the ball. He kicked it off the advertising board and caught it one-handed then grinned at the crowd like he was really smart or something.

Andy, though, had moved down to the corner flag and was waiting for him, rocking back and forth, inhaling, exhaling, and then – pow! – letting loose with 'YA DIRTY CHEATING SOAP-DODGING GEORDIE FUCKING BASTARD YE!!!'

The red-headed winger just laughed and placed the ball in the quarter-circle. He wiped his hands on the arse of his shorts before setting up to take the kick. He wasn't happy, though, and removed three blades of grass from in front of the ball and two from behind it.

'YOU WATCHING HIM, YA USELESS BASTARD. EVER HEARD OF TIME-WASTING?'

The linesman, though, wasn't listening to Andy, he was too busy concentrating on the jostling in the box. Should anyone fall down clutching their face, the linesman would be able to describe the incident and point out the guilty party. That was what got you mentioned. 'The linesman spotted an elbow . . . After consultation with his linesman . . .' Cause if you get mentioned folk got to hear of you, and if they heard of you they might just remember you when it came round to deciding who would be going over to officiate at the World Cup, the World Cup in the good old US of A. Yeah, spotting one of those was worth a million times more than whether or not you seen all those stupid wee deflections the crowd seemed to get so worked up about.

The red-headed winger was wiping his hands again. This time, though, he finished by pulling his shorts right up two reveal two fleshy, freckled buttocks.

And then:

i) Andy went spare.

ii) The red-headed winger swung over a head-high bullet which was met on the six yard line by his centre-half.

iii) In this, his 792nd appearance for the club, a club record, the centre-half scored his first ever competitive goal.

iv) The linesman, displaying a turn of pace somewhat at odds with his previous ability to keep up with the game, pelted back to the half-line.

v) The red-headed winger turned and made an ugly face and a rude gesture at the support.

vi) Andy, bawling and shouting, raced after the linesman but was prevented from entering the enclosure by the skinheaded steward, the one who had 'I kill' tattooed on his forehead.

*

'No, it is. Telling you, they're lethal. They're worse than the young ones. See my dad, right, he's the same speed wherever he goes.' Recca made like she was eyeballs out over an imaginary steering wheel. 'Forty mile an hour on the motorway.' Recca gave a sideways glance and indicated right. 'Forty mile an hour through the town.' Recca signalled another right. 'Then forty mile an hour up the drive. Telling you, guy's dangerous.'

'Mind when you gave mum those lessons?' said Carol to her dad. Her father nodded and Carol turned to Recca. 'Thing was, she wouldn't stop talking, and when mum was talking to you, mum had to be looking at you. Like this.' Carol took over the imaginary steering wheel. ' "So what is it I've to do now?", and, what a scream, if it was anything to do with the pedals she had to be sitting back like that, like she was looking under the table.'

Carol's dad laughed. He scratched behind his ear and said, 'She was never really that keen on the driving, your mother. We only went out the couple of times.'

'So,' said Recca, 'are you coming with us up to this quiz then or what?'

'Eh?'

'Up the quiz? Come on.'

'Och, no,' said Carol's dad, 'Don't be daft.'

Carol joined in. 'Come on, dad. Do you good.'

'Either that,' said Deke, 'or you can stay here and I'll thrash you at backgammon again.'

'Well, eh . . .'

'That's it settled then,' said Recca, 'you're coming with us. Tell you what, I'll give you a treat, you can pretend you're my rich sugar daddy.'

'Recca!' said Carol, then to her dad, 'Look, do you want to come up?'

Recca never gave him the opportunity to answer. 'Course he does. Anyway, men love being told what to do, saves them having to think. Not that they ever think, anyway, I suppose, but that's besides the point.'

'Hold your horses just a minute,' said Carol's dad. 'What I want to know is what's happening with this car? Are you wanting it?'

Deke shook his head.

'Look,' said Carol, 'you can leave it here the night, we'll take it back the morrow and see about getting your money back.'

'You sure, hen?'

Carol looked at Deke first. 'Yeah, we're sure.'

'Fair enough then. If that's what you're wanting.'

Deke went round collecting everybody's dishes.

'Listen,' said Carol's dad. 'I'll do that and stay here and look after the kids. You can all go up.'

'Deke won't come, dad. You know he never goes out.'

'Weirdo.' Recca shouted through loud enough for Deke to hear.

'We're late,' said Carol, 'better get a move on.'

'Cheerio then,' Deke popped his head back through. 'Au revoir! Auf wiedersehen! Buenos noches! Sayonora! Go! In the name of Allah, Go!'

Recca gave him the finger.

'Look,' said Carol, 'I'm going for a quick wash. Just two minutes. You needing anything?'

'Eh?' said Recca. 'Tell you what, toss us through your roll-on, will you.'

'I don't know what I'm letting myself in for here,' said Carol's dad. 'I just don't know.'

'Relax, you'll be alright. We'll look after you.'

Carol returned with the roll-on and Recca inserted it up the sleeve of her t-shirt and shoogled it about.

'Hey, you never know,' continued Recca, 'next week we might write off and get you all lined up for the Generation Game.'

Recca stuck the roll-on up her other sleeve and laughed. Carol's dad laughed too, but as to why he didn't really know.

'In the crying out for help stakes, that is what you call one serious fucking aria.'

While Andy was embroiled in deep half-time analysis with his fellow linesman baiters, Dunx was embroiled in going on about Andy.

Graeme, meanwhile, was taking his time searching through his pockets, hoping the extremely rich Eddie would oblige with the official half-time crash.

'Hey, boys,' said Gary. 'Do you think if I sang "She's too sexy for the police" everybody would join in?'

Graeme said, 'No, please, please don't' and took out his fags and gave one to Eddie.

'Andy's just out of order,' said Dunx. 'Just completely out of order. Acting like he's ashamed to be seen with us.'

'Speak for yourself,' said Eddie.

'Nah,' said Dunx, 'you know what it is? He's ashamed of himself, that's what it is. Watch him, look, he can't justify himself.'

'Would I be right in assuming you two've fallen out?' said Graeme. 'Just a guess, like.'

Dunx ignored him. 'It's all a sham, all this, that's all it is. It's all a sham. It's this woman, man. She is one major problem.'

'What the fuck is he havering about?' whispered Graeme to Eddie.

'Tell you later. You know what your trouble is, Dunky Dee. You are one jealous bitch.' Eddie gulped at his use of the word bitch.

'Fuck off,' said Dunx, 'I can't stand her.'

'Arsehole, I don't mean that, I mean you're jealous of her for taking away your wee bum chum.'

'Shite, Christ, your arse,' said Dunx. 'Hey, I'm going out with somebody, it's never affected the time I've had for my mates. Nah, she's manipulative that one, she's turning him against us.'

'Regardless, you're still a jealous bitch.' Eddie liked that word. 'Mind my going away day, you were giving it all your "Don't go, please stay, don't go, please stay". '

'Christ, I was pished, and anyway I'm not ashamed of that. We're your mates, we're your absolute best mates, you'll never take that away, I don't care how much you earn. You'll never have mates as good as us as long as you fucking live.'

Fucking pish, thought Eddie to himself, but never said anything.

'Go on,' said Dunx. 'Deny it, I dare you. D'you know what we're like? We're like women, man, we're like women.'

Eddie swallowed the biggest swallow of his life.

'Nah,' said Dunx, 'know how they always go on about how women are closer to each other than men are? Well, we're the crew, we're the generation, that disproves that 'cause everything we did, we did the gether.'

'I.e. Fuck all,' said Graeme.

'See,' said Dunx, 'I knew you'd come away with one of these wee wanky comments. I fucking know these things. I know everything about you pair, and I know everything there is to know about that wee shite down there.' Dunx nodded towards Andy.

'Eh, Dunx,' said Eddie, 'just to get back to the real world for a sec, just a second, like, there's a friend of yours over there looking for you.'

'What? Where about? God, it's not Fids, is it?'

Eddie laughed. 'Nah,' he said, 'over there, next the boys off Fat Charlie's bus.'

It took Dunx a few seconds to spot, focus and recognize. It took him a millionth of that time to react, though. 'Oh fuck. Oh, fuck off, will you. Don't let on we can see her.'

'This is fucking hilarious this,' said Eddie, ignoring Dunx' advice and waving over. 'Watch her. Oh, there she goes, back again. Telling you, Dunx, she is serious. She's studying every bastard in here. Oh oh. She's going the wrong way. No, no, those guys are telling her she's already been there, she's coming back again. This is what you call a search, Dunx, this is a search, this is what you call combing the area. Oh, hold on, Old Uncle Mel's got a hold of her. Oh no, Dunx, they're pointing over here. Old Uncle Mel's grassed you off, Dunx. What a fucking bastard.'

There was a ripple of applause and some cheers as she waved over and Eddie and Graeme waved back.

'Excuse me,' said Graeme, 'and just who the fuck is this?'

Dunx was leaning over the barrier, hiding his face. 'Some dozy cow at work,' he said. 'Her name's Heather. I was supposed to be seeing her the night. This is a total embarrassment.'

Heather, her name was Heather, the most beautiful name in the world. God was in his Heaven, Chaka Khan was singing 'This is my night', and the lassie with the cool threads was the lassie with the six-tube sunbed and she was called Heather.

Gary could hardly believe it.

Heather was done up in cream: fawn trousers, white shirt and a crushed linen fawn jacket secured over the shoulder with clear-varnished pinky. It would either have to have been that or the black, cause Heather hated colours. Colours were what ordinary folk wore. Ordinary folk with their lilacs and pastels in summer, purples and navys in winter. Ordinary folk that wanted to look like game shows or Australia; all brash and insensitive. Like trousers, like brain – all done down the same.

As lovely as cream was, though, it wasn't ideal for traipsing half way down the town to what she thought was the football ground only to discover it was something called 'a sports stadium' then having to take the dreaded Glenbow bus back with the dreaded Glenbowians, sat on a stinking, smelling seat next to a bloke that looked like he'd just returned from Mr Dodgiest-looking-bastard-in-the-universe with a winner's rosette.

Nor was cream the colour in which to shell out six quid to go wandering round this unfit-for-vermin crumbling stairway, and trying to avoid the eyes of individuals who looked like their parents were brother and sister, while all the while somehow trying to spot the hundred percent hunk of gorgeousness that was Dunx.

Consequently, Heather was flushed. She was aware of her odour, her discomfort and her confusion. Not that it ever counted for anything but Heather was good at things like that. She was aware she was moving when, by rights, by now she should have been standing still and drying off. This made things worse. The worry fuelling the movement fuelling the worry.

Heather looked around. It was like one of those pictures of car manufacturers' car parks displaying the brand new models, all bright and shiny and, wow, comes in, five, yes five, five different colours – but all exactly the same. Except these weren't cars – they were guys called Rab with severe speech impediments like her brother-in-law and the sub-humans that had helped with her flitting for whom personal hygiene did not mean soap and water but pints of aftershave and pawfulls of perfumed powder. If Halfords ever went into the clothing market they'd clear up: this lot would wear anything. For all their supposed lack of concern regarding all things sartorial the male of the species seemed drawn to the loudest of fashions: high-tops, shell-suits, baseball caps, shiny football tops. Tut tut, even the hair was getting longer again with all that attendant washing, drying and grooming.

'Hey, you! Hey, Boy George! Your boyfriend's waving at you.'

It took Heather a second to realize she shouldn't be looking for who had spoken, but looking for somebody, somewhere waving.

A second was long enough, though.

'Over there!' 'Other way, ya daftie!' 'Down at the corner!' 'Over by the stand!'

Somebody started singing 'I just don't know what to do with myself' but thankfully only knew the first line.

Somebody else said something about 'a tart in a trance' and that got a bit of laughter. As did the one when somebody shouted 'Sign her! Sign her!'

Heather, meanwhile, was on the verge of staging a raged exit when Old Uncle Mel – clearly rattled by this distraction and the correspondent drop in value for his money – grabbed a hold of Heather and swung her round to face him.

'Are you blind, hen, are you blind? There! There! Over there! Christ, hen, if brains were chocolate you'd struggle to fill a Smartie.'

Heather glared in reproach but was refrained from one of her favourite put-downs by the old fellow swinging her round so she was facing in the opposite direction.

'For Christ's sake, look!' he said. 'There! See?'

Heather looked – and there was the one they called Eddie, waving, another bloke was waving as well. And there was Dunx with his hands in front of his face. And there was Andy talking to some old guys further along. And there was . . .

Heather's heart went bumpity-bump-bumpity-bump. For she was looking at the boy from across the court, and, tonight, a vision in fawn trousers, white shirt and casual dress jacket – cream, of course.

The cartoon video had held their attention for as long as it had taken them to drink their juice, and now Joanne was off doing a series of cartwheels and Baby Joe was bombing about trying to build up speed so as to increase his kinetic energy, thereby enabling him and his walking frame to smash through the junction of the settees and investigate what lay beyond.

Nevertheless it had done its job and allowed Deke the time to skin up. He switched off the video with one remote, activated the CD with another then lit up.

'Where's my slippers?' said Joanne.

Deke laughed. 'Where you left them.'

'Where was that?'

'You're the one should know, dear. Trace back your steps from when you came in.'

Joanne sat herself down, arranged her legs like she was preparing for a session of Yogic flying and opened her gob like she was a fish.

Deke had a wee smile to himself. It was funny how kids were basically just thick adults. You could never quite remember what it was like being like that, being so different, the sensation of being different. There were four things that Deke felt held the key to understanding what was going on, what life was all about: number one was dreams, number two was being out of it, number three was senility and number four was children.

'You got it yet?' said Deke.

Joanne shook her head. 'How come you and papa don't get on?'

Deke laughed. Better luck next time. 'Who said we don't get on?'

'You don't, you don't get on.'

'It's not that we don't get on,' said Deke, 'it's just like, well; see men are always in competition with each other. They'll compete over anything and . . .'

'How?'

Fuck knows, thought Deke. 'Don't know why, they just do. Like one man'll say something then another man'll say something to better it. Say, like, if you've got one man and he says how his house is really smart then the next man'll say something that'll make his house sound even smarter.'

'Like what boys do?'

'A-ha, that's it, exactly. But even if the man says something to make his house sound really bad, then the next man'll come away with something that'll make his house sound even worse.'

Joanne shook her head, not through lack of understanding, but just at the stupidity of the species under consideration.

'True,' continued Deke, 'men like to be at the extremes. There's this thing called ego. Men have got big egos, great big egos. It's like the way you measure yourself.'

Joanne looked puzzled. 'But what's all this got to do with you and papa not getting on?'

'I'm getting to that, hold on, I'm coming to that. Cause, right, me and your papa are sort of in competition for your mum. Well, he is, I'm not, cause I've won so to speak. Your mum prefers me to him.'

'Papa says that if you and mum split up then me and Baby Joe and mum can all go and stay with papa.'

That was kind of him, thought Deke. God, that was kind of the old bastard to say that.

'That won't happen,' said Deke.

'But what if it did?'

'Then you, little lady, are coming with me.'

Joanne shook her head then said, 'You and papa should try harder to get on.'

'I try, I really try, it's him that doesn't.'

'Then you should try harder still.'

'Your papa's old, he's a bit funny 'bout things. He wants your mum all to himself. He makes out that she's still a wee lassie and how he's protecting her and how he's looking after her. But it's really him that's wanting the help. He's wanting your mum to do all his cleaning and make all his dinners for him. Your papa's old-fashioned, he thinks women should do all that kind of stuff.'

'Then you could go round and do all his cleaning and make his dinners then.'

'Why ya, come here, I'll. . . .'

Joanne made a run for it but Deke caught her in the corner. Just as he was about to pull her sticky-out ears off, though, there was a wee clatter from up above.

Baby Joe, who'd given up the penetrative approach, and was using his now lop-sided walking-frame as scaffolding to scramble up the arm of the settee, pointed to the ceiling.

'Oh,' said Joanne, 'can we go up to the loft and play with Scott? Please, pretty please.'

Deke checked the time. 'Okay,' he said, 'but only half an hour, half an hour then bed, alright?'

That was all Joanne needed to hear. Next thing, she was rushing away to get the broom to bang on the trap door so that Scott would let the rope-ladder down.

Heather was just standing there, nobody had spoken to her.

'Come on to fuck, ref. Last time I did that much shoving I fathered a wean.'

But then again they weren't really speaking to each other either.

'They do this the start of every fucking season. They start off with their smart new sweeper system, stick the one-foot wonder in the middle of the park and everything's fucking rosy, then what do they do, they go and lose four crappy goals.'

You'd think they'd have at least introduced her, though.

'Play to the system, play to the system   to feet, play to fucking feet.'

They were just sort of commentating or whatever it was you called it.

'That is fucking terrible that is! That is shocking. See that, that is absolutely shocking!'

All she'd got was a mumble from Eddie, a grudging half-smile from Dunx, complete with half-raised eyebrows to indicate some sort of surprise –

'Come on, a wee bit dig. Clear your lines, will you! A wee bit fucking dig.'

– and half a nod from Andy. The one that was smoking hadn't even looked at her.

'My fucking piles run faster than you, ya bastard!'

Neither had the guy from across the court – but he was definitely edging towards her, though.

'Should get Serial Killer on, and sort these Geordie fucking bastards out, man.'

He was swaying all the time and with each and every sway he was moving that wee bit closer.

'Who was that to? Who the fuck was that to?'

So Heather moved closer to him.

'Don't try to play football with it when you're in your own box; just hoof the flaming thing out the park!'

Her eyes caught his. The four eyes lingered, like fish in a fishmonger's window.

'See what you've done! See what you've fucking gone and done!'

Eye contact was serious, serious enough to exchange a knowing smile.

'Talk to each other! Talk to each other! Did they never ever teach you to talk to each other?'

But Heather didn't know what to say. This wasn't the time for dialogue, anyway. This wasn't the place for secrets. This was just a moment, the moment.

'Oh, come on, come on. What you playing at? You gave it away, you gave it afuckingway!'

Heather made a definite move; she moved a step closer. She didn't edge closer, she moved a whole step.

'I can't believe it. When was the last time we lost five goals?'

'Last season, reserve league cup, home to Arbroath.'

All that was needed was for something to be said.

'Boo! Boo! Boo! Fucking terrible!'

Heather said, 'Is that it finished?'

'No,' said Dunx. 'That's what you call a goal. Just a goal.'

Heather didn't much care for Dunx's tone of voice. 'Are these your friends?' she said.

'Mates,' said Dunx, 'these are my mates, aye.'

The one who'd been smoking gave a half-smile while the guy from across the court held out his hand.

'A-hem,' he said, 'Gary.'

'Heather,' said Heather.

'The only time I ever went to a football match somebody tried to stick their finger up my arse when a goal was scored.'

Recca gulped.

'One of my cousins,' explained Hazel.

Recca gave a rare glance of sympathy but was distracted by the next question, the anagram. Recca was the first to get it so they got maximum points which was a good thing cause Hazel's solo efforts had left Waster's Corner trailing in last place.

'How you enjoying it?' said Recca to Carol's dad.

Carol's dad wasn't listening. He was too busy studying the team of old guys and trying to place the faces.

'Dad,' said Carol, 'Recca's speaking to you.'

'Sorry, sorry, what was that?'

'I was just asking if you were enjoying yourself.'

'Aye, aye, it's fine.' Carol's dad laughed. 'Not that you'll get much help from me mind. It's true what they say, you know, the brain's the first to go. What about you, hen, you alright?'

'Yes, dad,' said Carol and glared at Recca like this was some really bad idea which suited no one and had nothing going for it.

Hazel gulped her drink. Never in all her days had she been so pleased to see folk she couldn't stand the sight of. One more stupid question and she'd've been out that door and that would've been the end of it.

The last of the anagrams was handed in by the Media Studies table and Recca shouted over 'Hey, you lot, what do Media Studies students use as contraceptives?'

Silence, a blushed silence.

'Do you give in?' said Recca.

No response, nothing.

'Come on,' said Recca, 'say something, at least tell me you give in.'

'Okay, if it'll shut you up we give in,' said one of them then brought up his glass to hide his face.

'Looks,' said Recca, 'they use their looks as contraceptives.'

The Media Studies students stopped what they were pretending to be doing and turned on Recca. They could handle being called thick 'cause they knew they weren't. They could handle being called virgins cause they'd got awfy good at pretending they weren't. But when a woman this beautiful passed comment to the effect that you were as ugly as the guy sitting next to you then it really fucking hurt.

The world sunk back into the comfort of the next question – films and naming the co-stars.

'Right, dad,' said Carol, 'this is your specialist subject.'

But Carol's dad only got a couple of the answers, and they were the easy ones. He felt a bit annoyed with Carol and Recca for pretending they hadn't known. He was also annoyed at not knowing any of those old guys. Not that it mattered, you couldn't know everybody, but it would be something to say. These blokes didn't look like they were from round here, though, they didn't look like they'd worked in the woodyards, they looked like toffs. Carol's dad laughed to himself.

'You alright, dad?' said Carol.

'Aye, just thinking about something.' He stopped for a second, seen that this was as good a time as any, then added, 'Listen, hen, I think I'll just away off down the road, eh. Let you lot get on with it.'

He was on his feet so he was going.

'You sure?' said Carol.

'Aye,' said her dad. He laughed and went on, 'No, I've enjoyed myself. Nice to see you out and about with all your friends. Eh, I'll see you the morrow then, the usual time, eh?'

'A-ha,' said Carol and with that he was off. Carol decided he was alright. If anything, he looked relieved to be going.

When Scott was at the loft-insulation with Martin, Martin who stayed across the landing from Scott, the pair of them joked about what they could do with all that space, all their new-found skills and with all that insulating and draught excluding material.

Then one day they thought – why the fuck not.

So in a very casual sort of way they put forward their proposal to Terry, who stayed through the wall from Martin, Moira, who stayed across the landing from Terry, and Deke, who stayed through the wall from Scott. Old Mrs Docherty, who stayed across the landing from Deke, and who thankfully was as deaf as a post, was not invited to give her opinions.

Everyone thought it was daft, but decided there would be no harm in giving it a try.

The first crop, though, the first crop had been a poor crop. What there was, and there wasn't much, had little effect other than stinking to the high heavens. So Scott did some reading and got a hold of some green halogen lights and rigged them up, on the understanding that growth required a sympathetic environment. And, by God, he was right. The second crop was better. Not exactly plentiful but a right sweet smell and a half-decent hit.

Deke latched onto Scott's train of thought and got a hold of a couple of second-hand fish tanks and a few old bean-bags (green, of course), and it was agreed that all the folk would spend more time up there, playing sweet music and chatting and the like, creating a bit of a mellow vibe.

And that did the trick 'cause the third crop had the top-floor residents of No's 25–48 Irvine Avenue bounding about like Big Bird out of Sesame Street.

Okay, so that was quality, top-flight quality as Scott so punningly said, now all they had to do was do something about the quantity. They'd did their best with all the materials they'd pockled for insulating the place but the temperature they were insulating was never quite high enough.

Portable gas heaters were clumsy, and the cylinders were expensive and attracted attention. Electricity was also problematic. It was either too hot or too cold, and there were all those cables to contend with. It wasn't a good heat, either, the plants told Scott they didn't like it.

Then the blessed council announced that the gas central heating for the block was to be upgraded.

Scott couldn't believe his luck – he'd served his time as a plumber, Martin had done an electronics ET and Terry fancied himself as a bit of a joiner.

Originally they'd just intended lifting the old radiators out the skips under the pretext of flogging them for a fiver to Second-Hand Dan the Garbage Man, but when they caught sight of all those bright, shiny new ones, Moira, who'd served her time in Cortonvale for serious thieving, said there was no point in settling for second best.

Once work began on the flats, the top-floor residents would stand about and monitor what the tradesmen were doing, then come the end of the day they'd rush up to the loft and copy what they'd seen. Things were made even easier due to the tradesmen leaving their tools in the folks' houses overnight on account of all the thieving that had been going on from the sites portacabins.

So that was that, a brand new heating system: clean, efficient, controllable and all available at the flick of a switch. Don't you just love being in control ?

But there was still a problem: the smell. The smell was a sweet smell and the smell was a downright lovely smell, but the smell was a also strong smell and the smell was a distinctive smell that travelled easily and could twitch a dopehead's nostril at twenty paces in a pet shop.

And the thing was all this had to be kept quiet or it wouldn't work. The top-floor residents were sworn to secrecy, the produce was prescribed for personal use only, no profit, so they had to do something about the smell.

Then another flyer appeared from the council, apologising for the delay in the installation of the extractor fans in the kitchens and bathrooms, and promising that they would be installed by the end of the following week.

Add, that's what happened, they were installed by the end of the following week, installed in the loft.

And a few fiddled meters, which was what Martin appeared to have specialised in with his electronics ET, and that was that, that was the loft-garden, first-class quality and all-year quantity. And when you were successful, what did you do? Why, you branched out, of course.

'What's that one?' said Joanne.

'That,' said Scott, 'that is what you call cambula or star fruit.'

'Psst,' said Eddie, 'Gary's nicked your bird.'

Dunx tutted. 'Talk sense, will you, she's not my bird.'

'Just thought I'd mention it, no need to get all bitchy.'

'Who's getting bitchy?' said Dunx, bitchily. 'And will you stop saying that word, it's stupid.'

'Now just you don't get all, eh, huffy and aggressive,' said Graeme.

'What was what? What did you say there? Ah, fuck it. Who cares, anyway.'

Dunx started rocking back and forth on the barrier. 'And what's all this "bird" nonsense, that one of your London expressions?'

No, thought Eddie, it's one of yours. But, fair do's, it'd been remiss of Eddie to use it, made a change from Simon digging him up.

'Wide! Wide! For God's sake, as least look. Oh, come on.' Dunx shook his head. 'Look, I just can't get into this game. Fancy just shooting off the now?'

'Now, come on,' said Graeme, 'you're only saying that cause you're upset.'

'Aye, that's right, well done, well spotted. Stroll on, will you.'

'I think he's upset,' said Eddie.

'Stroll on.'

'Look,' said Graeme, 'we're worried about you, we're your mates, are you sure you're not upset?'

'Stroll on. Stroll fucking on.'

'It's a shame he's not upset,' whispered Graeme.

'How come?' said Eddie.

'Cause he's a bloody scream when he's upset.'

Eddie and Graeme laughed.

'Christ,' said Dunx, 'did you not see me when she appeared? Like this I was, man, hiding my face. Hiding my fucking face. It was you that waved her over. It was you.'

'Just as long as you're not upset,' said Eddie.

'Stroll on, that's all I can say. Hey, and if you're so fucking smart, right, will you tell us why all these Geordie fucking bastards, man, why all of those cunts over there are singing "Ingerland! Ingerland!"? What the fuck is all that in aid of?'

Eddie and Graeme pondered this observation. They couldn't think of an answer but they did come up with a response.

'One Tommy Brolin! There's only one Tommy Brolin! One Tommy Brolin!'

'Like it, like it,' said Dunx. 'That's better.' Then he paused and added. 'The thing about this lassie, right . . .'

Eddie and Graeme groaned.

'No, the thing with the lassie, right, is you sit there in that fucking office all day, five days a week, that's all we ever do, and you just get so bored out your skull, day after day, you just get bored out your skull, and you think about anything. And I just thought about riding the lassie, right, no, cause, telling you, there's times when you'll ride anything, you'll ride fucking anything. That's all she was.'

Eddie gulped. At least she wasn't a "bird".

'Got to laugh 'bout Gary but,' continued Dunx. 'Look at him. That guy has been found out, that's his true colours, man, absolutely found out. Bet he doesn't even know what to do with a lassie. And I had first option on that, by the way. I had first option. Aye, stroll on. Stroll on, alright. He's welcome, he's welcome to her.'

'Listen,' said Eddie, 'are you sure you're not upset?'

'Stroll on, that's all I can say.'

'I think he is upset,' said Graeme.

'Aye?' said Eddie.

'Oh aye,' said Graeme, 'in fact I would go as far as to say I was positive.'

'Really?' said Eddie, 'and what makes you so sure?'

Graeme grinned and said, 'Well, it's kind of like the way his face is the colour of a skelped arse.'

'What's this I was hearing about you last night,' said Recca. 'Puffing at the party fags, I hear, and whacked out on the old wackiebaccie.'

'Recca!' said Carol.

Hazel just shrugged and sipped her drink. Just as she was about to put it back on the table, though, she changed her mind and took a decent gulp.

So much for trying to get on with folk. All they ever wanted was for you to be the same as them. And if you didn't choose to be the same as them, living their crappy wee lives, you were up for every little sarky comment of the day. Everybody had to be the same round here, and for everybody to be the same it was easiest if everybody was just crap. All Hazel had been trying to do had been trying to get on with them, but to get on with them you had to get in with them, and all they were ever doing was going on about how unusual it all was, and how different she was. Folk were only ever smart round here when they agreed with you, that was the way of it. It was crap to suggest that folk sought out things to challenge their prejudices, folk only ever interpreted things to suit their prejudices.

Hazel took another gulp. She was getting in a bad mood. She had to do something about it or she would end up doing something stupid. Hazel smiled at Recca. Recca smiled back. That was good. A pleasant exterior showed a pleasant interior. They'd got that at a seminar, it was Chinese or something like that. The guy had said something about how it took only half the muscles to smile as it did to frown. At the time Hazel had questioned, though, whether the exercise wouldn't ultimately be better for her, pointing out that moody bastards were better looking than geeks.

Cut it out, Hazel told herself. Go on, say something, say something to them.

'There's an old friend of yours back in town,' said Hazel to Carol, 'Eddie somebody-or-other.'

'Eddie! Christ, haven't seen Eddie in ages.'

Hazel looked interested. 'He might be coming round here a bit later on.'

Carol laughed. 'I shouldn't think so. If Eddie's back, the wee boys'll be out getting blootered, unless that is he's taken the pledge which, knowing Eddie, I rather doubt.'

Hazel was now intrigued. Deke and Carol were near teetotal and looked down on drinkers and pubs. Deke hadn't been in a pub for seven years, he'd said. 'Andy was saying that you and Eddie used to go out together.'

'No,' Carol laughed, 'Eddie's just a dear old friend, a dear and lovely friend.'

A dear and lovely friend, repeated Hazel to herself. What was that supposed to mean? Could be anything, you could never tell with these hippies.

But no, she decided, it was a lovely way to describe somebody, to be described as a dear and lovely friend, or even to have a dear and lovely friend. It was the way you'd talk of a beloved family pet, a lovely spaniel with big sad eyes. It was a helluva lot better than being prescribed an awkward little squirt, anyway.

'Listen,' said Carol, 'I know you're expecting Andy the night but I'd better warn you that, well, if Eddie's back in town then, eh . . .'

'No, he said he'd be here, he promised.' Hazel shook her head. Unless Andy wanted to go through life minus a spleen he'd be here alright.

'I know,' said Carol, 'I'm sure he did, I'm sure he did say that but, well, you know yourself what Andy's like. He can be a bit funny as regards time. I just thought I'd warn you, anyway. Eddie can get a bit carried away at times, and folk tend to get carried away with him.'

Recca was sniggering away to herself as she was writing down the names of eight post-war South American dictators who had more vowels than consonants in their middle names.

Hazel opened her bag. 'What do you want?'

'Sorry?' said Carol.

'To drink, what do you want to drink?'

Carol didn't want anything and Recca just wanted a packet of roast beef and mustard.

Hazel went up to get served.

'You made a right arse of that, Batman,' said Recca.

'Shut up.'

'Aye, it's a shame for the lassie, right enough –'

'Pack it in.'

'– young lassie like that.'

Recca laughed. Carol frowned.

It wasn't unusual for Gary to be heading home after a game and for somebody or other to enquire of Gary what the score was. Equally, it wasn't unusual for Gary not to have the faintest clue what the score was because, despite his trainspotter's attitude to his scrapbooks, Gary used football the same way Deke used his fish-tank, a calming and peaceful way to mull over all of life.

That was the norm, anyway. This, the Sunderland game, was far from the norm. Gary couldn't think, he just couldn't think. Hell, he couldn't even think of the sunbed. It wasn't that he daren't think of the sunbed, he just couldn't think of the sunbed. It was physically impossible to think of the sunbed. It was physically impossible 'cause all that was going on in Gary's head was still just Chaka Khan belting out 'This is my night/ I'm gonna do it just right/ I'm gonna let this magic shine' and in the mixing desk of his fevered mind Gary'd all but made the 12" redundant and created a whole new genre that would set the world of dance culture into pangs of pure delight.

Not that Gary was thinking that, 'cause Gary couldn't think about anything.

Likewise, he knew that this was a good opportunity to talk to Heather but dialogue required preparatory thought and since this was something Gary was presently incapable of, it would be a bit like making the dinner without any food.

She hadn't spoken either, Heather hadn't spoken, nothing other than her name, that glorious most wonderful of names.

If love didn't exist, Gary decided, then no one would have the gumption to invent it. Nah, it existed alright. That was proof. Everything in life derived from some sort of sense. Ears made sense, the nose made sense, the fingers made sense, even the brain made sense. Their functions, their forms and their positions all made some kind of sense, but to woo someone, to worship someone, to simply and utterly adore one and only one made no sense whatsoever. If you asked a really smart computer to judge the worthiness of love and define its purpose, the print-out would read a big fat zilcheroony. You wouldn't stick to the one place, to the one food, or to the one activity so why then should the prospect of a lifetimesworth of one partner be so overwhelmingly enthralling? No, love made no sense. It appeared so limiting, so rigid. Yet, it was the exact opposite. It lifted you, it transported you, it turned you on, turned you over, turned you inside out. It transformed you by lending a new freedom, a spiritual freedom, a new fulfilment, a new fabulousness, a new . . .

Gary shuddered. Chaka Khan wasn't singing anymore. Instead Gary could hear Dunx and Eddie and Graeme and everyone else, all shouting and swearing. Gary could make out what they were saying, all of them, all of what they were saying. Gary could smell things, disgusting things, he could smell pies and bovril and piss and beer. Gary was aware that he was aware, and the real world was staring him in the face like a pile of dirty washing. The moment had passed; shit, it had only been a moment.

Or had it?

Gary gave himself a shake. He felt remarkably clean, he felt cleansed. He also felt remarkably loose of limb, almost dizzy, like after a right good workout, but better, better than those. Gary felt good; Gary felt very good indeed. He felt like he could go on the pitch and run rings round everybody, and that was something you never felt when you were actually standing there at the games, normally you felt scared and stiff, but, Christ, that's how good Gary was feeling.

Thus the moment had not been a mere moment.

The moment had not been a mere moment cause the moment had been a door, a turnstile, an entrance, a door that had taken him, permitted him, accessed him, to a higher level of consciousness, a more profound level, a deeper level, a more fulfilled level, the level of love.

'Penny for them.'

The voice of an angel.

'Your thoughts,' said Heather, 'a penny for your thoughts.'

'Oh, eh, aye, eh, I've not really been thinking, like, as such, just had this song playing away, you know.'

Heather smiled. 'What song was that?'

Having gone through the door Gary felt pure and had this incredible desire for honesty. What the world lacked was honesty. 'It's a song by Chaka Khan,' he said 'called *This Is My Night.*'

Heather laughed. 'I've been playing Sibelius, the Karelia Suite.'

'I'll get it out the library,' said Gary, 'tomorrow.'

Hazel lowered her lids. 'You could maybe hear it the night.'

And through the door there was a room, a blue room. And in the corner of the blue room there lay a six-tube sunbed.

There were only two left.

Graeme took his finger out of his packet and his hand out of his pocket and applauded the award of a throw-in.

Eight since getting up, eight. Graeme put his hand in his pocket again.

'You wanting one of these?' he said to Eddie.

Eddie did so that was them. Good. Graeme would go up the quiz once the game was finished. He couldn't go with Eddie. No, that would be a major mistake. That wouldn't be temptation, that would be submission, like lying on the tracks of the Inter-city line of life. To be in that situation and not smoke would be impossible. Going to see the lassies would be a temptation, aye, but only a finite temptation and Graeme could control it. Oh yes, he could. And to be in a pub and not smoke would be some recompense for this day of sheer and utter weakness and patheticness.

The referee blew the final whistle. The visitors had won 7–3 with three sent off, two stretchered off and two missed penalties.

'What a boring fucking game,' said Dunx. 'Right, we off then. Come on, offski and bevski.'

'I'm fucking shattered,' teased Eddie. 'Just call it a day, eh?'

'What? Come on to fuck, man. Just the one.'

Andy returned. He was looking at his watch, near enough displaying it. 'Well, I'm away then, I'll see you later, okay.'

'Just hold on,' said Dunx, then to Eddie. 'Come on, just the one, man, just the one.'

'Oh alright then, you old arm-twister you. As long as you're paying.'

Dunx laughed. 'Hey, if I could afford to pay I wouldn't be bothering with asking you along, would I?'

'Well,' said Andy, 'I'll see you then.'

'Just hold on, I says,' said Dunx. 'Come on.'

Andy didn't understand, but, seeing as how he was going anyway, did as Dunx told him.

'I'm just heading over to see the lassies,' said Graeme, then to Eddie 'I'll come round for you the morrow. Take you out for your dinner or something.'

'Oh aye, spot the money bags.'

'That's me clearing two hundred a week now,' boasted Graeme. 'In my hand, like. Two hundred.'

Eddie laughed. 'I just got a raise myself. That's me on Grade 2, twenty-five grand a year. Clearing five hundred a week. In my hand, like.' Eddie beamed. Graeme didn't. 'Tell you what,' said Eddie, 'while you're over there tell Carol I'll come round and see her the morrow afternoon. Tell her to give us a bell in the morning.'

'Okay-cokey. See you.'

'Hold on,' said Andy to Graeme, 'tell Hazel I'll be there in half an hour. Tell her that, right. Be sure and tell her that I promised. Half an hour. Thirty minutes. I'll be there in thirty minutes. You got that?'

Graeme nodded. 'Message received and understood.'

'Eh,' said Gary, 'we're just going over to the quiz as well.'

Dunx scowled. 'What you telling me for? Fucking arsewipe that you are. You can do whatever the fuck you want, sunshine. Need my permission or something do you?' Dunx started laughing.

They went their separate ways. Graeme went with Gary and Heather but insisted they walk ten yards in front since they were both wearing the exact same clothes and Graeme explained how he'd feel rather awkward about walking down the road with two people who were wearing the same clothes. It would be a bit silly, like.

Andy went with Dunx and Eddie. This was him postponing the big break, he knew that, but anything to stop Dunx nagging him and going on at him. It wouldn't have made any difference if he'd just walked away, anyway. No, that wouldn't have been the end of it, he'd just have been playing it over and over in his head like a stuck record. No, the only way to get through this was to see it through and have it out. Andy would leave after the half hour. If it meant falling out with Dunx then so be it. If it meant killing Dunx then so be it.

Andy stopped in the middle of the street. He was having one of his panic attacks – reason being that that last bit, the bit about killing Dunx, had not been said by Andy's own thought voice but had been said by the fearful Charlie Endell.

Folk started to trickle in from the football. One of the women who was running the quiz okayed it with the bar manager then went over and shut and bolted the door.

Hazel knew the place well enough to know that the regulars would get in the back way but it just hammered home to her that she was bloody waiting again, she was in that state again, she was in a state again.

'You alright?' said Carol.

Hazel nodded so Hazel lied. Hazel was far from alright. If she'd only come here to enjoy herself then this wouldn't have been too bad, the evening would have been okay she supposed. But she'd come here to meet Andy, and she'd made such a big thing of that earlier on with Carol. Hazel couldn't hide the fact that she was bothered. Bothered about being let down, bothered about being made a fool of and bothered about Andy. For that reason alone he should at least have the decency to turn up.

'There's Gary,' said Carol.

'God,' said Recca, 'that's all we need. See if that prick calls me Rec, just the once, I'm going to make him rue the day his balls dropped.'

'Who's that with him?' said Carol. 'And why are they both wearing the same clothes?'

'Don't know,' said Recca, 'she just must be an arsehole as well.'

Hazel was watching the door. She seen Graeme enter but then – no more. Hazel took a drink then helped herself to one of Carol's cigarettes.

'Alright,' said Gary. He got a couple of chairs from a nearby table and everybody moved round so that him and his new companion could sit together.

'Who's your new friend, Gary?' asked Carol.

'This,' announced Gary, 'this is Heather.' Gary made the introductions, defining the women in terms of their men. 'Heather works with Andy and Dunx,' he concluded.

'I work too,' said Hazel, 'and I even get paid for it.'

'So do I,' said Recca, 'and I get to boss people around.'

Hazel and Recca exchanged a look of belated sisterhood.

Gary was a bit confused. 'Eh, well, aye, so –'

Graeme arrived. 'Listen up, I've got a couple of messages.' Graeme pointed to Carol. 'Eddie says he'll be round to see you the morrow afternoon. Says you've to phone him in the morning. Now you be sure and do that, right?' Graeme pointed to Hazel. 'Right, Andy says he'll be here in half an hour. Sorry, damn, got that wrong, try again, hold on, important correction, Andy says to say he *promises* he'll be here in half an hour. He absolutely and categorically fucking promises he'll be here in half an hour.'

Everybody laughed apart from Hazel.

'Well,' said Recca, 'stop standing about looking like a Media Studies student and get yourself a seat.'

'Actually,' said Graeme, 'since I just got promoted the day, I was going to share with you all my new found wealth and offer to fill your glasses. What are you wanting?'

'How much are you on?' said Recca.

'Eh, that's me on Grade 2, twenty-five grand a year, clearing five hundred a week. In my hand, like.'

'Aye, right,' said Recca.

Graeme smiled and repeated his offer. Carol and Recca declined but Hazel accepted. Gary opted for a low-alcohol and Heather thought that was a good idea and opted for a low-alcohol as well.

As Graeme left to get served, Gary said, 'Well, we winning, Rec?'

'*What?*'

'Eh, I just asked if we were winning, if you were winning, like.'

'No,' said Recca, 'it was what you said after that, what did you say after that, Gar?'

Geordies of all ages, Geordies of all heights, even Geordies of both sexes – but, noticeably, only Geordies of one shape.

'Hey,' said Dunx, 'how come all these bastards are so fucking fat?'

'Bad diet,' said Eddie. 'And too much of this.' Eddie inclined the elbow. 'Went on a course with a couple of them once. Fucking cases, they were.'

Dunx didn't seem too impressed. 'Thought they were all supposed to be impoverished down there, how come they can afford all this then?'

'Would've saved up for it, I suppose. These cunts're dedicated mind.'

'Aye, right,' said Dunx.

'No, they would've. Like you going down to Glastonbury, you saved up for that.'

'That's different,' said Dunx. 'And, anyway, I got a right good look at your Trevorland when we went down there, a right good look, and you know what it's like, you know what it put me in mind of – it's like Bridge of Allan. No, it is, every wee town you go through, you just look out the window and say to yourself "Fuck me, there goes Bridge of Allan again". Fucking Trevors are all spoilt bastards, man, spoilt fucking bastards.'

'Whaz tha sane, canny lad?'

'Whit?'

'Ah sez whaz tha sane boot Trevors, canny lad?'

Dunx turned to Eddie. 'Whit ih fuck's iss doss-cunt on aboot?'

Eddie translated. Dunx put his arm round the Geordie and said, 'Just a joke, big man, just a joke. You're alright, pal.'

'Baz,' said the Geordie, returning the embrace, and introduced his mates. 'Wor Patrick, Wor Stevie and Wor Christine.'

This embrace prompted one of Andy's brainwaves: if Dunx and Eddie were to get in with this lot then it would be easier for Andy to get away because Andy wouldn't be leaving just the pair of them, Andy would be leaving a crowd of them.

This was smart thinking. Andy checked his watch. Twenty-two minutes remained of his half-hour. He'd stay for nineteen. Three would be enough to get over the road. No problem, he'd have a minute to spare. Andy went over to get served some fuel for Dunx's friendliness.

Things went well and the next quarter of an hour went according to Andy's plan. Eddie'd got another round in and the Geordies were giving good crack. Andy was relieved, excited and confident. He could've left at any time without being missed.

To leave without saying, though, now that would've been impolite, and Andy was never impolite.

'Right,' said Andy to Eddie, 'I'll away then. Give us a bell the morrow and let us know what's happening.'

'Right,' said Eddie, 'see you.'

And that was it, Andy was off.

Just as he reached the door, though, his sleeve got caught in something, or rather caught by something.

'Where you going?' said Dunx.

Andy took a deep breath. 'Hazel.'

Dunx tutted. 'Come on, man, just stay, stay a bit.'

Andy tried to pull away but couldn't.

'Come on,' repeated Dunx. 'These guys are great, don't fucking go. Just give her a phone and let her know what's happening, she'll understand. You wanting 10p? Here you are, hold on, I'll have 10p for you, here it is. There you go, take it, it's yours, go on.'

Andy shook his head and started peeling Dunx's fingers off his sleeve.

'Hey, fuck off.' Dunx stepped back and squared up.

Andy, too, stepped back. Maybe Charlie Endell was right.

'What's going on?' said Baz. 'You want me to go and fetch the sheriff?'

'No, it's alright,' Dunx put on his best namby-pamby voice. 'Andy's got to run off to the little lady, got to get back under the thumb again.'

The Geordies were laughing.

'Christ, man,' said Baz, 'I never even told the wife I was coming up here. First she got to hear about it was when I phoned her up to tell her to mind and tape my fucking programmes.'

'See,' said Dunx. 'That's the way you treat them, got to show them who's the boss.'

'Too fucking right,' said Baz.

Andy checked his watch. Ninety seconds remained. He could sprint it in thirty. He just wanted one last act of defiance.

'Come on,' said Dunx, offering the 10p again. Dunx went over to the phone. 'Just pick it up, dial the numbers and say "Hello, Hazel, I'm having a really good time and I'm just staying over here. See you later. Bye." Simple as that. D'you want me to phone her for you? Right, I'll phone for you.'

Andy, though, went over and pushed Dunx away from the phone then walked over to the door.

'Right,' said Dunx, 'away you go then. Fuck off and away you go. But there's one thing, right, there's just one thing I want to say to you, just one thing. You listening? Well listen to this, listen to this one then. You know what you are? D'you know what you fucking are? I know a lot about you mind and I know what you fucking are. You want to know what you are? Eh? Ih? You want to know? Well, I'll tell you . . . You are a fucking woman, that's what you fucking are. You're a fucking woman, a fucking wifie. That's all I've got to say on the matter, a fucking woman. On you go.'

Andy just shook his head and headed for the door.

'Just hold on a sec.'

Andy turned round cause it was Eddie who'd spoken.

Andy watched as Eddie climbed up on his chair then up on the table.

'Talking of being a fucking woman,' said Eddie. 'I have an announcement to make . . .'

While Scott and the rest of them were enjoying a fairly serious game of Monopoly, Deke was in charge of containing, cleansing and clothing what was known to the loft-gardeners as the assembly-line.

The assembly-line comprised Moira's Baby Charlotte, Terry's Baby David and Deke's Baby Joe, along with one yellow baby-shaped baby bath, one basin of clean water, one basin for dirty water, one towel, one sponge, one cloth, one tin of talc and three sets of jammies.

It was a bit like washing the dishes only in this instance when the dishes were washed the dishes tended to run away.

Deke sat himself down and stretched out his legs, making a barrier to confine the toddlers. The thing was to get them in their jammies – once they were in their jammies they went to their sleep. This was what Deke called the 'bricklayers don't wear tutus' theory, i.e. clothes dictated behaviour. His reasoning was that if kids always, without exception, went to their beds to go to sleep then this was always what they would do.

Not that Deke was an expert or anything, but the arrival of Baby Joe had aroused within Deke a degree of parental gooeyness that he'd missed out on with Joanne.

When Joanne was born, Deke had stood back from things. The new arrival was very much an addition to Carol's family and very much Carol's production job. The fascination for Deke came as much from watching Carol's reactions, the glint in her eye, the gentleness, her pride and the way she coped with it all.

Deke had been working at the time of Joanne's birth and had

missed the actual event. For Baby Joe's first night, though, Deke was present throughout.

The calmness and serenity which had so impressed the nursing staff during the natal stage disappeared, however, when the midwife held aloft the brand new baby for its parents to inspect. Deke's reaction was to let out an almighty squeal and race across to the other side of the room, a look of sheer and utter horror on his face. Carol asked him what the matter was, to which Deke stuttered the immortal words 'That cunt looks like me.'

For poor Deke it was like one of those photos folk were always saying looked like him but which made him want to curl up and croak – and, God, this was just the start, Deke was going to have to put up with this for every second of the rest of his life.

By this time Carol herself was getting into a bit of a state. The midwife, though, told her not to worry and explained it away as being only 'a mild attack of post-natal doppelganger shock'. Carol was still alarmed, though, and asked how long it would go on for. 'Oh,' said the mid-wife, looking at her watch, 'be about six, maybe seven, call it seven minutes.'

And so it proved. Within the stated time Deke became a doting father, pointing out a cheeky familiar smile no one else could see, and describing bone structure and facial characteristics with an artist's relish. Indeed, Deke was a bit browned off when he was told that, no, he couldn't take Baby Joe away with him, not even when he promised he'd bring him right back. Nevertheless from that moment on Deke made a promise to himself that Number 1 son was going to have a Number 1 dad.

'Go and sign my homework book, please.'

It was Joanne. Deke held his hand out for the jotter. 'What did you have to do?'

'We were to say what we wanted to be when we grow up.'

'Oh,' said Deke, 'and what did you put?'

'Look and see.'

Deke flicked through the jotter until he found the page.

There then followed an attack of what Baby Joe's midwife would doubtless call 'post-homework doppelganger shock'.

On the top line of the latest page of her jotter Joanne had written her class and the date.

Then she'd missed a line and wrote 'What I want to be when I grow up.'

Then she'd missed another line and wrote the single word 'Cool'.

Under normal circumstances round the table silence was about as comfortable as a bellyful of indigestion. The thing about quiz night, though, was that it legitimised such behaviour under the pretext of application to the task at hand.

Take Gary, for instance – a picture of studied concentration. But if one of those folk who was always pestering Gary for the full-time score was to stop and ask Gary the question he was supposedly, and so apparently, in deep contemplation of, Gary would have to respond with the blankest expression this side of a mortuary.

Likewise, Heather herself would be unable to come up with the relevant piece of information. This was because Heather's brain was in a state of flummox over what Recca had said about Gary when Gary was away relieving himself. God, it couldn't be true, could it? But why on earth had Recca said it then if it wasn't true? Jealousy? Spite? Tease? Heather tried to reverse the roles. In these very circumstances, if she'd known what Recca had said to be true, to be genuinely true, then would she Heather have said what Recca said? Yes, she would, she would, she definitely would. Oh God, it was true then, it was true!

From the moment Recca and Carol had arrived Hazel hadn't paid a blind bit of notice to those stupid, bloody questions, and it was with a degree of dull inevitability that Hazel noted the arrival and prompt departure of Andy's half hour, been and gone without so much as a message or a call and Andy was now, to use the parlance of the day, in injury time. Hazel's state of diminished responsibility had brought on a petty urge to have a go at someone, and had prompted her to endorse what Recca had said to Heather about Gary when Gary was away at the toilet. Anyway, anybody big enough and daft enough to wear those clothes and choose that company was crying out for help to an extent that effectively encouraged ridicule.

Carol, meanwhile, hadn't been entirely happy about what

Recca had told Heather about Gary when Gary was away at the toilet. Before Carol had had a chance to say anything, though, Hazel had butted in and backed up Recca's comments, so Carol just shook her head and kept her trap shut. She had enough problems of her own to be going on with, anyway, what with her dad and that bloody car.

Not even in his wildest dreams could Graeme ever have anticipated it being so easy to sit in a pub without smoking. Admittedly his lungs were fully charged but overindulgence was usually accompanied by the craving of expectation. At this moment, though, he was so relaxed and in control, maybe even superior; Graeme the Conqueror. His superiority stemmed partly from his high-quality abstinence skills but also from the way in which Hazel, an avowed anti-smoker, was helping herself from Carol's packet. Watching someone who couldn't inhale properly or even hold the thing properly showed just what an unpleasant, anti-social and ultimately stupid thing to do it undoubtedly all was.

If Graeme felt smug then that was as nothing as to what Recca was feeling – because, well, who else in the whole wide world but Recca could rhyme off all the contestants in *Wacky Races* without even having to stop and think about it?

'Yeah . . . A-ha . . . Yeah . . . Just like you wanted, standing on the table in a macho, Scottish pub . . . I fucking did, ya wanker. Honest. Got half a ton of witnesses . . . Look, hold on a minute.' Eddie bunged in another couple of pound coins. 'Still there, aye? . . . Hey, guess what, though? This place is stowed out with fucking Geordies . . . Stowed out, mobbed, packed . . . No, they're up for a pre-season . . . 7-3 . . . Them . . . No, nobody's said anything . . . But that's them told so everybody'll know . . . What's with all the questions, anyway? This the Simon inquisition, is it?'

While Eddie was on the phone, the folk at the table sat by their pints. Even though Baz, Wor Patrick, Wor Christine and Wor Stevie had only just arrived on the scene, they were waiting for Dunx to react like they'd known him all their lives.

'Crikey,' said Andy.

Dunx scowled. ' "Crikey"?' he repeated. 'Fucking "crikey"?

That's all you've got to fucking say for yourself. That is the entirety of what you've got to say. The cumulative effect of all your tiny brain cells, all beavering away and all ganging up the gether, the effect of all that has come away with the great philosophical observation "crikey". Fuck's sakes, man.' Dunx paused. 'This is a major as, this is a serious major as.'

They were all quiet for a few seconds until Baz said, 'Major as what, canny lad?'

Dunx scowled and it was left to Andy to explain. 'It's an expression,' said Andy, 'like cool as or smart as. It's like the ultimate, the extreme. Not that I think that myself, of course.'

'Fuck off. Talk sense, will you,' said Dunx. 'Course it is, course it fucking is. Hey, remember that guy's showered with us, showered with us at five-a-side mind.'

'So what?' said Andy. 'Christ, everybody checks each other out, everybody sizes up.'

'That's different. Telling you, that was one thing he never did, he never sized up. Aye, too busy thinking about things, too busy fantasising. Aye, I've always had my suspicions about that bloke.'

Andy laughed. For Dunx to accept this would be a real major as – and Dunx was going to accept this because no one Andy knew of had ever exerted a greater influence over Dunx politics, tastes or humour than Eddie; a status Andy had long been jealous of.

Dunx never took anything from Andy, never agreed with anything Andy ever said or praised anything Andy ever did. Like anything new or different Andy ever said, bought or even laughed at was frowned upon by Dunx and made out to be an embarrassment by Dunx. Whereas if Eddie had been the source Dunx would be going 'Aye, aye, aye, a-ha, aye, aye, aye.'

'Cannot believe it,' said Dunx, 'just cannot fucking believe it.'

'You're just after saying you've always had your suspicions,' said Wor Christine.

Dunx scowled at Wor Christine.

Andy laughed again. God, he was loving this, loving it all so much he wouldn't miss it for the world.

'It's not natural.'

'Your arse.'

'Is it dan,' said Dunx. 'It is not fucking normal and that's the end of it.'

'What the fuck d'you mean by normal?'

'Jesus, normal's normal, it's what folk do.'

'Aye, you're just acting sideways cause I've never made a pass at you.'

'Aye, right. This is not funny, by the way. You're not Julian Clary, you're one of us.'

'One of what?'

'One of us, one of the lads. You're into the same stuff. You're into all the best of gear and all that. You go to the games. You're into good music.'

Eddie laughed. 'So?'

'So, so that's all, that's all I've got to say on the matter.'

'Can I still be your pal?'

'I don't know, I don't know about that. It's all about trust.' Dunx took a drink. 'What is this, anyway? I mean really what is all this all about? You been having women problems or something? It's all to do with Carol, eh?'

Eddie sighed. 'What you on about? Fuck all to do with Carol.'

'Aye, right. You and her were pretty close for a while there. Don't think I've forgotten. Don't think nobody noticed. Sneaking round when Deke wasn't there. You were fucking smitten, pal.'

'Listen, I was going through a bad spell, right. I confided a lot in Carol. Christ, this was eight years ago mind. I'd been dumped, right, and I needed someone to talk to. I had to see about some tests.'

'Tests?' Dunx looked puzzled. 'What, your exams, like? You were failing your exams so you went a wee bit sideways?'

'No, not that kind of tests.'

Dunx got half-serious. 'You mean tests tests?' Eddie nodded. 'This is serious,' Dunx slammed his drink down, 'this is fucking serious. It's fucking sordid all this, it's fucking sordid.'

'How's it fucking sordid?'

'Cause it is. It's not natural.'

'That's just fear talking.'

'Exactly, too damn right it's fear talking. I'm having none of that.'

'Funny, but that's the exact same words you used when we seen Skete Laird with Michelle Chapman, primary seven, Glenbow Primary. You were just like that back then. Anything you weren't involved in, you just dismissed it. Anything to do with lassies and you ran a mile. You were the guy that dogged it on the last day when we had dances at the school, that was you. Scared.'

'Fuck, everybody did that.'

'Nah,' said Eddie, shaking his head, 'only thee, me and Fat Fraze.'

Dunx turned his head away. 'The act, the act is still sordid. You saying that if I go out and suck the Pope's cock everything'll be alright?'

'No,' said Eddie, 'don't be stupid. I just want you to remember how you were back then, and how you are about a lot of things still, a lot of other things. It's just something different, and what I want to know is what fucking difference does it make to you or anybody, anyway? It's as daft as saying folk in Belgium shouldn't be allowed to eat chocolate biscuits. I mean how much do you know about life that you can turn round to me and say what is and isn't wrong? I mean we're all going to fucking die, right, I'm not hurting anybody, in fact I'm making somebody very happy. There's two of us that are very happy. There's . . .'

'It's sordid! I hate that whole fucking scene, man. It's all just so casual. I hate all this two hundred partners a year carry-on, I hate all that. How in the world are you supposed to develop a relationship living like that?'

'We're not all like that.'

'I thought you just said you had to go for tests.'

'That was a one-off, you go for tests even after a one-off. And, anyway, you're not exactly a symbol of fidelity yourself mind.'

'That's different, that's a macho thing. And I don't go to public toilets and stand there with my cock hanging out for forty minutes hoping somebody'll notice me.'

'Neither do I,' said Eddie, 'and then again I don't think it's any of your business if folk want to do that. And Dunx,' Eddie eyeballed Dunx, 'I don't just go with anybody for the sake of shooting off my load.'

'Shite. That's a pity that.'

Everybody looked up. It was Wor Patrick that had spoken. 'Hey, sunshine,' said Wor Stevie, grabbing Wor Patrick by the hand. 'Shut it. You're spoken for remember.'

'Why don't you ever bother about anything?'

He wasn't listening, or he was pretending not to listen, him that had never quite learned how to shave properly and always left those wee bits just under his nostrils and that bit of fluff on his bottom lip.

Hazel tried again. 'Graeme,' she said, 'why don't you ever bother about anything?'

'Eh, what was that?'

Hazel groaned. 'Graeme, you don't bother about anything. You don't get worked up.'

'I do,' said Graeme defiantly, 'I do so.' Then he shrugged a shoulder.

'Do you ever get really, really angry?'

Graeme thought about it then shrugged the other shoulder. 'Nah, there's worse off than me.'

'Do you really think like that? Do you really always think like that?'

Graeme shrugged both shoulders, realigned his buttocks and tried not to notice the empty itch, the veritable pang, that had just started pounding away between the second and third fingers of his right hand.

'Eh, no,' said Graeme, 'because I don't really think about it. Point of fact, to tell you the truth, I don't really think at all, I just get on with things.'

'What things?'

'My job, my life, my family. What d'you think?'

'Really? D'you really mean that? Do you not want for more?'

Graeme shook his head. Machine fags were two quid for a half empty packet, and asking Carol would be damn rude considering she only had a couple left.

'No,' said Graeme, 'I never think about having more. For most folk this would be more, this is the more they're all striving for.'

Hazel sniffed. 'I wish I could be like that,'

Me too – thought Graeme, and tried to concentrate on the scores on the teletext over the other side of the pub.

'Am I making you uncomfortable, Graeme?' said Hazel.

'No,' lied Graeme, 'I've got food in my belly, money in my pocket, Tranmere have won 2-0 away from home and my family are all well and healthy – how could little old you be making great big me feel uncomfortable?'

'But what about me,' said Hazel, 'does it not bother you that I'm upset, that I'm unhappy and that I'm lonely?'

'Nah, no really.'

Hazel said, 'Do you like me?'

Graeme rotated one shoulder one way and the other shoulder the other way. The all-night garage would be open. It meant a detour but that was no trouble. The way Graeme was starting to feel an all-night garage the other side of Fife would suffice.

'Well?' said Hazel.

'Not tonight I don't.'

'Do you fancy me?'

'Eh.' This was too much. Graeme whispered, like he was talking to a wee, wee lassie, letting her know that he was onto her game. 'That's a terrible, terrible thing to say to somebody.'

'Yes or no.'

Graeme exhaled. 'No,' he said.

'Why not?'

Graeme tried to act like he was irritated. 'Look, it's like going out for something to eat,' he said, 'you're not on the menu.'

'What if I was?'

Graeme sighed. 'I suppose so.'

Hazel kissed Graeme on the cheek. 'Thank you,' she said. 'Will you take me home, please?'

Carol butted in. 'The quiz'll be over soon. You'll get a run home with the rest of us.'

'No,' said Hazel, 'I want him to take me home. I'm going to the toilet then I want him to take me home, right.'

'Whoah! Get in there, my son!'

'Recca!' said Carol. 'This is serious,'

'Can I have a cigarette, please,' said Graeme.

Carol pushed the packet in Graeme's direction. 'Oh, Graeme, what's she playing at? God, I could strangle Andy, I really could. What you going to do, Graeme?'

Graeme lit up. The first hit was a lovely wee 'Ahhhh'. The second hit, though, confirmed the law of diminishing returns and just left a taste and a desire to cough a hair up from the back of the throat.

'Could you not just stick her in a taxi?' said Heather.

'I don't think that's what she wants,' said Recca. 'Just ignore her. She'll just blow up and storm off.'

'Oh, Graeme,' said Carol, 'you can't do that, you'd never forgive yourself if anything happened to her.'

'We'll come with ou,' said Gary.

The prospect of Gary's company was something Graeme normally looked forward to about as much as the close season – but, by God, Gary had just turned himself into the biggest hero this side of the bloke who invented the Mars Bar.

'Poor Graeme,' said Recca. 'Poor, poor Graeme.'

'Just one of these things.' Graeme shrugged. 'Probably be laughing at it the morrow.'

The door swung open and Hazel reappeared. Gary and Heather got up out of their seats and started putting their matching jackets on.

'We're just off as well,' said Gary. 'We'll get you down the road.'

'No,' said Hazel. 'No, just you stay and enjoy the quiz. Me and him have got things to talk about, in private.'

Right, that was it, that was enough. Graeme had had it. This situation was daft, daft enough to laugh at, not just next week, not just tomorrow, but at this very second this whole shebang was just a whole, gigantic joke.

Graeme let his face relax into a smile and chewed imaginary gum – cool as.

'Right,' said Graeme, 'come on then. Let's go. Anything for a quiet life. And, hey, don't you stop to worry your pretty little self for one second, not even for the slightests of seconds, about dragging me away from my friends, my dear friends, and thereby depriving me of a jolly good time and drastically reducing their chances of victory in this here quiz.'

'I'm not worried,' countered Hazel, 'No, I'm not worried in the slightest. Remember, you've got food in your belly, money in your pocket, Tranmere won 2-0 away from home and your family are all well and healthy.' Hazel rolled her eyes, raised her eyebrows and inclined her head. Touché.

Graeme kept his smile going, though. If he treated her like a kid, she'd be satisfied in letting him know she was a smart one – at least that's what he was telling himself to tell himself.

'Come on then,' said Graeme, his voice dry and cracking.

'Let's be having you,' mumbled Recca in a gruff sergeant-major's voice.

'What was that?' said Hazel.

'Nothing,' said Recca.

But Graeme looked back as they were on their way out, and there was Recca, Recca with her arms crossed so that her fingertips were on her shoulders as she mouthed a long, slow kiss.

And that was how, with his hand on the handle of a half-open door, Andy came to see Hazel and Graeme heading off down the road. Hazel with her arm through Graeme's, and Graeme with that smile, that smile that excluded, that smile that excluded Andy.

'Jees-oh,' said Dunx, releasing his grip from Andy's sleeve. 'There you go then, eh. I told you, didn't I. Didn't I tell you? That is what that woman is like, that is what she's like. Now will you believe me? She is no good, no good at all. Just fucking dump her, just fucking finish with her and that's that. Should never have got involved with her in the first place.'

Those exact words were the exact words Andy was saying to himself. And then some – should never have got involved with women in the first place, should never have been born in the first place, should never have been anything in the first place.

No, Andy wasn't one for blowing up or storming off when things went wrong – Andy just fell to pieces.

Dunx put his arm round Andy, asked him to stop crying, then

helped him back over to the table and explained to the others what had happened.

'Graeme, eh,' said Eddie. 'Christ, always thought he was one of us.'

'Hey,' said Dunx poking Andy, 'that'll be the next stop for you, you'll end up one of them.' Dunx quickly stopped laughing though, when he realised no one else was. 'Sorry, sorry. Better stop saying things like that, I suppose, eh. Sorry.'

And here endeth the homophobic asshole, noted Andy with no little irony. If there was one thing that would be guaranteed to change Dunx, to eliminate a prejudice, it was the transference of said prejudice to something else, that was always the way of it. Folk were always like that, and Dunx was more like folk than anybody. Andy was now the Number 1 nadir, the lowest of the low.

'So what you going to do now?' said Baz.

Andy indicated his drink.

'Would Graeme no just be seeing her home?' said Eddie.

Andy shook his head.

'Nah,' said Dunx, 'you want to have seen them, like that they were, laughing and joking. Telling you, him and Gary have shown their true colours the night, wankers. Tell you a thing or two about those two . . .'

While Dunx slagged Gary and Graeme, Andy turned in on himself to face his demons. Yes, tonight may well have been his fault but he'd only brought forward something that had been bound to happen, something that always happened, something as inevitable as death – Andy getting dumped before the six-month mark.

As much as Andy was pissed off at Dunx there was one fact that was undeniable – what Dunx had been saying all along had been proved to be true. He had a strange way of showing it at times but Dunx really cared about Andy and would always be there for him, and that had to count for something.

The doors flew open and in came Elephant Man, Serial Killer, the One-Foot Wonder and a few of the Sunderland side. A roar went up from the Geordies and Elephant Man grabbed the red-headed winger in a head-lock and made like he was battering fuck out of him.

Andy laughed along with the rest of them. It was good to be reminded that there was something else that would always be there for him, something that would be there every Saturday for nine months of the year for the rest of his life, something that that represented him, who he was and where he was from, something to share with folk, something to get worked up about, yes sure something to look back on, but mostly something to look forward to, something to look forward to with fear, with expectation, but always with anticipation and always with hope, always with hope . . . and with hope . . . in your heart . . . you'll ne- . . . -ver walk . . . alone . . . alone.

It was Andy's turn to get on the table.

'Walk on! Walk on!'

'You still bothered with your posters coming down all the time?'

'Eh?'

'Your posters, Graeme,' said Hazel. 'Last time I was speaking to you you were saying they kept falling off your walls all the time.'

'Oh aye,' said Graeme, like he'd just realized something. 'Aye, I suppose so, suppose you could say that.'

Whatever confidence Graeme had deluded himself into thinking he'd had had just been found out for the fake it undoubtedly was with that distinct (leading?) reference to his one and only home.

Graeme tried not to think about it, trying instead to think about how he could start to get in control of this situation.

The thing about getting folk down the road was that it was normally such a piece of piss on the old communication front, like it was really easy to talk or to pretend you were listening, just to blether away. It was like being on the works' phone, you could make faces or you could look at other things while you were just stood there or just sat there, or in this instance just walking there, and haver away; as long as there was no eye contact there was no pressure. That was it – haver.

'Thing is see,' havered Graeme 'in summer you open up all your windows and all the things just get blown down – and then when winter comes round you go and put on all your heating and that dries up all the sticky stuff so everything just falls down, cause there's nothing sticking it up, like.'

'Sounds like a big problem, Graeme.'

'Nah, don't be silly, course not. It's just a kind of nuisance, that's all you could call it. As big a problem as I want mind.'

Hazel laughed. 'Do you like it here?'

'Ih?'

'This town,' said Hazel, 'this place.'

'Oh, aye.' That wasn't what Graeme thought she'd meant. 'This place, aye. Eh, it's alright. Never really been anywhere else to compare it with, I suppose.'

'D'you think you'll always be here?'

'Suppose so. Here or somewhere like it.'

They walked a whole two and a half paces in silence before Hazel said, 'D'you like Andy?'

Graeme sniffed. 'He's alright, I suppose. Don't really know him.' Graeme thought for a second, trying to think of a sentence that didn't have the word 'suppose' in it. 'He's too serious, Andy is, he's way too serious.'

Hazel nodded. 'What is it that you're always thinking about?'

Graeme thought.

'I mean,' said Hazel, 'how come you always know what to say?'

Graeme laughed. 'I don't. Take just now, I don't have a clue. Honest, I don't have a clue what to say.'

'But you can always say things that make folk happy. I can't do that, how d'you do that? Everybody likes you.'

This was news to Graeme.

'They do,' said Hazel. 'Everybody thinks you're funny and nice.'

'Believe it or not,' said Graeme, with no little pride. 'I try to be.'

'But how do you do it, though?'

'What? Saying things that keep folk happy? Years of practise, hen, years of them.'

'How, though? How do you know what to say?'

Graeme laughed. 'If it keeps you happy, I'll let you in on my secret. Right, if I'm talking to somebody, right, I just remember what they said and rearrange it. That's all I do. Everybody knows more than me so I just keep them happy by going on about the things I know they'll agree with 'cause it came from them in the first place.'

'Really?' said Hazel. 'But what if it's somebody you don't know.'

'Ah, well, then I just use the bits that are appropriate. All my opinions are other folks' opinions.'

'You're funny, though,' said Hazel. 'They're not funny.'

'As I said, I try to be.'

'No, you are. I mean you don't say much but everything you say is really interesting. Everything I've ever heard you say is really interesting, Graeme.'

Graeme gulped. That was the nicest thing anyone had ever said to him in his life since Wilko Donnelly, presently holding down the right back position in the Clydebank third eleven, said he had a half-decent left-peg.

The ice-cream van which played The Fall's *Mixer* made itself heard and Graeme tried to work out where it would be and how quickly he could get there.

'What d'you know about me?' said Hazel.

Graeme thought for a second then whispered, 'Just what my Auntie Recca's told me.'

'Ha ha, very funny. No, but what do you know about me?'

'Well,' said Graeme, 'I know your job, I know your boyfriend, I know your . . .'

'HEY YOU, JUST HOLD ON THERE!!! WE'VE BEEN ASKED TO HAVE A FUCKING WORD WITH YOU, SUNSHINE!!!'

The tone alone had been enough to burp Graeme's bowels but when he turned himself round to find himself facing five tattooed-knuckled black shell-suited famously psychotic Regal-smoking Bampot Brothers, the burp went straight to Graeme's guts and he thought he was going to die before the season had even got under way.

'Shit,' said Recca, 'four behind. Got to go for it.'

'Who's winning?' said Heather.

'Who d'you think?' said Recca. 'Those grave-dodging old bastards with their halves of shandy. Shh.'

They all went quiet so as they could all hear the last question. It was a 'Who am I?' Twelve points would be awarded to anyone getting the answer from the first clue, ten from the second and so on.

'Who am I?' said the woman. 'I was born on . . .'

Recca was busy writing down all she could think of when Heather grabbed the pen and pad and wrote down a name.

'Could be,' said Recca, 'but could be a lot of folk.'

'No,' said Heather, 'it is, it is, it's right. I know it's right. Listen, that's my birthday. I know who shares my birthday.'

'Any offers?' said the woman.

'Take it up,' said Heather. 'Go on.'

'Hold on,' shouted Recca, 'just hold on, just hold your wee horses, I was just checking my spelling.'

The ten-point clue narrowed it down to the occupation. Recca still couldn't be sure, though. The old guys submitted an answer. If they were right, Recca would lose.

The eight point clue described the subject as female and there was a groan from the old guy's table.

'Yeah,' said Recca. 'Got them. Stuffed the old bastards. Taxidermied them.'

The six-point clue confirmed their answer, describing as it did the subject's marriage to the poet Robert Browning.

By now all the tables had submitted answers, and soon the final totals announced that Waster's Corner had indeed won, and by a clear five points from the Kelman Court Crusties, that really nice couple with the matching wax jackets and the Alkies at the Bar with the old guys' table trailing a further point behind. In the overall league table, for which two tickets to Miami were supposed to be the prize, they'd leapt back up to second place but were still way behind the old guys.

Egged on by Gary, Heather accompanied Recca for the presentation of the three bottles of wine.

'Come on,' said Recca, 'just gloat.'

And gloat they did. Not that anybody seemed to bother, mind, in fact, everybody seemed quite pleased for them. One of the old guys even grabbed a hold of Recca and said, 'Well played, hen.' Recca was a bit miffed at that. Why couldn't they be like normal folk and storm off in the huff, or demand a recount, or complain about slanted questions?

'Party?' said Gary.

'Yeah, party,' said Recca and turned to Carol, 'Back to your bit, eh?'

'Oh, come on,' said Carol. 'The kids'll be in their beds and Deke's got an early rise.'

'Be alright,' said Recca. 'We'll be nice and quiet. Just give the old man a bottle of vino and he'll be happy.'

'Excuse me.'

It was one of the Media Studies students.

'What you wanting, bozo?' said Recca. 'Come to bask in the presence of genius?'

'Eh,' said the guy, 'sort of, I suppose.' Then he took a deep breath. 'Listen, what it is is, right, I've drawn the short straw and been delegated to come over to tell you that there's one of the guys at our table who actually thinks that you're really funny, and, well, he'd like to know if there was a chance maybe that you would go out with him sometime.'

Recca's mouth dropped. 'What?'

'I said . . .'

'I heard you, I heard you.' Recca went over to the Media Studies table. 'This some kind of joke, ih?'

They all shook their heads.

Recca walked round the table, laughing her head off. 'I can't believe this, this is a classic. Well, who is it? Come on, I want to know.'

There was no response.

'Oh, come on,' said Recca. 'This is the biggest laugh of my life, please tell me. Come on, pretty please. Pretty, pretty please, please tell me.'

Still there was no response.

'I know,' said Recca, 'I know who'll tell me.' Recca went back over to her table and said to the guy who'd come over in the first place, 'Hey you, bozo, you tell me, you tell me which one it is. Come on, I want to know.'

The guy sighed then pointed with his index finger going round all the Media Studies students and then back again.

'Come on, you,' said Recca. 'Cut it out. Stop arsing about. Which one is it?'

It was then Recca realized the guy's finger was no longer moving but had stopped – and was pointing at himself.

'Well?' he said.

For getting her homework right Joanne was rewarded by being allowed to stay up and join the loft-gardeners for a game of Junior Trivial Pursuit, but only on the condition that in between shots she would keep a lookout for Carol coming home.

'There's Recca's car,' said Joanne.

'Right,' said Deke, 'top gear it, bed.'

'Hold on, there's other folk there.'

'Shit. It's not Fids, is it?'

'No,' said Joanne, 'Gary's one of them but I don't know the others.'

Deke went over to have a look. It was Gary right enough. And there was some lassie wearing the same clothes as Gary. And there was a guy as well, some bloke with a beard that Deke had never seen before, but who looked a total straight.

What the hell was going on? Deke had to be up in exactly seven hours and twenty minutes. How the hell was he supposed to sleep when there was folk going about the house?

There was no point in making a thing out of it, though. And, anyway, seeing as here he was keeping Joanne back from her bed, something that would set Carol fuming, he wasn't really in a position to lecture anyone.

'Do you want me to pretend I'm sleepwalking,' said Joanne, 'and come through and call Gary a wanker again?'

'Eh,' said Deke, 'no, not the night. Some other time maybe. Come on, we better shift.'

They made their way down the rope-ladder, Deke with the sound asleep Baby Joe over his arm.

Deke put Baby Joe straight to his bed then said to Joanne, 'See when your mum comes through to check on you, right, don't squeeze your eyes shut, just have them closed really softly, just so. And breathe really softly as well, really slowly and really softly, slowly and softly. Okay? Got that?'

'A-ha.'

'Give it a try then.'

Joanne gave it a try.

'Wee bit deeper,' said Deke. 'That's it, perfect. And another thing, don't lie there all squashed up and tight, relax yourself, loosen up, like you're in the bath, like a banana. Okay?'

'Okay,' said Joanne. 'Eyes: closed softly, not tightly. Breathing: slow, soft and deep. Body: loose, like I'm in the bath, like a banana.'

'Magic, that's my girl. Goodnight.'

Deke put their big light off, their wee light on then went through the bathroom to practise a few of his whacked out and weary expressions. Actually, Deke noted, going by the look of him, he wouldn't really have to try that hard.

'What you wanting, ya shower of fucking plebs? No out breaking into some poor old dear's the night?'

'Shut up, you,' said Rab, Boaby or Robert. 'Shut up, right, just shut up and fucking listen.'

'Fuck off,' said Hazel. 'Come on,' she said to Graeme, 'just ignore them.'

But Graeme couldn't ignore them because they were blocking his path. And if he moved he'd come into contact with them. So Graeme didn't ignore them and Graeme didn't move. He did, however, take the opportunity to wonder, and chose to wonder as to why it was that they were on at Hazel? And more to the point, why was it that Hazel was on at them? You didn't talk to folk like that like that – and they didn't talk to you, they just killed you then chopped you up into poly-bags and took the polybags over to that house over the old town.

'Fucking stay there and fucking shut up, right!' Rab, Boaby or Robert had a hold of Hazel by the shoulders. 'We've been told to have a fucking word with you so we are going to have a fucking word with you, right, so you're going to stay here and you're going to fucking listen, right.'

It was for a time such as this that Graeme had made a mental note of the immortal words of national hero Group Captain,

Douglas Bader: 'Could never be bothered with this women and children first nonsense'. Graeme kept stumm.

'You listening?' repeated Rab, Boaby or Robert, shaking Hazel by her shoulders.

'I'm listening,' said Hazel.

'Right, your old fellow, your old fellow, right, says we've to have a word with you, says you've been hanging out with all the hippy wankers, says you've been up to no good, says we've to keep an eye on you, like, says we've to check these scum out, says, if need be, we've to sort these scum out.'

The mention of 'old fellow' had certainly stirred in Graeme a sense of curiosity. The vision of the good old blood-soaked polybags returned, however, somewhere around 'sort', 'scum' or 'out'.

'I can look after myself,' said Hazel, freeing herself from the grip. 'I don't need you arseholes babysitting me.'

Rab, Boaby and Robert decided this was funny and started laughing. Graeme's sense of self-preservation was such that out of a sense of wanting to blend in with the crowd, he started laughing as well.

'What you laughing at, arsehole?'

Graeme stopped laughing.

'Hey, that's the cunt that shits at the church, eh? Eh, you're the cunt that shits at the church, eh. That's you, eh?'

Graeme was saved from having to answer the most difficult question of his life when Hazel said, 'Leave him alone! Just leave him alone, right.'

'Oh,' said Rab, Boaby or Robert, 'you hear that, we've to leave Choochy-face alone. Poor wee Choochy-face.'

Choochy-face? Choochy-face! Okay, Graeme could live with that.

'Look, you lot,' said Hazel, 'I can look after myself. Now why don't you all be good little arseholes and leave us alone.'

'What? You going to shag him, like.' It was Stuart, the Bampot from work, who'd spoken. 'Hey, you still taking the line-ups?'

They all started laughing. Graeme didn't laugh. This was like being back at school again. One minute terrifying, the next minute pathetic.

'Funnee,' said Hazel, 'Funnee. Only time you lot ever get a ride is when you get a job as a bum-boy up the Bar-L.'

'Hey,' said Stuart. 'I was out last night, out with Pam and her five sisters.' The guy put his hand to his crotch and made like he was chugging.

'Come on,' said Hazel, 'I've had enough of this. Don't bother about them, let's go.'

Graeme had been well brought up, knew when to take a telling, and so followed Hazel.

'Oh, and hey, Mr Bossman,' shouted Stuart. 'By the way, you can stick your job up your jacksy. Nothing worth nicking there, anyway.'

As they walked away, Graeme looked back to check they weren't being followed, and it was then that Graeme saw something which kind of explained why the work hadn't burnt down earlier on. For what Graeme saw was all the Bampots stubbing their wee Regals out on their hands and swallowing the subsequent butts.

They were in the kitchen cleaning mugs for the wine.

'Hey,' said Carol, 'have you really smoked all that bit?'

Deke patted his pocket.

'Tch. She knows you're at it, you know. She's not stupid.'

'No, she doesn't know,' said Deke, 'she doesn't know for sure. Without proof, she can never really know. Anyway, her bit's big enough for all of us, and she can afford it, her and her new boyfriend.'

Carol laughed. 'What d'you make of Neil?'

'Seems alright.'

'He teaches Media Studies and English. He's on twenty-two grand a year.'

Deke made a face to show how much that really hurt. 'How was your dad?'

'Okay, he left early, though, don't think he was into it too much. Listen, there's something I've been meaning to tell you about dad but I've been putting it off. And I'm only telling you now because we've folk in.'

'What?'

'Promise you won't blow up.'

Deke turned away. 'I won't blow up, promise.'

Carol took a deep breath. 'Dad had been drinking again yesterday when he brought Joanne home from school.'

Deke didn't blow up he just laughed. 'Well, hen, you'll have to get her the morrow then. I'm not fucking having that, no way, not having that at all.'

'Look,' said Carol, 'I'm having a word with him the morrow, I'll tell him then, I'll tell him straight. I'll give him one last chance, he does it again and I'm collecting Joanne. One last chance, okay?'

It wasn't the time for an argument, Deke knew that, that's why she was telling him now, but Deke had had it up to here with Carol's dad, way up to here.

'Look,' said Deke, 'it will happen again, you know it'll happen again, so you'd be as well just to start collecting Joanne yourself, and be as well just starting the morrow.'

'One last chance,' said Carol. 'Listen, I know my dad, I know he'll do as I tell him. I'm all he's got here, Deke, he won't want me turning against him. He couldn't take that. That would be the end of him.'

There was a part of Carol Deke would never get to know, a part that he could never quite fathom and that would never belong to him. And if you didn't understand something then you . . . stood back. Deke dipped his hands in the basin then held them up.

'Thanks,' said Carol, 'you're great' and kissed him on the cheek.

'So are you,' said Deke, '99% of you.'

'Come on back through,' said Carol. 'They'll be wondering what's going on.'

'Back to hear what Gary's bird's got to say for herself.'

'Don't,' said Carol, 'she's a nice lassie, do him the world of good.'

They went back through and Deke's eyes near popped out their sockets; because Neil was not only skinning up, but Neil was skinning up from the biggest bit Deke had seen since Gaegs had got back from liberating Kuwait.

'Fucking hell,' said Deke. 'You can call anytime, pal, anytime at all. Where the fuck did you get that?'

'Contacts,' said Neil, 'contacts.'

'Aye, right,' said Deke.

'Just wait till you get a hit off it.'

'I'm waiting,' said Deke. He turned to Heather and said, 'Telling you, hen, you made a big mistake, this was the man you should've gone for. This man is a fucking hero.'

Heather smiled. Her head was pounding, the room was spinning and she'd have stabbed to death the residents of a home for sick children for a whiff of fresh air, but apart from that she'd never been so happy in all her life.

'Never knew you were related to the boys.'

'Funny,' said Hazel. 'My wonderful cousins.'

Graeme checked to make sure they were well enough out of earshot. 'That must be, eh, interesting.'

'No, it's not, it's not interesting, not interesting at all, Graeme.'

'Come on,' said Graeme, 'the family get-togethers must be a riot.'

Hazel scowled. 'Can we just drop it, please? They're my family, they're just something I'm always going to have to live with, right?'

Graeme was enjoying this. 'Nutter families are really close, eh? You must all be really close.'

'What?'

'They are, they're really ... close. They're all into all this sticking up for each other and all that malarky. Mind when the old granny there snuffed it, there was about half a million turned up for the service. It was like the Gala day, all these folk you've never seen before stoating about the town.'

'Look, I don't want to talk about my granny, and I don't want to talk about my family. We were talking about me, remember. Were you staring at my legs yesterday?'

Graeme gulped.

'Well, were you?'

'Were I what?'

'You heard. Yesterday, when I went for my dinner. You and numbskull, were you staring at my legs?'

Graeme thought for a second. 'No,' he said.

'Oh – why not, Graeme?'

'Cause, Hazel, I was doing something else. If I recall right I was stubbing out a cigarette in fact. Anyway, I don't do things like that.'

'Do you want me to walk in front for a bit so you can stare at my legs just now?'

'For fuck's sake!'

'I'll do it if you want me to, Graeme.'

'No,' said Graeme, 'I don't want you to.'

'Does this change the way you feel about me?'

'What,' said Graeme, 'the legs, the family, the fact you've started smoking, the way you've . . .'

'The family.'

'Aye, course it does, too right it does.'

'How?'

'Just does. They're fucking mad, they hurt people, they've stabbed folk. They're a bunch of seriously bad bastards.'

'But I'm not like that.'

'Aye, right.'

'I'm not!'

'Still,' said Graeme, 'it's like you're deceased or something, you're kind of soiled, that's what it is, soiled.'

Hazel sniffled. 'I don't think I like you anymore, Graeme.'

Graeme shrugged. He hadn't really meant what he'd said to come out that way but, well, the desired effect had been achieved and they were now only twenty paces from her door so Graeme should've been feeling a wee bit better. He should've but he wasn't, instead he had this incredible desire to apologise.

'Hey, look, I'm sorry,' he said. 'Mind, you're putting me in an awkward situation here. One minute you're related to the Mad Mental Chungy Team, the next thing you're on about your legs, then you're all aggressive, and now you're off in the flaming huff holding back the waterworks.'

'You got a big stiffie, Graeme?'

Graeme opened up his mouth for a good three seconds before he said, 'No.' A truthful response – but only truthful to the extent that Old Todd could never be described as big.

'Well, that's you,' said Graeme, 'delivered, safe and sound, and, by Christ, I'll tell you I'll sleep all the better for knowing that.'

'Do you fancy coming in for a coffee?'

'Uh-uh.'

'Because you don't want to, or because you feel you shouldn't?'
Graeme shook his head.
'Well?'
'I think we've had enough, don't you? It's been nice, really nice.
Interesting as well, damn interesting.' Graeme leaned forward and
whispered, 'Even though I think you've been bloody rotten to me.'
Hazel screwed her face up. 'Is that what you think? Is that what
you really think?'
Graeme nodded. Hazel sighed.
'I've not,' said Hazel. 'I've not. I have not.'
Hazel leaned forward and kissed Graeme, a slobbery one.
Graeme could taste the B&H.
Then he did something daft, he kissed back, a proper one, well,
what he thought was a proper one.
Then Graeme put his hands on Hazel's hips, partly to keep her
at a distance so she wouldn't be aware of any bulge, but mostly
because he wanted to.
After a few seconds they came apart.
'Oh,' said Graeme, 'I've winched a Bampot.'
Hazel sniffed. 'Better watch you don't go and catch anything.'
'Nah, should be alright.'
Graeme ran his finger down Hazel's nose. 'Mind when you
were at the school,' he said, 'and you were always taught that when
you divided a number by nothing then you were always left with
nothing?'
Hazel looked puzzled.
'Well,' continued Graeme, 'believe me, you were. Well, how
come then when you divide an apple by nothing, you're not left
with nothing, you're left with an apple, you've still got your apple.'
Hazel smiled. 'Is this some great mathematical breakthrough of
yours?'
'Nah,' said Graeme, 'just the way I feel. See you later, alright.
Look after yourself.'
'Bye . . . Goodnight, Graeme.'

Baz had had an attack of the Indians and once they'd managed to
extricate a tearful Andy from a confused Elephant Man, Andy

embracing Elephant Man and telling him how much he loved him and all he represented blah blah blah, they'd ended up at Mr Vaudeville's Vindaloo which came as a surprise to Dunx who thought it was still called the Take Your Nose Off Tandoori. Eddie, though, pointed out it had been under new management on his last visit, then proceeded to go through all the changes he'd seen on this visit: new phoneboxes and bus-shelters, new railings and fences, new buckets and drying areas and, of course, the precinct pot-plants.

'It's like a new place every time I come here,' said Eddie. 'It's like they do it up especially just for little old me. It's awfy good of them.'

'Same down ours,' said Baz, 'all these little changes that are supposed to be some kind of improvements but don't amount to a flake of shit when it comes to anything.'

'Oh, here we go,' said Dunx, 'the Trevor's pleading poverty. You see that one of yours that was on the telly the other night? Oh, man, he was doing my head in, going on about this being a recession, like how things were supposed to have been better a wee while ago there or some joke like that. Aye, right. Guys haven't a fucking clue, you know that. That's what really bugs me. There's folk round here in their forties, in their forties, never had a proper job in their fucking lives.'

'Same down ours,' said Baz. 'No bloody chance of getting one either.'

Dunx pointed at Eddie. 'Hey, twenty-five grand a year. Don't come it.'

'London's different, lad,' said Baz, 'do you not see all the kids out smashing up the streets, all the riots and that? That was ours.'

'Nah,' said Dunx, 'funny, I didn't actually, all I ever saw was a shower of spoilt bastards with all the best of gear on out enjoying themselves.'

'Christ's sakes,' said Eddie.

'You know how you never get riots up here?' continued Dunx. 'Folk are too fucking scared. Imagine going out rioting with some of the arseholes you get round here, you'd need to be off your fucking head. Telling you, any cunt sees you out on the streets and that's your house done over like that. Either that or you'll get one of them fucking bastards standing next to you, and that's it, out the

game, those cunts'd fucking stab you soon as look at you. Telling
you, if there was folk like the Bampots down there, you'd never get
any of your poxy wee riots.'
  Baz laughed. 'Sounds a bit like the Craigies down ours. Twenty-
seven of them in the one house, scary bastards. The old mother,
she's in her fifties, and all her bairns, like, they're all her's alright
but there's about seven different fathers so all the kids they're all
into shagging each other, like. Fucking mad, they are. Dangerous
bastards. They'd eat your Bampots for breakfast.'
  'Nah,' said Dunx, 'up the braes, they fucking invented inter-
breeding up there, been going for generations they have. Some
seriously deformed folk you get from up there, freaks. And, anyway, I wasn't saying the Bampots were the scariest round here,
cause they're no, they're fucking arsewipes – get them on their own
and they're fucking arsewipes, fucking nothings. I could take them.
Nah, the scariest cunt round here is Callum fucking Harvie. Telling
you, that guy ever comes down your way the whole of fucking
Trevorland'll shit itself.'
  'Aye?' said Baz.
  'You want to know what he fucking does? I'll tell you what he
fucking does – he bites folks' noses off. He bites them right fucking
off. And that's without a drink in him. You ask anybody. That guy
is fucking crazy. And he's a really nice guy, too. That's the thing.
But he bites folks' noses off.'
  Baz nodded. 'Scariest bloke I ever came across were a bloke
called Spinelaw Kenmore.' Wor Patrick, Wor Stevie and Wor
Christine nodded. 'Had a run-in with the Craigies once, 'bout ten
years ago, a run-in with the whole flaming lot of them. Supposed
to have said, "Send me your top man, one on one, in a locked room
for ninety minutes and I'll show them what's for". And that's what
happened and to this day nobody knows what went on but telling
you anything Spinelaw wants the Craigies get him.'
  Everybody was seen to be thinking the same thing, then Eddie
spoke for all of them. 'Eh, what could he have done that would
have needed ninety minutes?'
  Baz shrugged. 'You want to ask him?'
  The cultural exchange continued with Baz and Dunx topping
each others' childhood poverty, violent acts witnessed, murdered

acquaintances etc etc until Eddie got bored and said, 'Where you folks stopping the night?'

Baz shrugged. 'The car, I suppose.'

'Just crash back at my bit,' said Dunx. 'Get a few cans in.'

'Sure?' said Baz. 'What about the missus?'

'Nah, no problem, Recca's alright. Probably get a smoke off her. Anyway, that place is as much mine as it is her's, if she doesn't like it she can lump it.'

And with that reassurance they were off. On the way, though, they stopped at a site over the town where there was some building work going on. Baz was particularly taken by a pile of bricks, about the size of a wee mini-bus, and went over to have a look at them.

'What's up?' said Dunx.

'Telling you, canny lad, I've had me such a great time the night I feel like . . .'

'Captain what?' said Neil.

'Captain Trip, best band ever.' Deke switched on the machine and the music came out of the speakers: muffled tribal drumming; mumbled tribal vocals; a really loud guitar that sounded as if it was recorded best part of half a mile away; and a bass that appeared to have been set up all of two inches from the mic.

'Fucking brilliant, eh,' said Deke.

Neil gave a serious nod like he was into it and said, 'Bit like Can.'

'One of our influences,' said Deke. 'Mostly we just made it up, though. Well, us and the drugs, like.'

'Listen,' said Gary, coming in at just the right moment so as to drown out his famous missed beat, 'we've got to do something and get this thing going again.'

Deke shook his head. 'Nah, it's gone, Gary, finished. Had to be of its time. Let the bastards catch up and then we'll fucking show them.'

'Oh, come on,' pleaded Gary.

Deke turned to Neil, though. 'Listen to this,' he said, 'just listen to this, listen to it. This was a 12″ before there was a 12″, this was rave before there was a rave, this was baggy before there was a baggy. Listen. Telling you, I'm hearing all this new stuff, and it all sounds fucking familiar to me, you know, and I just goes back and plays the old tape, and, bang, there you go, there it all is, it's all there. Listen to this bit.'

Neil listened. 'Nirvana?'

'Exactly,' said Deke. 'We were Nirvana, we were Nirvana years ago, years ago, we were doing all that grunge stuff years ago. We were Nirvana before they even knew they existed, and they've made millions out of that, by the way, millions. That three and a half seconds there, that's their fucking career. Hold on, this bit?'

'My Bloody Valentine?' said Neil.

'There you go. More fucking millionaires. Telling you, you want to have seen the reactions we got when we were on stage. The kids just loved us.'

'Mind Kirkcaldy?' said Gary.

'Mind it? Come on, how am I ever going to forget Kirkcaldy?' Deke turned to Neil again. 'You ever heard of anyone getting themselves a life-long ban from the Kingdom of Fife? No? Well, wait till you hear this one . . .'

Hearing his past so gloriously described almost made Gary forgive Deke for not wanting to get the band going again. Maybe though it was for the best to consign all this to the past, not to want to recapture it but, like Deke said, to move on, to go for the future.

Gary took Heather by the hand. She looked happy that he'd done that. This was Gary's future. This gorgeous, wonderful woman was his future. For the first time in his life Gary really wanted to get up in the morning and go out and get himself a job. A job that would enable him to clothe, feed and house this fabulous woman. A job would be needed to rear their children. Gary was overwhelmed. He wanted to go to the nearest church and thank the lord for sending this woman to him, he wanted to take her to meet his family, he wanted to take her to a school reunion and show her off, he wanted to . . .

It was just then the door squeaked open.

'Hi-ya,' said Deke. 'What you wanting? You coming in? Come on, then, come in and say hello to everybody.'

Baby Joe swaggered in, rubbing his eyes, and pulling at his jammy bottoms.

'Oh, he's lovely,' said Heather.

'Come here,' said Deke.

Baby Joe looked a bit frightened and shy of all the new faces, and went and hid round behind Deke's chair.

Everybody laughed.

'It's okay,' said Deke. 'Nobody's going to harm you, son.'

Baby Joe didn't look too sure, though, and shook his head.

'What's up, son?'

Baby Joe pointed to Gary and said, 'Dad! Dad! It's the Wanker Man!'

Hazel switched it on at half-load.

Doing a washing wasn't exactly going to keep her busy, but it gave her that wee bit of time to think about things before going to her bed.

The head was starting to go its dinger so Hazel took a couple of aspirins and tried to down a mug of water in a oner. She managed it but nearly choked in the process.

Hazel filled the mug again and sipped from it. When the washing was done and the water was drunk she would go to her bed.

Andy had always said they would never go to bed not talking, if there was a problem then they'd stay up till it was sorted out. Well that was two nights in a row they'd nailed the jelly to the ceiling on that one. Andy'd always said communication could solve any problem in the world. Last night, though, they'd failed when they'd tried and tonight he hadn't even bothered.

That was what really hurt Hazel, the fact he hadn't even tried. And where the hell was he, anyway?

He could be anywhere, anything could have happened to him, anything.

But if something had happened to him somebody would have got in touch with her, by now somebody would have got in touch with her. No, that's not what had happened. He'd just not come round, he'd chosen not to come round, he'd made that choice, and he'd made Hazel feel rotten. Everything was just rotten.

And then there'd been that stupid nonsense with Graeme. He shouldn't have kissed her like that, and he shouldn't have held her like that.

But then she shouldn't have kissed him, she shouldn't have, and she shouldn't have dragged him away and went on at him like that.

Okay, granted, that was her fault, a bit of it was her fault, but it was all nothing, anyway. It was as much in the past as anything ever could be. It had nothing to do with Graeme, it only had to do with Andy.

She'd planned around Andy. She'd more than pinned her hopes on him, she'd nailed them, she'd stapled them, she'd glued them, she'd done everything. For all her making it out like she'd been cold and calculated in choosing him, making out how he was nothing more than the perfect donor for her children and the perfect partner for growing old, for all that, that front she'd kidded herself with, it was only now that she could admit to herself that things ran a whole lot deeper, they were a whole lot more instinctive, a whole lot more basic, a whole lot more base. She loved him.

That's what all this was about. It wasn't about role-playing, it wasn't because she hadn't got her own way, and it wasn't because she was all huffy and petty. It was about being in love with someone who didn't seem to feel the same way, or share the same commitment, or . . .

Hazel sniffed and sipped her water.

Well, if that was the reality then she wasn't going to go on like this, she wasn't carrying a torch for no one. There was no way she'd put up with it, going through this like it was the norm.

Hazel started worrying again, worrying that he really had been in an accident. If they'd all been in a car or something then there would be no way they could get in touch. Nobody would know to . . .

But, no, she shouldn't think like that. Hazel closed her eyes and everything was spinning, like it was when she'd had that smoke over at Carol and Deke's. She didn't fight it, though, she'd learnt not to fight it, and just gave into it, feeling the warmth on the hairs of the back of her arms.

Hazel decided she'd stay like this for a few minutes then get her stuff ready for her work in the morning.

Within a few moments, though, Hazel was asleep.

*

'Did you put Baby Joe up to that?'

'Uh-uh. The wee fellow made it all up himself.' Deke got into his bed. 'What you doing?'

'Joanne's got her gym the morrow. Just be a couple of minutes.' Carol snapped the ironing-board into place and Deke did a double-take of the clock.

'Gary was alright the night, though, eh.' Carol tested her iron with spit. 'Here, I think he's fair smitten with that lassie. See the look on his poor wee face, oh was that no a picture, a pure picture? And her, she was just as bad. No, I think she'll be good for him, though. Mind you, they'll have to work at it all the same. That's the trouble with folk these days, they don't work at it. Just like our Recca, she's going to have to work at it, if she's serious about Neil she's going to have to work at it alright. I mean she never gave that stint with Dunx half a chance, did she? Not that myself, personally speaking, that I ever thought it stood a snowball's, but, Christ, she's got to learn to work at these things, got to work at them. I like Neil, though, he's nice, got money as well, a blooming teacher. Do you think they're like us, Deke, folk like that, folk with money, I mean brainy folk? I mean I know Recca herself's got money, but that's different. I mean folk that've got like proper money, that live off better things, folk that go out and that? They must be, eh? They're different to us. You want to have seen him the night, though, the neck of him, gee whiz, I've never seen the likes of it. Just comes right over, bold as you like, and just asks her out, just asks Recca out. Telling you, there was all of us just waiting for her to come away with one of her comments, you know one of her sarky specials, and she's just standing there with her gob wide open no saying a thing. So he comes away and asks her again, asks her out again, and then he starts this talking, and he's over at our table telling us all about himself. He's dead brainy, he's a doctor, like. Well, he's got the degree, the doctor's degree, he can put the letters in front of his name, like, no that he ever does, though. So, anyway, he keeps talking away, saying as how he's no a media studies student at all, he's actually a Media Studies teacher, a lecturer. And he's saying all these really nice things to her, to Recca, just keeping going on and on, and eventually she just says, "Okay", that's all, she says just "Okay". And so she asks him if he wants to come back with the rest of us, and he says "Aye" and the next thing we're piled in the back of the car then back here, and he's still telling us all about himself. Like it's a joke like, like he's selling himself. He's divorced, he says, says she ran away with another man. He was saying that she's away from him now as well. Apparently she's awfy bothered with that depression. That can be a bad thing that, awfy bothered with her nerves. Isa Rodgers was telling us that her Janie's going a bit sideyways. No going out the door at all these days. Says she's on that many pills she rattles more than the bus. Aye, and that's her that's always on at us for having a wee smoke. Probably flogging them. Wouldn't put it past that lot. Oh, and I never said, Eddie's back, aye, Eddie's back. I've to phone him the morrow. I never seen him, though, it was Graeme that was telling us. Oh here, you want to have seen this the night with Graeme and your pal Hazel. Oh, see poor Hazel, right, she'd been waiting all night for Andy to appear. And did Andy appear? Did he hell as like. Telling you, see that laddie. Anyway, Andy never shows, so Hazel, she gets all uppity and demands that Graeme takes her home. You want to have seen the look on Graeme's face, you'd have thought he was going to get raped. Heh heh. He was terrified. It's a shame for the lassie, though, young lassie like that. It is. Andy's needing to give himself a bit of a shake or he's going to lose her. First bloke that turns her head and, wheech, she'll be off. I didn't like the look of dad the night, Deke. No, he was a bit funny, a bit edgy, a bit too keen to get going, you know, couldn't wait to get out of that place. Deke, I'm worried about him. I know he's been causing us a bit of bother of late and that but he's still my dad. He's not getting any younger. Well, right, that's me done. Just switch this off and put these through in the room for the morning.'

Carol went through with the clothes then returned and un-plugged the iron, leaving it where it was to cool overnight.

'Right, your alarm set, aye? Right . . . Hey . . .'

Carol went round to the other side of the bed.

'You asleep? . . . You been listening to me?'

And there he was – sound, with his eyes closed softly; his breathing soft, deep and quiet, and his body relaxed, loose and cosy, like a banana in a bath.

*

Recca took a toke and considered.

He'd said he wasn't perfect, but then he would say that, wouldn't he. Fact he'd said he wasn't anywhere near perfect, and that there were plenty who would testify as such. He'd said he had a problem with punctuality, other folks' punctuality. And he'd a thing about money as well, his money and how he didn't like parting with it.

Recca shook her head – these were flaws?

Sure, Neil had said, these were things that got up folks' noses. He'd said you were supposed to spend what you earned and that you were always supposed to be so cool and so laid-back that you were never on time. Recca couldn't believe all this. For the first time in her life she'd even admitted to someone that she'd a couple of bank accounts stashed away that she'd never ever told anyone about.

Neil hadn't said much about his wife. All he'd done was to give a little history.

They'd been students and he'd been infatuated with her, overwhelmed by her. They'd got hitched when they were twenty-two. In terms of being in love with her, he'd said he was over her, he'd been over her for a while, but he still cared about her, though, he still worried about what would happen to her.

As Recca had suspected she was a bit of a looker alright, but as for her personality and her problems, Neil hadn't gave much away, all he'd said was she could be a bit tiring, that folk like that could be a bit demanding.

It was nice the way he talked about his wife, there was no secrecy, just a respect for her privacy. He still got on with her folks, her parents and brother, and went to see them from time to time. As much as he couldn't understand her, what was wrong with her, he'd made a good job of explaining it all to Recca. Recca had said maybe that was why he was so organized, not wanting to get too involved with the unknown again. He hadn't denied that. Then again, as Recca realized about two seconds after she'd opened her mouth, that was a pretty obvious observation to have made.

Then came the moment of dread, the moment he'd asked about Recca.

Recca concentrated on her family and her job, even going to the extent of giving Uncle Denny and Auntie Jessie in Canada a mention. Eventually, though, she'd gotten round to it, and admitted that she was at present living with somebody.

Neil just burst out laughing.

Recca'd told him it wasn't funny and went on to explain that although it wasn't the biggest mistake of her life, it was certainly the stupidest. She'd told Neil how it was all over, all over apart from the gathering of his clothes and the throwing out. She'd said she'd been too busy of late with the shutdown and everything and had just been waiting for the right moment. Now, she'd realized, any moment was as good as any other.

Recca had felt a bit cheap going on about all that in front of Neil, it sounded a bit desperate, like she was dumping on Dunx because Neil was better. Compared to what Neil had been through it must all have seemed pretty stupid and pretty petty. The guy had been good about it, though. A problem was a problem, he'd said, and a mistake was a mistake.

When he'd introduced himself at the quiz, he'd really played on his nerves, but the more he'd opened up, the more he'd been relaxed and the more confident he'd got. That had helped Recca. She hated all that deliberate coyness.

Recca took another toke.

There was no denying that he was handsome, even with that tickly beard he was still handsome.

Recca'd laughed and told him about the Holy-holy who'd stopped her earlier, going on about Christ being her lover. He was a bloke with a beard too, wasn't he? Neil had just laughed, though. He'd said his beard was more for the academic look than wanting to come over as some kind of prophet. If you looked the part you acted the part. He said he'd even got himself a pair of horn-rimmed spectacles and a battered old briefcase to complete the effect.

Yeah, Neil was a nice man, but was he perfect?

Well, if he wasn't, he was pretty close. He had so much going for him: he had the looks, he had the money, he was nice, he was loaded, he was available, he rolled a good smoke and for the last forty minutes he'd been at the cunnilingus, and didn't look like he was going to stop till a week on Tuesday.

*

They were all in the kitchen, washing the blood and the brick-crumbs from their hands.

'That was fucking mad,' said Dunx. 'Never in my life have I ever been a part of anything as sheer and utter mad as that, never. Telling you, that was unreal, that was a bit deranged that was.'

Baz shook his head as if it was all the same to him. 'Any toast?' he said.

'Eh, I don't know, have a look, see if you can find any. Just help yourselves, anything you fancy just help yourselves, alright.'

Eddie went through the living-room where Dunx's clothes were still lying about all over the place. 'See you've still never learned how to use a cupboard, Duncan.'

Dunx laughed. 'Mind how I was telling you we got this smart new mirror and how I was trying all the stuff on, well . . .'

'Can't find any toast,' said Baz, 'alright if we have these pizzas?'

'Aye, sure, on you go, just help yourselves.'

'Got any vaseline?' said Wor Patrick.

'Eh?'

Wor Patrick held up his scratched and torn hands.

'Eh, oh aye, aye. Eh, don't know, have a look, just have a look, right. Just help yourselves to anything.' Dunx turned to Andy, 'Hey, you alright, pal?'

Andy nodded. He'd been the hardest working of the monument builders and had ended up with hands that looked like somebody with their best cherry reds on had been using them for a half-hour trampoline practise. Andy was peeling at the loose flesh. It was agony, but it was what he wanted to do, what he was compelled to do.

'Come on, cheer up,' Dunx put his arm around Andy. 'It's not the end of the world, man. You're starting a new life. Look on it as a start. It's all for the best. You've always got your mates, you've always got us, you'll always have me, you know I'll always be there for you.'

Andy just stared with Sicilian eyes.

'You sure you're alright?'

Andy gave in. 'My hands are sore.'

'Well, Christ, come on then, come on over and I'll help you get them washed.'

And so Dunx helped Andy over to the sink and ran the warm water over Andy's hands.

'This is a major turn-on, this,' whispered Wor Patrick to Eddie as Dunx gently washed then pat-dried Andy's fragile fingers with one of Recca's clean dish-towels.

Eddie slowly nodded as the vaseline went on, over and in between the delicate digits. 'Wish I'd a camcorder,' he said, 'wish I'd a fucking camcorder. You know he won't remember a thing of this, a fucking thing.'

'Come on, he's just pissed,' said Wor Patrick.

'I know,' said Eddie, 'I know that. I'm not saying anything, I'm just wishing he could see himself like this.' Eddie was also thinking that how he wouldn't mind Simon seeing this either.

'Hey,' said Baz, 'thought you said you'd see about getting us a smoke.'

'Right,' said Dunx, 'a smoke, aye right, hold on. I'll just away up and see Recca. See if she's got a bit.'

'And straight back down mind,' said Baz, 'no staying up there for your wee bit nookie, straight back down.'

Dunx blushed. Everyone was laughing at him but Dunx wasn't bothering. It was great being the centre of attention and having all these folk round, all your old mates and all your brand new mates, feeding them and looking after them and laughing and joking with them. Yeah, this was the life alright, this was the life.

Baz rubbed his hands in expectation. 'That was quick,' he said. 'You get the blow?'

Dunx didn't say anything, just stood there, looking a wee bit funny.

'You alright?' said Eddie. 'What's up?'

Dunx pointed to the ceiling and tried to say something but couldn't.

'Is Recca alright?'

The state of shock gave way to a trickle of rage.

'Alright?' said Dunx. 'Alright? I'll give you fucking alright, alright.'

Eddie couldn't farthern this. 'Is Recca up there, aye?'

'Aye, she's up there, she's up there alright, she's way up there, she's way up there in the fucking clouds.'

Dunx was gathering up all his clothes and flinging them onto the same chair. He said, 'Fucking hell, man' then stormed through the kitchen.

'Eh, what's going on,' said Wor Patrick. 'This anything to do with us?'

Eddie shrugged. 'Shouldn't think so.'

Through the kitchen two cupboard doors slammed and one drawer slammed before Dunx reappeared with two black bin-liners and started piling in his clothes.

Eddie was starting to feel a bit like a panellist on What's My Problem? 'Eh, is Recca up there on her own?'

Dunx stopped what he was doing. 'What do you think? What do you fucking think?'

Eddie did as was suggested and thought. 'Is she up there with another man?'

The tapes and the records were now being subjected to an indiscriminate rummage, the bulk of them ending up in the bin-bags with Dunx vigorously mumbling away to himself.

Although the mumbles weren't intelligible, the absence of an articulate response didn't refute what Eddie had said, so for the time being at least Eddie accepted what he'd said to be true.

Wow!

Wor Patrick whispered to Eddie, 'Look, should we just not piss off or something?'

Eddie shook his head. 'Might as well just stay. Not going to make any difference, is it?'

'Coming?' said Dunx to Andy.

'What?'

'You coming, you coming with us? Find somewhere to kip. Come on.'

Andy shook his head. He'd given all his rage to the monument and all he was up for was fuck all. Maybe death. 'No, I'm stopping here. I'm not moving.'

'What?' Dunx flung down his bags. 'You're joking? Do you know what's going on up there?'

Nobody did, but they were all kind of curious, so they all moved in that wee bit nearer.

Andy shrugged. 'No, I don't know, and I couldn't care less.'

Dunx went eyeball to eyeball on Andy. 'Do you know what she's letting him do to her?'

Everybody moved in closer still as Andy shook his head. 'I said, I don't care.'

Dunx picked up his bags and then leant forward so that the tip of his nose was touching the tip of Andy's nose.

'You don't fucking care,' said Dunx, 'you don't fucking care and she's up there . . .'

Everybody leant forward as the tears flowed down Dunx cheeks.

'. . . letting him do, letting him do . . . letting him do dirty things!'

As much as Gary'd hoped they'd be heading back to Heather's home of the sunbed, the lure of the Captain Trip scrapbook had tipped the balance, and they'd ended up back at his bit.

'Why's your telly upside-down?' said Heather.

Shit, Gary'd forgotten about that.

'Eh,' said Gary, 'oh, I was just fixing it. It wasn't working right. It's working all right now, though.' Gary went over and put the telly the right way up. 'There you go. Just forgot to put it back the right way, that was all.'

'You've got some amount of videos.'

'Aye,' said Gary, 'football mostly, and some groups and that, you know.'

'I love old films,' said Heather, looking through the titles, 'old black and whites. You got any of those?'

'No, eh, no, just the football. I like the old films myself, like, but I never tape them, just the football and that.'

Heather continued looking around. Gary tried to think of things he wouldn't want her to see. Kitchen? No, safe. Could take the calendar down, though. Bedroom? A mess, but saved by the lack of lightbulb. Bathroom? Mags in the cistern. Should be alright unless the plumbing does a wobbly. Spare bedroom? Binoculars. Yikes, the binoculars!

'Be back in a sec,' said Gary. 'I'll just stick the kettle on.'

Gary hid the binoculars in the fitted wardrobe – they'd be safe enough in there – then he got down and did twenty right-arm press-ups, then twenty left-arm press-ups, then curtain-towelled his armpits and went through and stuck the kettle on.

'Tea or coffee?' he shouted through.

'Tea. Milk and three sugars.'

Milk and three sugars? That was the same as Gary took. Was there anything that was wrong with this woman?

The kitchen was looking a bit bare so Gary got a few things – cereal packet, egg box, margarine tub, a couple of foul-smelling bean tins that needed a rinse – from the bucket and placed them at the front of the cupboard. Good, that looked better.

There was still the problem of what to eat, though. All there was was half a loaf, a packet of cheapo digestives he was saving for Friday night's telly, and a precious bit of cheese Gary was saving for Saturday night's telly.

Hell, Christ, what was he thinking, if this wasn't a special enough occasion to break into everything and upset his routine then there never would be one.

Once he was ready Gary put everything on the tray, took a deep breath and went through the living-room.

Wherein he discovered that Heather had managed to put on the telly, had worked out how to use the video and was now watching the Cyrus twins, Sally and Cally, symmetrically tongueing King Dong's King Dong.

Heather was sitting there, agog, her mouth wide open to an extent almost undignified.

Gary was standing there, agog, his mouth wide open to an extent almost cavelike.

'Are all your films like this?' said Heather, her eyes glued to the screen.

'Yes,' said Gary, in the repentant tones of one who wants other offences to be taken into consideration. 'Every last one of them.'

'Wow,' said Heather. 'We've got to watch them all, we've got to watch every last one of them.'

Gary gulped. 'There's a lot of them, an awful lot. And they're all on long play.'

'Who cares,' said Heather, 'who fucking cares.'

Gary poured the tea and gave Heather the cleanest mug. He

gave her a plate of toasted cheese then sliced the packet of biscuits
and gave Heather half.

Heather accepted and started munching away.

'This is amazing,' said Heather.

Gary laughed. 'You know sometimes,' he said 'there's some bits
are even better when the telly's turned upside-down.'

And folk wondered why Graeme never went out.

What a fucking carry-on, though. Jesus fucking Christ almighty
bastern fucking shite, man what a fucking carry-on. All he'd
wanted was a nice wee quiet nicotine-free evening seeing some
friends, and he'd ended up with enough guilt to keep Latin Amer-
ica on the go for another millennium or two.

That was what you got for being Mr Nice Guy, that was what
you got for being Mr I'll-see-you-home-safely, that was what you
got for being Mr Yeah-I'll-be-a-potty-for-all-your-pish-darling,
that was what you got for being Mr . . .

But, by Christ, that was it, though, Graeme was never going out
again, ever. Okay, he would still go to the games, but he'd come
straight back – likewise, when he was going to his work, it would
be straight back. He'd still have to go up the town as well, of course,
but he'd only go up the town when he was going for something,
and if somebody stopped to talk to him and started coming away
with pish then Graeme would be off before they could even say
'Do you want to look at my legs?'

Graeme was really wild, he put a whole teaspoon of coffee in
his mug.

God almighty, what had been going on back there? What had
really been going on back there? . . . Other folks' girlfriends, that's
what had been going on back there. Aye, other folks' girlfriends,
alright.

Graeme tapped the side of his mug in that really aggressive way
folk have of doing when they're too intense to think about anything.

. . . other folks' girlfriends . . . other folks' girlfriends . . . other
folks' girlfriends . . . other folks' girlfriends . . .

That was it, alright, other folks' girlfriends. And if it was other folks' girlfriends, hey, then it was other folks' problems. Too fucking right it was. There you go, it was nothing at all to do with Graeme, he could just sit back and laugh at it.

Graeme sat back and forced a laugh. Ha bloody ha ha. What a right laugh it all was. There you go, that was better. Graeme lit a fag.

Shite and fuck and bugger it, that's how disoriented he'd been. Imagine lighting up a fag half way through a coffee, like forgetting to take your clothes off before you got in the bath.

Oh no!

Graeme squirmed with shock.

Oh fuck!

Graeme bolted upright in shock.

Oh fucking fuck!

Graeme held his head in shock.

God no, what about the Bampots? God, those fuckers would be stoating up the town all the time; was Graeme supposed to speak to them? Oh no, maybe they would want to talk to him, maybe they would ask him for money, maybe they would ask him for protection money, maybe they would want to be pals.

That did it, the parka was making a comeback, zipped right up to the fucking snorkel, and when he wasn't going to the games or going to his work, he'd only go out when it was raining, and he'd walk really fast with his head down. No, Christ, that was daft, a wee bit too stupid, he wouldn't walk really fast at all, he'd walk with a pronounced limp the same way every other fucking bastard in this town walked, he wouldn't be wanting to draw attention to himself, like, would he.

Right, that was that sorted. Graeme put on the telly – but the telly wouldn't work, though. Before Graeme started crying, he noticed the telly wasn't coming on because the video was off. Now why the fuck was the video off? . . . Christ, how could he have forgotten, the afternoon's Paul Morley Show. Imagine forgetting that, talk about disorientation. Graeme put the video on, rewound the tape to zero then pressed play and settled back.

Paul havered on for about six minutes about what happens when we die then paused a long, cool pause and said, 'A pleasure? An obsession? An accessory? Either way statistics tell us that millions of us do it, and millions of us want to stop.' The camera went in close-up. 'Later on,' continued Paul, 'we'll be speaking to Winona Carlson, a lady from Hastings, Nebraska. Now the thing is Winona Carlson is a really quite remarkable lady who claims to have developed a hugely successful technique for stopping; for stopping us do what we do with these.'

The camera pulled back to show Paul holding up a cigarette.

'Wow,' said Graeme.

'The even more amazing thing,' went on Paul, 'is Winona Carlson's success rate.' Paul paused for dramatic effect. 'A success rate she claims of one hundred per cent.'

Heather was still confused. All these films could either confirm or refute what Recca had said at the quiz about Gary when Gary was away at the toilet.

Heather probed. 'Tell me about Recca,' she said, 'what's she really like?'

'Our Recca?' said Gary. 'Well, she's a nice enough lassie I suppose but she's had her fair share of problems of late. She makes a bit of a mess of her life, like.'

'You live and learn.'

Gary laughed. 'Recca doesn't, Recca just lives. Like, she's got this thing going with Dunx the now but it's never going to work out, doesn't stand a chance.'

'She seems so straightforward, though. I mean she's very straight talking.'

Gary nodded. 'She is that, alright, granted she says what she thinks and she says what she knows. Mind, though, that's no always necessarily a good thing.'

Heather swallowed. She needed time to think about this. 'What about Hazel and Andy?' she said. 'What's going to happen to them?'

'Well,' said Gary, 'there's a lot of unhappiness there obviously, a lot of problems, external things. Hazel comes from a bad family, and Andy, well he doesn't have a family, he's only got us. He's too dependent on us. It all stems from when . . .'

And that was Gary off, going on about everybody, telling

Heather all about Graeme and all about Carol and Deke and all about all their families, and all about Captain Trip.

Gary was fair into this, talking about folk. Point of fact Gary had never really went on like this with anyone before. No, well, hold on, Gary talked about folk all the time. But Heather, though, she was being attentive and appeared to be genuinely interested and appreciative of what Gary had to say, and nobody had ever done that before, nobody'd ever credited Gary for his ability to understand folks' problems and everything that was going on, how he was good at things like that.

As Gary finished so did Christians in the Scud and Gary went over and put on Vanessa Del Rio Volume 3: The Bare-Arsed Boxing Years.

'What about you?' said Gary. 'Tell me about all your friends.'

Heather sighed. Heather hadn't had any friends since she'd left the school, near enough half her life ago. Since then she'd just drifted away into her own wee world. A world where she always protected herself by . . .

'I'm divorced,' lied Heather. 'I got divorced a couple of years ago.'

'Oh,' said Gary.

'A-ha. I don't like to talk about it, though. His name was Tom, Tom Clancy.'

'Don't know him,' said Gary.

'No, he wasn't from round here. We stayed over the water. He was a soldier, a soldier with the RAF.'

A soldier with the RAF? Gary thought about that. But since she didn't want to talk about it Gary let it drop.

'What about now?' said Gary. 'What do you do now?'

Heather thought quickly. 'I'm hoping to go to the Americas sometime, I'm hoping to get a job as a nanny.'

Gary was just about to follow that up with asking about Heather's family when there was a knock at the door and Heather damn near jumped out her skin.

Gary just laughed. 'It's okay, it'll only be Fids.'

The door went again.

'At this time of the night?' said Heather.

Gary checked the clock. 'Aye, it'll be Fids, alright. Sleeps during the day, stoats about at night.'

There was another knock, louder, almost angry.

'It's okay,' said Gary. 'Don't worry. He'll go away.'

Heather saw this as being as good an opportunity as any to get the conversation away from herself. She ran her fingers through Gary's hair and said, 'Tell me all about Fids. I love it when you talk about your friends.'

Gary laughed. 'Fids? Fids is the saddest bastard in the world. He's got this flat, right, and he's got absolutely nothing in it, nothing. He's got no carpets, just a couple of smelly old rugs. He's got one chair and it creaks all the time. Oh, and he doesn't have a cooker, he's only got a kettle and one of those things for making toasties. Oh aye, and he's got this great big fishtank and in the five years he's had it it's . . .'

. . . never once been used cause he's never once had the money to get anything for it. In the same way that he's never had the money to get the broken telly fixed that Heinz had given him, or the broken hi-fi separates that other folk had given him. Folk were always giving Fids things that were broken, and Fids was always grateful, knowing that when the day came and Fids finally got himself sorted out, he'd be able to get everything going and that would be him off to a good start for getting the place kitted out.

Fids lit a fag from the single-bar fire then pulled his blanket around his shoulders.

The fire was raised at the front by a couple of books so that the heat was directed right at Fids face. The only light in the room was coming from the fire and from the incense burning away on the window ledge.

Fids had got into the habit of staying up late over the winter months cause, despite what folk said, Fids's bones told him that in winter the nights were warmer than the days. And from there Fids had grown addicted to sitting like this all year round in front of the fire, his body nice and cosy under the blanket, his legs toasting at the side of the fire and his face all tingly. This was Fids's treat.

Fids moved down from the Braes because of a job, but before he'd had the chance to get himself settled, he'd lost the job. Fids then tried his hand at getting on with folk, getting in with them.

He'd spent twenty quid on that fish tank because everybody had fish tanks, he bought clothes like everyone wore, and he even bought bloody expensive red lightbulbs. Fids bought music as well, the same sort of sounds everybody else was into. Trouble was Fids only ever bought the stuff that came at the end of things, the imitators and the bandwaggoners, the stuff of the bargain bins. Like his clothes out of Poundies, this was the stuff that nobody would ever admit to liking.

The only thing Fids had to play his music on was his Walkman, complete with a gimmicky wee external speaker he'd nicked from Clydesdale because his headphones weren't too clever.

Through the night Fids had his radio and Fids had his library books, thrillers mostly and some poetry, modern poetry.

All the folk Fids went to see treated him the same. He'd tried to set himself up as a dealer for a while there but that hadn't worked either because dealers never went out, folk got in touch with dealers, and nobody ever got in touch with Fids. All Fids ever got to sell he ended up just giving away when he went round trying to find customers. Nobody ever bought any because nobody ever had money – or so they said – and Fids felt sorry for them and gave them a smoke. Not that Fids was bothered. All he wanted was the company.

Fids wasn't bitter that folk took a loan of him or took him for a fool. There were loads of folk who would swap places with Fids: folk that were starving in Africa, folk that were battling all the time. Even round here there were folk worse off than Fids, folk with kids, folk with debts, folk that used needles. Fids's neighbours were all worse off than him, bawling and shouting, and screaming and smashing things. It always sounded like somebody was getting murdered. Funny thing was, as Fids told folk, the time there was the murder there was only the one scream. There was a kind of sense to that, he supposed, there was even a kind of sick humour to it. There was a sick humour to life period, like the one that always got to Fids – the one about being brought up to take a telling and to do what he was told. All the time that's all he'd ever got. And now here he was with nothing to do, let alone anybody telling him how to do it.

It was the same for everybody, of course, but folk never did anything about it, they never communicated. They hated each other more than they hated their problems. Sure, they talked and they confided but they never helped, they never organized. Hell was private, hell was in the huff, hell had a do-not-disturb sign on the door.

Fids lifted the fire and held it as close to his face as he could without burning himself.

In the heat Fids could see a landscape, an empty landscape with bright blue water, pale blue sky and white sand, with no people, no features, nothing.

Fids, as he did every night, would stay like this until the tingling on his face turned to a sting and then he'd go to his bed.

That plan fell through, though, following the knocking of Fids's door, an event so rare and unexpected as to cause Fids to drop his fire and set his blanket ablaze.

'. . . and there's still the baggage of a decadent glamour, isn't there? I mean, it's not just the advertising, it's seen as a definite aloofness, a definite intensity. You know, the thing that's always fascinated me is the attraction for those two groups of people with whom you immediately associate it: the grotty, grubby, shell-suited under-class and the artisans from the Sunday supplements; you know, captured in sensitive soft focus, the smoke gently billowing up from between their fingers . . . Well, Winona, what do you think? Smoking's hard, isn't it?'

Clad in what looked like Auntie Lena's best curtains, the eigh-teen stone of hippychick that was Winona Carlson had done more chatshows than a politician's mistress. 'Listen, Einstein,' she said, 'you folks are paying me good money to come here and do a job, not to sit and listen to the biggest pile of crap this side of the Chappaquiddick County sewage works, so let's cut the mumbo-jumbo and let's work! Okay, padre? Is everybody ready?'

The audience was hollering. Paul beamed. This was the stuff of true telly, the surprise takeover. One more 'crap' and the switch-boards would be jammed then the tabloids would be on to them and Paul would be on the morrow morn's front cover.

Winona turned to camera. 'Okay, you lot, listen up. Get your lung cancer sticks, get yourselves some sellotape, get yourselves some scissors, and get yourselves a move on, I haven't got all day.'

There was lots of rummaging as the camera panned round the audience. If nothing else it would be a good laugh, so Graeme went and got scissors and tape as well.

'Now here's what I want you all to do. Now, watch the lady.' Winona wrapped the tape around the packet. 'And, hey, listen, this is important, don't throw them out, don't give the packet away, and, hey, don't hide the packet. Sure, stick them out the road in a drawer somewhere, but don't hide them. Leave them somewhere you'll come across them from time to time. Got that?'

There were still seven left, which seemed a hell of a lot to Graeme, especially since he'd walked halfway round the town to get them, so he took three out before applying the sellotape.

'Right,' said Winona. 'Dim the lights and bring the camera in. Come on, closer, closer, closer, closer, closer, closer – close enough so you can see the flakes of my favourite cheap foundation.'

The cameraman and the lightingman did as they were told and soon there was silence and near-darkness as Winona's face filled the screen.

'Okay,' Winona's voice dropped to a slow, barely audible whisper, 'read my lips: no new baccy, no new baccy, no new baccy.'

The audience took up the chant. 'No new baccy, no new baccy, no new baccy.'

Graeme joined in the chant, hopping round the room in a Red Indian style.

Then suddenly Winona went quiet again. A few moments later, though, and without moving her lips, Winona started a new chant. Something that went to the tune of 'You're going to get your fucking heads kicked in', only slower. The words derived from no new baccy but they weren't distinct words. There was an n sound, a b sound, and a k sound but they were only sounds and although Graeme chanted along he couldn't really make out what it was that he was saying.

This new chant was going on for ages, a good three minutes at least, Winona's face still filling the screen, like some test card from Hell. Graeme lit one fag from the other and kept chanting along.

After another minute, Winona put her hands across her face

then asked Paul to tell the floor manager to put the lights on and to pull the camera back.

Winona looked drained. 'That's it,' she said. 'Done and cured. Pay the lady.'

'That was incredible,' said Paul. 'Tell me now, why were all those people chanting?'

'Because I told them to.'

Paul laughed. 'But you never said anything.'

'Sunshine,' said Winona, 'the people could hear me, those in need could hear me. That right, people?'

'This is mad this,' Baz was getting his jeans off. 'Here I am in somebody's house, somebody who just happens to be up the stairs, somebody whom I've yet to meet, somebody who doesn't even know I'm here, and I've just polished off two of her pizzas and now I'm going to crash out on her sofa.'

Wor Patrick was equally confused. 'Look, are you sure it's alright for us to crash out in the spare bedroom?'

In the last thirty-six hours the only sleep Eddie had mustered had been a couple of hours over at ET City. Since then he'd had too much to drink, too much to eat, he'd talked too much, he'd listened too much and then he'd gone and built a bloody monument.

Eddie just gave a wave of the hand like a ref turning down a penalty, pulled the cushion off his chair, lay down on the floor and made loud snoring noises.

'I take it that's goodnight,' said Baz. 'Sweet dreams.'

'Fuck off,' said Eddie.

Wor Patrick and Wor Stevie went up the stairs. Eddie and Baz were soon asleep. Wor Christine returned from the kitchen.

'Alright?' she said.

Andy shook his head. This was the story of Andy's life, at every turn there was a new woman, another bloody woman.

The first thing Andy and his mortal coil ever did was to get left in a cardboard box at the Banana Bridge. The woman who found him was the woman who adopted him. If it hadn't been a woman who had found him then everything would have been different. But, no, it had to be a woman because women were obsessed with

Andy. Every time a woman finished with Andy – they always finished with him, they always dumped him – Andy would take himself away to some pub or party, and Andy would find himself in a corner and Andy would get paralytic, and when Andy got paralytic Andy got intense, and when Andy got intense Andy got a woman. There was always some poor wee lassie who would take pity on him and listen to the sad and pathetic tale that was Andy. A tale that brought forth sympathy, understanding, empathy and ultimately a shag. This was how he'd met Hazel, this was how he'd met everybody. She was just the same as the rest. As much as Andy had hoped and as much as Andy had even prayed she was going to turn out different, she'd just turned out to be the same, the exact bloody same as all the rest. In the football game of life Andy could win possession and Andy could string the passes together but when it came to the final third of the park and sticking the ball in the back of the net Andy was a pure numpty.

And now it was Wor Christine. This poor lassie was going to hear this story and this poor lassie was going to surrender herself just like all the others. Same old story. Blah blah blah. This poor lassie was going to fall for him, and this poor lassie was going to love him, love him emotionally and love him physically. She'd start by touching him, then he'd touch her, then she'd hold him, then he'd hold her . . . same old bloody story. Blah blah blah.

And Andy had to tell this story, Andy had to go through with all of this. He had to go through with it all because it was all he had.

Andy picked up the last two cans and offered one to Wor Christine. She shook her head and said 'Look, are you alright?'

Andy opened his can and took a big gulp. 'It all began when I was born.' Andy laughed. 'No it didn't, it all began when I was conceived. My mother, my natural mother, was an opera singer, my father was either Sean . . .'

It was three hours later, when Andy reached the age of sixteen and his second engagement to the heavily pregnant (although not by Andy) Lorna Ingham, before Andy realized that Wor Christine wasn't listening at all but was in fact lying sound asleep cuddled up to Baz.

Charlie Endell was pissing himself.

*

Fids was in agony. All he could think to do was to smother the blanket and wriggle about. Consequently, he'd managed to put the fire out but in the process had ruined his jumper, his shirt and his t-shirt and scalded his hands and chest.

Clatter! Clatter! Clatter!

That was the knocker going this time. Christ, it was some brave bastard that would create such a commotion in this close at this time of night.

Fids tried to work out who it could be.

It wasn't the Feds; no, the Feds had their standard knock, the rat-a-tat-tat – that was part of their training – then they did the two loud and lazy clatters of the letter box then they waited two-and-a-half seconds and then they just kicked the door in. No, it wasn't the Feds, there was a degree of agitation about this.

It wasn't the neighbours either. They never stopped when they were at the door, they just went knock-knock-knock, clatter-clatter-clatter, boot-boot-boot, usually all at the same time, until they got an answer. No, it wasn't the neighbours.

Somebody was shouting through the letter-box, shouting his name, shouting Fids' name.

No, the likelihood was that it was somebody wanting money or somebody claiming that Fids owed them money. Folk were always claiming that Fids owed them money, which was rotten: the only money Fids owed was from years ago, and these folk didn't hassle him for it anymore. Fids kept his money to himself these days. Never borrowed from anybody, never loaned to anybody. No, Fids wasn't answering the door, no fucking way.

There were voices out on the landing. Fids crawled over to the living-room door so as he could hear better.

One voice, a loud voice, definitely a neighbour, was saying something about 'racket' and 'weans'. Then another voice, a quieter voice, a drunken slur, said something about fucking off to somewhere. The loud voice, the neighbour's voice, said something about 'getting a skelp'. The quiet voice replied with something along the lines of 'Fuck off, ya arsehole, and mind your own business.'

There then followed the distinctive sound of fist on bone through skin.

Fids gave a start. The next thing he heard was running feet and the close door slamming then the neighbour's door slamming.

Fids crawled over to the window. He raised himself up so as he could look out.

There were no police cars or council vans. The only cars there were the cars that were always there: the Capri without the wheels, the Montego without the windows and the upside-down Jaguar next to the lock-ups that folk said was something to do with the Bampots and was supposedly booby-trapped with a couple of sticks of dynamite. That was what folk said, anyway.

Nobody was going about, though, only the fox every cunt called Freddy rummaging through the bin-bags.

Fids crawled back over to the living-room door, removed the draught-excluder from his diy spy-hole and looked along his lobby and out onto the landing.

It was quiet. Whatever had being going on was over. Fids went out into his lobby and then along to the front door so as he could look out on to the landing just to check there wasn't a corpse or anything lying out there.

No, it was okay, no blood-splattered walls or severed limbs.

Fids relaxed, and went back to the living-room and the smell of burnt blanket. Fids didn't want to wake up to that in the morning so he opened the window.

And it was then that Fids saw a very strange sight – a guy with white jeans and a green denim jacket was running away with two of their bin-bags, and was being hotly pursued by three cats, five dogs and the fox every cunt called Freddy.

That was it. They'd watched every last film, including the best bits upside down, they'd been through the Captain Trip scrapbook; Christ, they'd been through every scrapbook (apart from 'Death', Gary hadn't shown her that) and they'd been over every one of Gary's family, friends and neighbours.

Gary opened the curtains. 'Well,' he said, 'that's it, that's me.'

Heather shielded her eyes from the daylight. 'I wish my life was so full,' she said.

'Oh, come on now.'

'It isn't. Believe me, it isn't.'

'What you got in your place?' said Gary. 'What's special to you?'

Heather shrugged. 'Just odds and ends.' Heather didn't want to go on about her home and all those wrong things: the wrong curtains, the wrong furniture, the wrong mugs, the wrong colours, the wrong everything . . . and then there was that stupid bloody sunbed.

Gary laughed. 'You've hardly said a word about yourself.'

Heather smiled. Going on about herself wasn't something she ever cared for, it wasn't something she'd ever had any practise at, all she ever did was lie. She lied when she applied for jobs, she lied to her family, whenever she opened her mouth she lied.

That was what had been so good about all this, she hadn't had to say anything so she hadn't had to lie, apart from saying she was divorced she hadn't lied once. But Gary and his friends were always going on about the past, their pasts, and what they'd been up to. It was as much a part of them as their partners.

Which brought to mind another problem – what Recca had said about Gary at the quiz when Gary was away at the toilet. If that was true then all this would count for nothing, only a memory to add to a list of bad memories.

It was now or never.

'Listen,' said Heather, 'there's something that's been bothering me . . . Look, is there something you should have told me?'

'Eh?' Gary was worried.

Heather was watching him, interpreting his look.

'What you on about?' said Gary.

Heather sniffed. 'When you were away at the toilet earlier on Recca told me something about you.'

Inside, Gary squealed.

'What did Recca say?'

'Are you sure,' said Heather, 'that there's nothing you should tell me?'

Whoever said it was better to have loved and lost had never been in Gary's slippers. This was the worst. This was worse than anything. This was worse than dropping your fish supper in a puddle.

'Well,' said Gary, 'there's probably a lot of things. . . .'

'No,' said Heather. 'Not a lot of things, just one thing, just one very important thing you should tell me.'

Everything in life had a price, everything in life you had to pay for. For every good thing there had to be a bad thing. And something really good, something this good, could only be matched with the worst, the worst of anything. The most wonderful time of Gary's life was going to end, he knew it, he fucking knew it, it was going to end by being the worst night of his life.

'Just tell me what Recca said,' pleaded Gary, 'and I'll try and explain it all to you.'

'She said there was something wrong with you.'

'What?' Gary was nearly crying. 'What's wrong with me? What did she say was wrong with me'

'Look,' Heather took a deep breath. 'Recca said you didn't have a penis.'

'Wakey! Wakey! Rise and shite!'

They didn't stir, not as much as a twitch so Recca switched on her hoover.

'What the fuck?' said Baz.

'Exactly,' said Recca. 'Exactly, what the fuck indeed.' Then Recca kicked the still unconscious Eddie on the legs but to no effect, so she emptied the remnants of last night's teapot over his head.

'Jees-oh! Christ alfuckingmighty, no need for that.'

'Aye, there is,' said Recca. 'I'm on an early so you lot are going to have to find somewhere else to make a mess of. Come on, move it.'

'Five minutes,' said Eddie, curling up again, 'just five more minutes.'

'Five minutes, your arse.' Recca picked up the teabag and squeezed it over Eddie's nose. 'Fifteen minutes,' she said, 'fifteen minutes to get this place cleaned and fifteen minutes to get out of here.'

'That makes thirty minutes,' said Baz.

Recca scowled. 'Fifteen! And who the hell are you when you're at home?'

'Baz,' said Baz, 'here, any chance of a smoke?'

Recca smiled. 'I gave the lovebirds up the stair a bit, you'll get a smoke off them.' Recca turned to Andy. 'You alright?'

Andy shrugged. He hadn't slept a wink, just spent the night sussing out Hazel, life, death and everything in between then forgetting it all, then remembering it all, then forgetting it all, until he reached the point where he didn't understand anything about anything.

'Should've seen your Hazel last night,' said Recca. 'She was not a happy wee lassie.'

Andy sniffed. 'Looked happy enough when I seen her.'

'Eh? When d'you see her?'

'Going down the road with Graeme.'

Recca laughed. 'Look, Andy, son, she didn't have a clue whether she was coming or going. Andy, she was as pissed as a fart.'

Recca explained everything that had happened.

Considering how he'd been feeling, Andy achieved something he'd thought himself never ever again capable of – he actually felt worse.

'It's all my fault,' said Andy, 'it's all my fault.'

'Too fucking right it is,' said Recca, 'and don't you forget that.'

Neil came in with Wor Patrick and Wor Stevie.

'Alright,' said Neil. 'Listen, I'll stay here and keep an eye on this lot till it's time for me to go to my work. There's no hurry.'

'Sure?' said Recca.

'Yeah, no problem.'

Recca did a quick survey. Baz was skinning up, the rest were tidying up. 'They look trusty enough, I suppose,' conceded Recca. 'But, look, there's one thing I don't understand.'

They all stopped what they were doing and paid attention.

'Could you tell me,' said Recca, 'what the fuck you've all been doing with your hands?'

The thing was huge, man, it was fucking enormous. It was bigger than the bloody trees. And what the fuck was it supposed to be, anyway? I mean, all anybody was ever going to think was that it was a massive ten-foot high brick willy with two massive bricked-up balls.

'Hello, hello, hello. And what d'you know about all this then?'
Graeme turned round. It was Shug, or PC Meikeljohn as he was
with all his gear on.

'Is this what I think it is?' said Graeme.

'Nah,' said Shug, 'it's a rocket. We're sending a Bampot into
space.'

'Aye, right; that's what I was thinking. Best place for them.'

Shug got out his notebook. 'You haven't seen a bloke with a, eh,
green denim jacket carrying two bin-bags on your travels, have
you?'

A green denim jacket? Nah, couldn't be. 'No,' said Graeme, 'no
seen anybody with two bin-bags.'

Shug made a note. 'Seems he slept here last night. A couple of
our boys tried to catch him but he ran over to the old folks' houses
and just disappeared. If you hear anything you'll let us know, aye.'

'Aye,' said Graeme, 'sure.'

Shug put his notebook back in his pocket. 'You still working up
the Avoninch?'

'Aye, early start. Got promoted yesterday so they want me in
earlier.'

Shug shook his head. 'That's the thing with work, you make a
cunt of it and everybody's on your back, you do a good job and
they give you more.'

Graeme laughed. 'What's going to happen with this thing,
anyway?'

'Fuck knows,' said Shug. 'It's evidence, mind. You don't tamper
with the evidence.'

'Here,' said Graeme, 'be great to stay here all day and watch
everybody seeing it, eh.'

'Aye, funny for some, I suppose, only muggins here's been
delegated to cover the thing up. Just waiting for Boots to open so
as I can go in and ask for a twelve foot johnny.'

'Aye, right. Any idea who done it?'

'Nah,' said Shug, 'had all those diddys up from Geordieland
last night, that's all anybody can think of.'

'Must've been them,' said Graeme. 'This is pure class this.
There's nobody up here with the brains for this.'

'There's nobody up here with brains period. Anyway, I better get this thing under wraps before some old bint comes along and has herself a heart attack.'

Graeme started laughing.

'What's so funny?' said Shug.

'Over there,' said Graeme.

Shug looked, and saw six folk heading toward him: two with boom microphones, two with video cameras, Cathie Galbraith (the 'Under the weather' girl) and the one who did the news bits on the Paul Morley show.

'Smile, Shug,' said Graeme, 'you're going to be on the telly.'

'Dun-can . . . Oh, Dun-can.'

Great Auntie Bella gently tickled Dunx's toes.

'Duncan, can you hear me? Listen, Duncan, I've got to go out for a while, now are you wanting anything to eat?'

'No,' mumbled Dunx, ' 'malright.'

'Now are you sure, Duncan?'

Unlike the rest of him, though, Dunx's nostrils were wide awake and working. 'You been making toast?'

'Would you like a bit of toast, Duncan?'

'Would I like a bit of toast? Too right, I'd like a bit of toast. D'you know when the last time I had a bit of toast was? About three or four days ago, man.'

'Marmalade?'

'Nah, got any cheese?'

'Okay, cheese it is. Now, how many slices?'

'Eh, four, and mind plenty of pepper, and you got a tomato? You should slice up a tomato. That's really good that is.'

'Right you are, Duncan.'

Great Auntie Bella went through the kitchen and immediately returned with a tray adorned with four slices of heavily peppered cheese and tomato, toast, a pot of coffee and a glass of fresh orange juice.

'Oh, magic,' said Dunx.

'I had a funny feeling you might be hungry. Now, is there anything else you'll be wanting. I've got some of your clothes in the wash, but it'll be needing another load. I should have them ironed by the night.'

'Nah,' said Dunx, 'can't think of anything, just you do what you think you should.'

'Right, now let's see your hands.'

Dunx showed his hands.

'Christ, laddie, they're in some state. What were you up to?'

'Eh,' Dunx's brain was starting to wake up. 'Oh, I was helping a mate with some building work last night.'

'And your eye? What happened to your eye?'

'What eye?' Dunx put his hand up and touched his eye. 'Ouch! Ya fu . . .' And the rest of last night all came back to him: all that running about trying to find someone who would put him up for the night; Graeme hadn't been in (probably still away with that Hazel); Dunx's folks had been out; Dunx then tried Gary's – well, it was all his fault, anyway – but Gary hadn't answered his door; then there was that fucking psycho up Fids's bit; then that fucking pack of wolves; then the boys in blue and all; and then . . . Recca, Recca and that bloke.

Dunx held his head in his hands.

'Are you alright, Duncan?'

'Yeah, I'm okay. Just my eye that's a bit sore. Bit of a shiner, eh?'

Great Auntie Bella nodded. 'Right, I'll leave something out for it for when you decide to get up, and I'll leave the cream out for your hands. Now, are you sure there'll be nothing else that you'll be needing?'

Dunx shrugged. 'Nothing that I can think of, no.'

'That's a nice jacket that,' said Great Auntie Bella eyeing the Levi. 'Where'd you get that one from?'

'Eh,' Dunx paused, as if trying to remember. 'Oh aye, a lassie gave it us. Aye, she gave us it. Pretty smart, eh?'

'It's nice, it's nice right enough. I seen somebody with a red one on the other day. I thought the red was nicer.'

'Aye, you're right. The red ones are better, they're smarter.'

Great Auntie Bella studied the jacket. 'I think I could manage to dye it for you if you wanted.'

'Could you? Oh, that would be great that.'

'Should be straightforward enough.' Great Auntie Bella inspected the stitching. 'No, there shouldn't be any problems. Tell you what I'll do, I'll put it in the bleach just now and I'll dye it when it's ready, will I?'

'Aye, brilliant. Be really smart that. Thanks, Auntie Bella, you're a wee smasher, so you are.'

Great Auntie Bella smiled. It was nice to be called a wee smasher again – it was also nice knowing that that young policeman could spend the rest of his life looking for that green denim jacket and still never find it.

'Sorry, folks,' said Neil, 'but that's your time up. I've my work to go to.'

'Lucky you,' said Baz.

Eddie threw a cushion at him. 'Away and shut your fucking cakehole, ya moaning, greeting-faced Geordie bastard. Get enough of all that carry-on from this shower of losers up here.'

'Charming,' said Baz.

'Well.'

'You never think of moving back?' said Wor Christine.

'Ha, you must be joking. That's what this lot are always on about.' Eddie put on his namby-pamby voice. ' "When you coming home? So is that you moved down there for good? Ah, but you'll miss it here, though, eh?" Fucking no, no I don't. Expecting me to come back with my shirt out my trousers and my tail between my legs. No chance. No fucking way. I have not stayed in this town for twelve fucking years mind, twelve fucking years.'

'You'll be back,' said Andy, 'you'll be back.'

'Uh-uh.' Eddie shook his head. 'This is sad bastard city, man. Takes me all my strength to hold back the tears. Know it's no folks' faults, like, but, Christ, I hate them, I hate poverty. See the money I spent last night plying you cunts with drinks, be just the same for the next three days and all. Costs me a fortune to come up here. No that I grudge it mind, just pointing it out, likes. Nah, only reason I'm here is 'cause Simon told us. I fucking hate this dump: I hate all the lying, I hate all the cadging, I hate all the thieving, I hate all the whingeing, and I hate all that macho crap. Tell us, is there any other place in the world that would sell its major soft drink with the slogan "made from girders"? Do real Belgians read the *Record*? Do you get real Belgians? And is there any other country in the world where you're brought up to believe that smoking's cool and that Runrig's cool?'

Eddie lit a fag. 'But it's your town,' said Andy, 'it's your team.'

Eddie sighed. 'Granted, I miss the team. I miss the team and I miss Baggio's chips, but that's your fucking lot.'

'I'll never leave,' said Andy. 'I'll never leave the team.'

'And you'll never get a job, a job. Sign on! Sign on!' Eddie counted on his fingers. 'And neither will Gary, and neither will Dunx, and neither will Fids, and Deke'll always be getting paid off, and just you watch 'cause Graeme'll be getting laid off as well. That won't last. It's a fucking tragedy. Some cunt deserves to get shot. And I mean that.'

'Folk are still folk,' said Baz, 'it's the folk that count.'

Eddie shrugged and rubbed his fingers.

Baz got up. 'Well then, missus, we've had our wee dose of the middle classes feeling sorry for us. Time to go back and pick up the bairns.'

'Come again?' said Eddie. 'What you meaning "missus"?'

Wor Christine nodded. 'Five years. How, is that a problem?'

'Nah, don't be daft. I just thought . . .' Eddie bit his lip. He'd made a boo-boo on that one, but Baz did look old enough to be Wor Christine's father.

'It's the folk that count,' repeated Baz. 'You've got your Simon and I've got Wor Christine. Maybe don't have your money but. . .'

Andy interrupted. 'Hey, wait a fucking minute, you said last night you'd been phoning your wife, telling her to tape your programmes.'

Baz laughed. 'Just taking the piss, pal. Sorry but you've got one of those faces that's just asking for the piss to get taken out of it.'

Andy looked stunned.

'You need to stand up for yourself,' said Wor Christine. 'You need to decide what you want and you need to go for it. You wanting Hazel?'

Andy nodded.

'Then dump everything,' said Baz, 'and go for her: change, beg and go for her. Good boys get, bad boys don't.'

Andy massaged his scalp and brow. 'You don't understand,' he said.

'Don't understand what?' said Baz.

Andy lowered his head.

'Don't understand what, lad?'

Andy mumbled something.

'What was that? If you've got something to say then speak up so we can hear you.'

Andy looked up and Andy spoke up. 'You don't understand, Charlie Endell says I've to kill her.'

It was like the place had been hit with some new kind of bomb that left buildings and limbs intact, but did a fair job of destroying folks' souls.

Deke had been fleeing round all morning hoping to meet somebody, somewhere who'd tell him it was all a hoax and that everything was alright.

He'd even went to see the bosses, the works' bosses. They'd confirmed it, though, saying it was all true and that it was all to do with it being reclaimed land and the consequent problems that they'd be having with the foundations. Surely to God, Deke had said, they'd had all that sussed. They'd said they thought they had but that their last set of results had put the wind up the insurance folk. Now they would have to go through all the palaver of finding another site – all the testing, all the purchasing, all the planning permission – and all that would take at least a year, a year at least before the big contract would be getting off the ground.

Deke had left them to it and gone back to his pump and his hoover and the midgies from Hell before he started mouthing off and landing himself in some kind of trouble.

It was all just a joke. They'd have got that land on the cheap, thinking they could get away with it. Anybody with half a brain could see that there was going to be a problem with the foundations, any cunt could have told them that. Some poor bastard would get it in the neck for all this but that wasn't going to help Deke. The cleaning gig only had another eighteen working days to go then it was back to filling in another B1. It would be eight to ten weeks before another part of the work was shut down. All Deke had to hope for was that he would get on that, and that couldn't be guaranteed. There were some of them that got on every contract but there was a tendency to take on diddies, guys that just happened to call round at the office at the right time on the right day, and these guys ran off and told their mates, and that was that, the places were filled before anybody got to hear of it.

Deke and Willie stopped for their break.

'Alright?' said Willie.

Deke shook his head as he accepted one of Willie's polos. 'Nah, feeling like shite.' Deke didn't even bother with sucking the mint, just snapped into it. 'You never think, Willie, you never think that should be getting on a wee bit better at this life thing, you never feel that things are just mounting up against you, that everything's going too fast, and that you're no getting anywhere?'

Willie laughed. 'Thought you were the one that was supposed to have it all sussed.'

'Aye, right. No, but d'you no, though, d'you no think that?'

Willie shrugged. 'Don't know. All I'm waiting for is the weekend, and me and the brother-in-law heading up teuchterland and getting rat-arsed at the fishing.'

Deke laughed. 'Think I'll join you. Telling you, Willie, I really feel like doing a runner. I really feel like just chucking it all in and just running away.'

Willie laughed. 'Think I'll join you.'

For the rest of the break Deke and Willie went on about their imagined travels, how they'd be getting there, what they'd be needing and what they'd be getting up to. It was all just daft blethers but they got a good laugh out of it, topping each other's stories.

All this got brought to a halt, though, when Deke heard his name being called out.

It was Recca doing the shouting and from the sound of her something was wrong.

Deke rushed over to the side of the tank and shouted down, 'What is it, the kids?'

'No,' said Recca, 'the kids are fine, but, listen Deke, Carol was just off the phone, her dad's not answering his door and his curtains are still drawn.'

'. . . and Eddie, he was saying as how he's got a Charlie Endell and all. No, listen, listen to me, please listen, so I wasn't wanting to kill you after all 'cause Eddie was hearing the same voice, only his was saying no to bother with telling folk that he was a poof, sorry that he was gay, 'cause of all the hassle and 'cause he's never really been that good at things like that, being honest with folk. It's when your thought voice takes on a different accent, that's what Eddie says. It was the same with Wor Christine, she was saying how with her and Baz, 'cause of the age difference, like, that well, you know, it was all maybe just a big mistake and how she didn't know what was the right thing, what she was supposed to do. And, oh aye, Neil, he was saying he was a bit guilty about shagging Recca 'cause of his wife, 'cause he'd never been with anyone since the divorce, like, and he was saying to himself "Ach, well, I don't know, maybe never made a good enough go of the marriage". And Wor Patrick, he was saying . . .'

Hazel raised her hand. 'Just hold on a sec and slow down a bit. You're saying that Eddie's a, that he's gay. You were telling me last night that he had a thing about Carol.'

'I know,' said Andy. 'I was well off the mark with that one, well off. He was saying that he confided a lot in Carol, though, that's why he was always going round there.'

'Right,' Hazel nodded. 'I think I understand. Now, who's this Neil?'

Andy laughed. 'That's Recca's new boyfriend.' Andy explained what had happened.

'So that's her finished with Dunx,' said Andy. Andy shook his head. 'I'm finished with Dunx. We're not speaking. Never again. Honest.' Andy nodded his head. 'Promise.'

Hazel groaned. 'Listen, I don't want you not to speak with Dunx. God, you make it sound like it was a choice between us, between me and him.'

'No,' said Andy. 'No, no way. There wasn't a choice, there was never a choice. I didn't mean that at all. Nothing to do with that.'

'Well, don't make it sound like that then. You know, that's what really upsets me.'

'I won't,' said Andy. 'Sorry, I won't do that again.'

'And who are all these people with the funny names?'

'What?'

'The War People.'

'Oh, the Geordies, sorry the Makkums, you call them Makkums, the Makkums n Takkums. Hey, they were saying we've to go and see them, they all want to meet you.'

'But who are they?'

'They were up for the game.' Andy laughed like it was the most obvious thing in the world. 'Who'd you think they were?'

Hazel shook her head.

'Listen,' said Andy, 'can I have a shot of your phone? I need to phone Stan.'

'Stan?'

'You know Stan, Stan-Stan-the-supervisor-man.'

No, Hazel didn't know Stan, but at least she'd heard of him. 'On you go,' she said.

Andy dialled. 'Alright there, Stan-the-man. How's it going? Listen, I'll no be in the day . . . No, sickness and diarrhoea . . . What's that? . . . No, no seen anything of Dunx or Heather . . . Eh? . . . Aye? . . . You're joking! A pair of caked keks in the bog bucket? . . . Nah, don't know nothing about that. Nah, mine just started this morning . . . Listen, Stan, I need to go again. I'll see you the morrow, right. See you.'

'So?' said Hazel.

Andy looked blank.

'So why didn't you turn up last night?'

'Oh, aye, eh.' Andy stopped. Shit, that was the bit he'd forgotten about. 'Well,' he said, 'it's a long story but there's no story good enough. I could've made it. It was just well with Dunx holding me back, he was really holding me back, like, had a hold of my arm, like that, really tight,' Andy demonstrated on Hazel's arm, 'and well then with Eddie telling us what he was telling us, and then when I seen you and Graeme walking down the road I just flipped, I just caved in. Look, I'm sorry, I'm really sorry.'

Hazel could see that he was sorry alright. What she couldn't understand was why he was so excited. For somebody who should have been in fear of his life, and who had a history of doing a runner even when there was a lightbulb needing changed, he was either taking her for a mug or he was on some dodgy new tablets that gave him a couple of qualities he'd never been noted for, namely confidence and enthusiasm.

Anyway, with all that, and the fact that Hazel had even surprised herself at just how pleased and relieved she was that he was alive and that he was okay, for the time being at any rate, Hazel was letting him off with it.

'Okay,' said Hazel, 'we'll try again but, listen, there's one thing I need you to explain to me?'

'What, what's that?'

'Could you tell me,' said Hazel 'what you've gone and done to your lovely wee hands?'

Deke had prepared and even prayed for this moment: the end of having Carol and the kids turned against him, the end of seeing presents appear which Deke himself couldn't afford, the end of having the old bastard turning up half-cut expecting to be fed and pampered, the end of hearing about all those aches and all those pains and all that threadbare existence, the end of having to listen to him going on like he knew everything and how everything he did was right and how everything Deke did was wrong, the end of so much that was bad, so much that was disruptive and so much that was just a plain bloody nuisance.

There were a million specific reasons why Deke hated him but mostly it was just that attitude, that selfish, superior way of his. Okay, so it was born out of loneliness and the way he'd been brought up, and there were certain ties between him and Carol that Deke would never be a part of, and when you got to that kind of age you'd somehow earned the right to be a cantankerous old bastard, but the guy played on it, he played on it something rotten.

Deke had wished him dead alright, he'd wished him dead often enough and for long enough, but when Recca pulled into his street and Deke saw Carol, her sister and a couple of the neighbours chatting away with Carol's dad on his doorstep, Deke simply said, 'Thank God, thank fucking Christ.'

'Okay then,' said Recca.

Deke shook his head. 'I don't think she's ready for that again. I don't think she could handle it.'

'You're never ready for it,' said Recca.

They pulled up outside the house.

Carol's dad was laughing. 'What's this, the seventh cavalry coming round to rescue me?'

'Aye,' said Deke, 'heard there was some dozy old cunt no getting out his kip. Got the fucking jack leads in the boot to get him going.'

'Know what it was,' said Carol. 'Know what the old bugger was up to? He was sleeping on his good ear. He'd never have heard that flaming door if you'd took a pneumatic drill to it.'

Carol's dad was still laughing. 'Don't know what all the fuss is about,' he said, 'I was having a great time.'

'Dad, stop it, it's not funny. You shouldn't have been sleeping till this time of the day. You bloody well frightened the life out of me, you know that.'

'Aye well, take it easy, hen. All's well that ends well. I maybe had a wee bit much last night, a wee bit too much of the old hard stuff. I'm sorry, hen. And I'm sorry, son, to hear about the job no coming off. A couple of the boys down the club were on about it, that's fucking tragic that.'

'Oh no,' said Carol.

Deke nodded. 'A year they're saying, a year at least.'

'They're scum, son, they're just scum, no even bothered with the likes of us, no bothered one wee bit. They're building all these new plants so they'll be making the place more efficient. But do they no realize that when they're making everything more efficient they'll no be needing the men? Do they no realise that? Are they just plain daft? It's all just a joke, son, it's just a joke.'

'Aye, that's all it is.' Deke thought for a second then added, 'Listen, about this car of yours, well if you're still offering it to us likes, well then . . .'

'Aye, of course, sure, son, on you go, it's yours, take it.'

'What's brought all this on?' said Recca.

'Don't know.' Deke laughed. 'I just had this daft and crazy notion to run away – for all of us just to run away.'

Partly because he wanted to see the monument again, but mostly because he wanted to have a look through all the papers, Graeme had taken himself on a wee detour on his way for his dinner.

And sure enough, there she was, on every tabloid cover, Winona Carlson in all her glory.

The papers were all saying there'd been thousands of folk ringing up to say they'd stopped. Of course, they'd dug up a dodgy MP and a mickey mouse celebrity testifying that it hadn't worked for them, and there was some bloke from the medical world going on about how it was all just a load of old bollocks and how there was no basis upon which to believe a word of it.

But the thing was, it was true, Graeme knew it to be true because he'd stopped, he'd finished. He didn't want one, he didn't want one because he felt like he'd just had one half an hour ago. This was what Winona said would happen. She'd said it would be like this for the next couple of weeks until the system was cleansed and then the craving would just collapse, like taking off the perfect stookie.

And it was great. Everything was fantastic. It was like going into Ali's when he was putting the out-of-date milk chocolate Hob-nobs in the reduced-to-clear trolley. The whole world was just magic. Even up the work things went better than Graeme could ever have hoped for when, just like he'd said, the Bampot boy hadn't turned up and, because it was what he was paid for, Graeme picked up his courage and picked up his phone and dialled the family home.

It was the lad's mum, the legendary Aggie, who answered, Aggie who got the not proven for the 'murder-by-plasticine' of her second husband. Aggie'd said that Stuart wouldn't be in today or any other day come to that because he'd been lifted last night for breaking into the handicapped houses down Jenkins Street. Aggie had went on and on about how it was wrong for the lad to break into 'the poor things' and about what she was going to do to him when she got a hold of him. Graeme had been fair impressed by this show of displeasure, but suspected that if it had been Graeme himself who'd been done over then Aggie would've seen that as fair game.

So that left a wee problem – an opening at the work.

Graeme told Phil he'd take himself a long dinner break and offer the post to one of his mates, thereby saving them all the hassle of advertising, interviewing and all that carry-on.

The trouble, though, was who to choose.

As he left Menzies Graeme seen one of the possibles studying the monument, and laughing and joking with Hazel. Andy was alright in his own wee way, and would do a good job, but Hazel and her legs and her cousins were not something Graeme particularly wanted reminding of or, even worse, to have to go over at some point or other. Nah, so that was Andy off the list.

The next of the candidates, Dunx, was in a somewhat relaxed mood, apparently deciding that this was the day he wanted to sunbathe out the back of his Auntie Bella's with his walkie, his shades, some juice, some crisps and with a pound of steak over one eye and his hands all covered in white paint.

Dunx was never the easiest of folk to fathom and while Graeme pondered a car tooted at him. It was Deke. Graeme waved back. Oh, that was great. Deke must've got himself on the big contract and got himself a car to celebrate. Graeme was really chuffed. For as long as Graeme had known him Deke had only ever wanted to do the scaffolding, anyway. Graeme knew that he could cross Deke's name off his list without the slightest hint of guilt.

Graeme continued on his journey and next up was Gary, Gary whose curtains were still closed and Gary whose windows were all steamed up. Probably up there chugging away to one of his films. No, decided Graeme, the company of Gary wasn't something Graeme wanted to share for eight hours a day, five days a week. It was a shame for the laddie, right enough, young laddie like that, and the lad needed a break alright but let somebody else give it to him. So that was Gary off the list.

Graeme saw Fids coming out of the Health Clinic with his wrists bandaged up. The crying out for help had reached the old slashed wrists stage. It was so sad.

Had Graeme been the sort of bloke who fed every charity tin and every hungry-and-homeless bunnet, he'd have rushed over to Fids and offered him the job right then and there without even bothering to think about the others. But Graeme didn't: instead he hid in the bushes next to the car park and wondered what he should do now that Fids had joined the others and was crossed off the list.

That left an empty list . . . so Graeme had to go back to the list
. . . or Graeme had to add to the list.

It was then that Graeme had a brilliant idea, an idea that would
make somebody very happy indeed. It was no wonder Graeme got
promoted when he could come away with crackers like this.

So Graeme went round and chapped the guy's door.

'Alright?' said Graeme. 'Listen, what it is is, got a wee proposal
for you, right. See, there's one of our guys, one of the boys at the
work, like, and well to cut a long story short he'll no be coming
back, having been detained at her majesty's pleasure so to speak.
So, there's now an opening at our place, and, well, I know how you
go on about how you hate the town and all that, going on about it
being crap all the time. But, hey, you can't fool me, I notice things
about you – oh aye, I can see it in your eyes – and I know you'd
love to come back, back to the old town. Anyway, all I'm saying's
the job's yours if you want it. So what d'you reckon then? How
about it?'

There was no reply, just a kind of stunned look.

'Come on,' said Graeme. 'How about being a season ticket
holder again, and how about me as your boss?'

Eddie just laughed.